THE
BLOOD
PROMISE

ALSO BY MARK PRYOR:

The Bookseller

The Crypt Thief

A Hugo Marston Novel

THE
BLOOD
PROMISE

MARK PRYOR

SEVENTH STREET BOOKS™
AN IMPRINT OF PROMETHEUS BOOKS
59 JOHN GLENN DRIVE • AMHERST, NY 14228
www.seventhstreetbooks.com

Published 2014 by Seventh Street Books, an imprint of Prometheus Books

Cover image © 2013 Media Bakery
Cover design by Grace M. Conti-Zilsberger

Inquiries should be addressed to
Seventh Street Books
59 John Glenn Drive
Amherst, New York 14228
VOICE: 716–691–0133
FAX: 716–691–0137
WWW.SEVENTHSTREETBOOKS.COM

18 17   5 4 3

Library of Congress Cataloging-in-Publication Data

Pryor, Mark, 1967–
    The blood promise : a Hugo Marston novel / Mark Pryor.
        pages cm.
    ISBN 978-1-61614-815-7 (pbk.)
    ISBN 978-1-61614-816-4 (ebook)
    1. Americans—France—Paris—Fiction. 2. Treasure chests—Fiction.
3. Murder—Investigation—Fiction. I. Title.

PS3616.R976B56 2014
813'.6—dc23

                                                            2013031881

Printed in the United States of America

To Natalie, whose bright eyes and kind heart bring me joy every day.

AUTHOR'S NOTE

As much as I love Paris, I have been forced to take occasional liberties with its history and geography. Events have been created and streets invented to suit my own selfish needs. All errors and misrepresentations, intentional and otherwise, are mine and mine alone.

CHAPTER ONE

PARIS, 1795

The man moved from the upstairs window to his desk near the fire. He sat slowly; the damp and cold that had saturated Paris for two weeks had stiffened his back and legs, all the more irritating because it was supposed to be summer. The fire in the grate hadn't made a dent in the chill just yet, but its crackle and spit were good comfort, and soon the flames would roast the stone of the fireplace to warm up the room—and him.

Once seated, Albert Pichon smoothed a hand across the blank page in front of him and picked up the quill that his new *domestique*, Laurence, had prepared. He grunted with satisfaction when he saw that the young man had obtained, without having to be told, a feather from the left wing of the goose; Pichon had many eccentricities, and this was one, but if pressed he would insist that the curve of this shaft fit his hand better than a right-winged feather did. And if he was willing to pay a little more for the left wing, wasn't he entitled to his quirk?

This letter, however, was no mere whim. It was perhaps the most important thing he'd ever written. In fact, he wasn't unnecessarily scaring himself by thinking that more than life depended on it. The man who would receive his communiqué, along with the small box that would accompany it, was one of the most influential men in the modern world—and gaining influence by the day.

Out of habit, Pichon reached for the small knife that lived in his waistcoat pocket, opened it with some trouble, and grazed the blade across the quill's tip, perfecting the arrow-point and checking the tiny splice that would draw up the oak gall ink.

Rituals completed, he sighed, reminded himself of his opening lines, and began to write, all but the salutation in English.

Cher Monsieur,

I hope this dispatch finds you in good health and, please, do forgive me for dispensing with further formalities but time presses in on me and I have come to think that perhaps more than this one life depends on your receipt of, and trust in, my words. One life, for certain.

He wrote with more care than flourish, the muscles in his hand loosening as he worked. In the quiet of his study, the steady scratch of his quill whispered to him like the words of an earnest friend, plaintive and promising. It was an ordered liturgy of sorts, the dip of his pen into the inkwell, the dab of his blotting cloth, and the gradual birth of his sloping letters, and together they mesmerized the old man as he worked such that his desperate message flowed easily onto the page. Slow and steady, they fell, words of hope and promise, yet leaving behind a wretched taste as he brought them to life with his hand and mouthed them with his dry, cracked lips.

Once, he was startled when a burst of wind shook the glass in his window. A tiny drop of dark ink fell wayward from his quill as he jerked, and he dabbed at it like a nurse sopping blood, the only unwanted stain on the paper. Fortunately, it was not enough to require him to start again—as if he had time.

He was more than halfway through when a gentle knock interrupted him, but he didn't mind because it heralded the arrival of his nightly serving of wine. Laurence waited for the command to enter before letting himself in and placing the open bottle and empty glass in front of his master. Beside the bottle he placed a small wooden box, three inches long, plain and unadorned, its small hinges of brass simple but strong. It would hold what Monsieur Pichon and Laurence had taken to calling "the gift," *le cadeau.*

"You don't want to put *le cadeau* in with the letter, monsieur?" Laurence asked kindly. "I can fold it well, it will be safe. That way they can't be separated."

Pichon sighed. "You are kind, but I think the box will be better. If only that reaches him, I think he will understand. At least, I hope he will."

With a respectful nod Laurence went to the fire, adding two logs and nestling them into place with his boot. He turned to Pichon and asked, "Is there anything else you need, monsieur?"

Pichon smiled. "You are doing well, Laurence, I thank you for the attention you pay to me."

"It is my good fortune to work in your household, monsieur."

"*Bien*. I need to finish this, I don't have much time."

"An hour, monsieur, you have another hour, almost. When he gets here I will show him in, and even then, if he has to wait I'm sure he won't mind."

"Perhaps not. And perhaps the urgency is all mine but . . ." He sighed again. "Are we doing the right thing, Laurence? We are playing with one life and two entire nations and yet somehow that one life seems so much more . . ."

"Because it's the one you are closest to." Laurence gave his master a gentle smile. "History will judge these days, monsieur, it is not for us to do so. We must only live them the best we can."

Alone again, the man gently cleaned away the ink that had crept too high up the quill's shaft and continued to write. The rhythm took over again, scratching, dipping, blotting, scratching again. By the time he had finished, two sheets were filled with his words. Leaning back to relieve the ache in his shoulders, he read the letter aloud to himself once, then again.

Satisfied, he had one last thing to do, something that would, he hoped, convince the recipient of the letter and *le cadeau* of his sincerity. He found a clean corner of his rag and with slow, gentle strokes he cleaned the ink from his quill. With a dry mouth and a slight tremble in his fingers, Pichon rolled up his left sleeve. That done, he took two deep breaths, gritted his teeth and picked up his knife. He placed the blade against his skin and watched, almost from a distance, as the hairs on his arm parted under the sharp metal and opened up a thin red line. The pain took a moment to reach his brain but when it did, it was a streak of fire erupting from and scorching his arm. He dropped the knife as his stomach rose into his chest and he gripped the edge of the table to avoid fainting.

As the dizziness receded, he took deep breaths to quell the bile that soured his throat and, once under control, he realized that he was gripping the table so hard that his right hand was aching. He released his fingers and flexed the stiffness from them, then picked up his quill, and dipped its tip into one of the rivulets of red that trickled down his arm.

He ignored the pain, concentrating instead on putting on the paper, letter by letter, his elaborate and intricate signature. Two more dips, the sharp quill stabbing like a torturer's instrument, and he drew a quavering line under his name, managing a delicate flourish.

He bandaged his arm, wrapping it like it was someone else's sickly child, wincing as the rough bandage touched his open wound, but relieved as the fire eased into a fierce, insistent throbbing.

As he waited for the ink and his own blood to dry in the now-warm air, his eyes fell to the small wooden box on his desk that would travel with the letter. He ran his hands over its smooth top and then opened it to look inside, his fingers hovering over the contents, *le cadeau*, as though he might by his touching somehow reduce its power or contaminate its authenticity.

He took a final look, hoping that the wisp of a message it contained was enough, and closed the little box for the last time.

He folded the letter and secured it with his wax seal, then placed it on the desk and turned back to the tiny box. With the steady hand of a surgeon, he rotated it in his hands as he dripped red wax along the seam made by the lid. The box was too small for a lock, for one with any significance certainly, and the contents weren't valuable enough to steal, not in *that* way. But the seal would tell the man who received it that he was the first to open it, that the treasure within came untouched from its source.

That and his letter, Pichon knew, were about the only assurances he could offer his distant ally.

He rose and walked around his desk, taking the letter and sealed box with him, and knelt in front of a wooden chest, a small strongbox that he'd acquired from a dealer on the Ile de la Cité. "Barely used" had been the promise, which meant its owner had probably died of the plague or, more likely in this case, under the knife of a pirate. This chest was more ornate than the traditional sailor's chest, made from walnut not oak, with strong brass hinges and ornamental inlay of the same metal, golden and polished bright by Laurence. And this chest had other attributes, too, secret compartments revealed by sliding wooden panels in the lid and sides, the front itself entirely a façade that folded down and allowed the secretion of larger items. The cleverness of the chest was that it let you think you'd found everything and even now, a year after buying it, Monsieur Pichon had a sneaking suspicion it contained a compartment or two he'd not discovered. Nor would he, not now.

The strongbox already held an assortment of clothes, folded small and tight along with a pair of new, if petite, leather boots. Pichon buried his hands into the box, shoving the clothes aside and pressing his finger into a raised knot of wood that doubled as release. A square of panel gave way, and with great care he slid the small wooden box into the space and let the cover fall back into place; the fit was perfect.

The old man's fingers then moved to the front of the chest and fiddled with the hole where the latch would fall when the lid closed. Pichon poked around in the tiny space until he found the brass tip that slid left-to-right, letting the front fall open. He placed the letter in the space above the hinges and closed up the false front of the box, two treasures hidden away with a satisfying click.

A knock at the door. *Laurence with his guest?*

"Come in," Pichon said.

The man in front of him was barely thirty, and had a tired look to him exacerbated by his unshaven face and wild, dark hair. "Monsieur Pichon, *comment ça va?*"

"I'm well. You?"

The man didn't answer, just looked around the room and then down at the chest.

"Is everything ready?" Pichon asked, suddenly wary. "How is ... *he?*"

"He is still quite sick."

The man's eyes had flickered in a way Pichon did not care for. "Sick? *Il n'est pas mort?*"

"*Non*, monsieur, he is not dead. But sick."

The man finally met his eye and Pichon chose to believe him. "The chest, it's ready."

"That's it? Everything is in there?"

"Yes," said Pichon. "You will send it ahead and follow as soon as you can?"

"*Oui.* As soon as I can." He gave a weak smile. "I should take it, and go."

The man made his way out into the street, the heavy wooden chest in his hands. He felt more than a little guilt as, behind him, Monsieur Pichon watched from his doorway. The young man was not a good liar and took no pleasure in it, and he suspected that old man Pichon had sensed something was wrong.

Wrong indeed, the young man thought as he climbed into his carriage. Every man has his own agenda and sometimes circumstances change, requiring honest people to choose a different path.

He placed the chest on the leather seat beside him and left his hand on top, thinking about another box at his home, one not much bigger than this. A box more simple in design and more commonly used, a rectangle of oak that flared out at the sides and contained the lifeless remains of a child.

CHAPTER TWO

Hugo Marston walked into the embassy's security offices with one hand behind his back. His secretary, Emma, a handsome woman who was never anything but perfectly attired and coiffed, looked up from her computer screen.

"Good morning and happy birthday," he said, "to the most efficient and wonderful secretary an RSO could have."

"Oh, Hugo, you remembered." She took the bouquet and inhaled. "You are a sweet man."

Hugo picked up a stack of mail from the corner of her desk. "I know."

"Although as regional security officer, you seem to have forgotten some basic training."

"Meaning?"

She nodded toward the closed door of his office. "You should lock it at night."

"If it's who I think it is, he has a key."

"I suppose he would," said Emma, "being the ambassador."

"Did you make him coffee?"

"No, I made it for you, but I have no doubt he's drinking it."

"I better get in there, then." He opened the door to his office and entered, smiling at the rotund, bald man who sat with his polished shoes on Hugo's desk, sipping at a cup of coffee. "I suppose I should be grateful you're not using *my* chair."

"Wouldn't want to," Ambassador Taylor said. "It looks like something out of *Star Trek*."

"It's ergonomic, and it's better for your posture than sitting with your feet on a desk."

Taylor patted his stomach. "I'm way past anything a chair can do."

"And I may have mentioned this before." Hugo sat down. "But if you let me out in the field now and again, I wouldn't need a space-age chair."

"Every time you go out in the field, someone gets shot. And being the observant fellow that I am, I've noticed that the person getting shot is never you."

"That's because I duck." Hugo reached for the coffee pot. "So, are you here for the beverages or do you have a new stack of papers for me to read, sign, or otherwise shuffle?"

"I have a special assignment for you, as it happens. In the field."

Hugo perked up. "Oh yes?"

"We're having a surprise visit from Charles Lake."

"The senator?" Hugo asked.

"Yes, but more specifically the presidential candidate. Or about-to-be presidential candidate, I can't keep up."

"That season already, is it?"

"Seems like it's always that season. Point is, and bearing in mind he'll either fire me or be my next boss, I want my best man on it."

"If he's a presidential candidate, he should have Secret Service help."

"He will. When you're around they'll defer to you; their presence is a courtesy rather than a necessity. But yes, they'll be here with him."

Hugo groaned. "So I'm the babysitter, not security."

"Correct."

"I did that in London not too long ago. A movie star, that time. Did you hear about that?"

"I did. A gruesome business, if I recall correctly."

"Precisely. With that in mind, you want to rethink the assignment?"

"Quite the opposite. No doubt you learned from that experience and will be even better at it this time around."

"No doubt." Hugo poured himself coffee from the pot. "So when and why is he coming? And why aren't you babysitting your own future boss?"

"I plan to meet him and feed him when he gets here, but you get to have him when there's actual work to do."

"And what work is that, exactly?"

"You've been reading up on the whole Guadeloupe Archipelago thing."

"That fuss?" Hugo sat back. "It's a pile of rocks in the Atlantic, I don't get why anyone cares."

"People care, don't you worry."

"How much? Are the French planning to invade or something? Are we?"

"Invade?" Taylor sipped his coffee. "Can't imagine anyone's that upset about the place."

"I know, but the whole thing reminds me of the Falkland Islands debacle. You know, a few sheep-strewn rocks nearer to Argentina than England, but somehow English territory. The Argentineans invaded and the Brits invaded back. Same here, Guadeloupe is closer to the United States than to France, and yet is somehow French, so I wondered if the troops were massing."

"Guadeloupe has pineapples, not sheep."

"We wouldn't fight over pineapples?"

"We only fight over oil," Taylor said. "Nevertheless, the fact that Guadeloupe's inhabitants have petitioned to become part of the United States has strained relations with our French friends."

"I expect it has, but I don't see how that's our fault."

"We're Americans, everything's our fault, especially where the French are concerned. Actually, I agree with you but as far as I can tell fault doesn't matter in politics, it's the *appearance* of fault that carries weight. Either way, I'll worry about Guadeloupe, you worry about Lake."

"What is there to worry about?"

"Well, for one thing, he wasn't supposed to be coming. Head of the Foreign Relations Committee Jonty Railton was the original choice."

"Oh, yes, I remember reading something about his tires getting slashed."

"Yeah, and not known to the public were some fairly specific messages he was getting. Threats, to be precise, telling him to stay out of France."

"From?"

"No one knows. Anyway, he's one of our more spineless politicians, which is saying something, and he has decided to do as those anonymous notes told him."

"So he chickened out and we get Lake instead."

"I don't like the guy, but he has a decent 'fuck-you' attitude, and he's not likely to be bullied."

"Yeah, I gather he's a handful. If the newspapers are to be believed."

"Twenty years ago the guy was probably wearing a white hood and burning crosses. His current incarnation is as our nation's leading isolationist. He's free-market, anti-government, and anti-foreigner."

"A lot of people are. You think he has a real chance to be president?"

"Yes, otherwise I wouldn't be so upset." The ambassador leaned forward. "He's very smart and comes across like a nice, all-American guy. I think he's done a good job burying his true feelings and beliefs, although," Taylor smiled wryly, "there's an outside chance I'm making him sound worse than he is. Maybe he just rubs me the wrong way."

"Politicians can do that."

"Damn right. But for crying out loud, the guy has even made fun of the British. The *British*. Who doesn't like them? They've been our allies in every war, economic crisis, and trouble spot since we gave them the boot three hundred years ago."

"What's his problem with them?"

"Again, trying to be fair, I think it comes down to the monarchy, the idea that someone can be born into royalty and have all those trappings for life, no matter what."

Hugo shrugged. "He has a point."

"Maybe he does, and he's also been very critical of the class structure back home, the sons and nephews of our nation's leaders stepping into their fathers' and uncles' shoes, and not making it through their own merit."

"The more you talk, the more I like him. And he can't be such an outlier to have gotten this far."

"Maybe he's not such an outlier, is all I can think. And he has this, 'I am who I am' shtick going. Doesn't try to please everyone all of the time and seems to relish finding his foot in his mouth, just says that people need to take him at face value as a man who doesn't play the Washington games other politicians play."

"If he means it, I'll give him credit for that, too."

Taylor narrowed his eyes. "You a secret Lake supporter or something?"

"Don't know the man," Hugo said. "We can discuss after I've met him. I just know that sometimes you get a bee in your bonnet about things and people—"

"He's a hypocrite, too," Taylor interrupted, sounding a little like a pouty child.

Hugo tried not to smile but said, "Fine, I'll indulge you. Why is he a hypocrite, Mr. Ambassador?"

"Because he's just like any other politician. He has his cadre of rich backers, a half-dozen or so, who've latched onto his isolationist claptrap for their own purposes and he's happy as can be to take their money while acting like he's his own man."

"You know, it is possible to take someone's money and not be at their beck and call, to have a mind of your own."

"Not in Washington it's not."

"Maybe. But to get this far, he must have some redeeming qualities. He grow roses for old people or play with kittens a lot?"

Ambassador Taylor grimaced. "He does have a certain . . . charm, I suppose." He waved a hand. "Ah, you'll see for yourself, you can make up your own mind."

"Why thank you." Hugo frowned. "I guess my main question is, if he's such a—"

"Xenophobe?" Taylor offered.

"—*isolationist*, I was going to say. What's he doing in our fair city? What's his stake in the Guadeloupe business?"

"Trying to establish some foreign policy credentials. Other than, you know, 'screw the outside world.' People in Washington know he's on the way up so he's been given a chance to dial back his anti-Franco image and solve a massively unimportant crisis."

"I'm so glad I never went into politics," Hugo said. "I'll never understand who gets to do what, or why."

"Count yourself lucky. My guess is that as many people are waiting for him to screw it up as solve it. From here, though, it's a little hard to tell who's on whose side." The ambassador rose. "And sometimes I like it that way. Well, have fun with it, his schedule's on your desk. Excuse the footprints, and thanks for the coffee." He turned to leave but stopped at Hugo's question.

"Hang on, when's he coming in?"

"Oh, right. There's a dinner tomorrow night at a chateau just outside Paris, where the talks will be held. Fancy bash for those involved in the negotiations, you know, French foreign ministers and bureaucrats. You'll be driving him there. And dining."

Hugo raised an eyebrow. "Tomorrow?"

"Told you it was a surprise."

"You did, but how can I prepare a safe itinerary in less than a day?"

"You can't." Taylor smiled. "Remember, you're not security, you're the babysitter."

CHAPTER THREE

Several times a year, Hugo woke up between three thirty and four in the morning and knew immediately he wouldn't be going back to sleep. It was an affliction that began at his first post in London and continued ever after. He'd fought it the first few times, tossing and turning for hours only to fall out of bed at six o'clock rumpled and grumpy. For the past couple of years, though, he'd embraced it. Perhaps it was Taylor's promise of spending the next few days with a blowhard politician that did it, but the day after their meeting, Hugo woke on the dot of three thirty and knew that his night was done.

He rolled out of bed and dressed slowly, opening the large window looking over Rue Jacob to test the air. Cool and a little breezy, but the autumn hadn't swept away the summer entirely; a perfect morning for a walk.

He checked his watch as he closed the door behind him. He had a good two hours until he needed to be back, and the best bit: at least one hour before the rest of the city started waking up.

The sky was still black as he headed north toward the River Seine, alone on the quiet streets until he passed a bakery as its metal grill clattered up. The magnetic aroma of fresh bread enveloped him, a taunting siren call that he resisted by promising himself a reward on the other side of the river. He crossed the Seine on the Pont Des Arts, stopping midway to lean on the balustrade and watch the water. To his right was the facade of the Institute of France, built as a college three hundred and fifty years before and on his left sat, part of it anyway, the ever-impressive Louvre, once palace, now palatial museum.

He looked down at the water, blacker than the sky above him, running slick and fast beneath his feet. His eyes adjusted to the deeper darkness and he turned his head a fraction to watch the jumble of swirls and eddies at each bank where the current slowed, snagged and ruffled by the barges that were lashed to the impenetrable stone banks. Beneath him, movement caught his eye and he watched several heavy logs, dark brown and greasy, sweep past. Images forced themselves into his head, conjured from the darkness that was real and memories that were recent, and he shivered as he saw the human forms that this treacherous river had swallowed and spit out, the *bouquinistes* who'd been his friends, gentle men and women doing no more than selling books, posters, and postcards, making their meager living beside the river when they were targeted for death.

He shook away the image and walked on, turning his eyes to the waist-high crisscross of wire that made up the sides of this bridge, almost every strand holding onto a padlock. He didn't know when this had started but it had caught on, for locals and tourists alike. Padlocks of all description, many heart-shaped, each one with the name of a couple in love. Most were written in permanent marker but some, quite a few actually, had been professionally engraved. The idea, he'd been told, was to affix the lock and then toss the key into the water, thereby securing one's love forever. It was, Hugo thought, a charming if touristy place of semipermanent whimsy, and as he came to the end of the bridge he knelt and looked more closely at some of the locks. He smiled at the names *Natalie, Henry, Nicola*, on one side, their parents' names on the other. *English*? he wondered. *American*? Beside them, another quandary, a mix of Welsh and German: *Glynn and Elke*.

A thought bubbled up and he indulged it, wondering if he'd ever lock his name to the bridge and, if so, who'd be there with him. His first wife, yes, the love of his life who'd been killed in a car accident. She would have locked their names together and kissed the key before dropping it into the river, laughing all the while.

What about Christine? He'd married her hoping to fall in love again, wanting to, but found himself with a cultured and, it turned out, somewhat spoiled woman who was either unable or unwilling to temper her lifestyle for someone else. A woman who had replaced him with the shrink who'd taken Hugo's money to address that very issue. No, Christine would have found this bridge mildly amusing and rolled her eyes at any suggestion of a padlock for them, even for fun. She didn't do silly.

And Claudia? Hugo ran his fingers over an empty square of mesh and thought about Claudia. They'd met while he was hunting for his friend Max, the first of the *bouquinistes* to go missing, a chance encounter that had bloomed and then seemed to wither, their natural attraction and compatibility held back by . . . well, he thought, mostly by circumstances.

The gentle growl of an early morning barge reached his ear, the world starting to come alive, and he watched the long boat press its nose into the current, resolute and determined. Claudia, he thought, was fun and spontaneous, yet as a journalist she'd forged her own career and she'd been the one to pull away from Hugo just when they'd been falling . . . getting close, anyway. Being locked into anything wasn't Claudia's nature, it seemed, but on the other hand he'd seen her do silly.

Hugo stood and watched the barge pass under the bridge, aware now of a strip of misty yellow that had breached the horizon. The late-September morning making its way toward the city, and the thousand padlocks that faced the coming day seemed to glow in its soft light. Watching them, Hugo smiled to himself. The truth was, he had absolutely no idea what Claudia might think of this bridge and of the romantically naïve custom that had swarmed it.

Hugo looked at his watch and was surprised to see how long he'd spent on the bridge, recalculating his path to account for the lost time and the empty feeling in his stomach. He waited to cross the main road toward the Louvre with a new objective in mind: coffee and croissants.

As his foot hit the sidewalk, the phone in his pocket buzzed. He checked the number but didn't recognize it. He answered anyway.

"Hugo Marston."

"Marston, Charles Lake. Wasn't expecting you to answer—I'm an early bird so I hope I didn't wake you. Early bird yourself, eh?"

Lake's voice was gentler than Hugo had expected, not the harsh and angry rasp of a divisive politician.

"Sometimes, yes. How can I help?"

"Wanted to get with you to discuss the schedule. I'm not really planning on being here longer than I have to," Hugo heard a smile in the man's voice. "You've probably heard that about me. The wine's OK but the breakfasts suck, so when you're free, come by the Hotel Crillon and we can get this show on the road."

"Yes, sir, will do."

"And sooner rather than later, eh?"

"Absolutely," Hugo said. "See you in a little bit, Senator." He hung up and smiled to himself. *I like the breakfasts here, so it'll be right after coffee and croissants.*

Charles Lake was on the phone when Hugo spotted him in the lobby of the Hotel Crillon, the closest hotel to the US Embassy and one of the finest in Paris. Two dark-suited figures stood behind the seated congressman and watched Hugo approach, edging toward their charge as Hugo got closer.

He pulled out his embassy credentials and the Secret Service agents, a man and a woman, visibly relaxed.

"Mr. Marston," the woman said, checking his identification.

"Call me Hugo."

"If she doesn't, I will." Lake tucked away his phone, rose to his feet, and grinned. "And you can call me Charles. Not big on formalities."

"You'll have to rethink that if you become president," Hugo said.

"Well, until then," he said, offering his hand. "The young lady is Agent Emma Ruby, the fellow is Agent Charles Rousek."

Hugo nodded at the agents and shook hands with the congressman. Hugo appraised his new charge, trying to forget most of the things Ambassador Taylor had said. He'd seen Lake on television a few times, Hugo remembered now. Lake was over six feet, maybe an inch shorter than Hugo, and had the body of a long-retired boxer. Heavy, running to fat, he'd long ignored the advisors who'd told him voters preferred their candidates slender and fit. Rumor had it he'd slapped his belly and promised, "This is the only pork you'll see from me in Congress." Whether this story or Taylor's complaints were true or not, Hugo suspected that any reputation for speaking frankly would win him more friends off the Hill than on it. His receding hair, swept back on his skull by meaty hands rather than expensive hairdressers, served to emphasize his best features, a pair of wide-set and intelligent brown eyes and a frequent and artificially whitened smile.

"Welcome to Paris," Hugo said.

"Thanks, first time. Last, too, if it all works out."

"That'd be a shame, it's a wonderful place."

"So I've heard, but so's America and I think I like being there better. Still, the coffee's good, I just ordered some." Lake gestured to the plush seating. "Sit, join me."

"Thanks, I fueled up already. I have some questions about the schedule, though."

The two men sat while behind them the Secret Service agents walked small circles, eyes moving constantly.

"Fire away," Lake said.

"Just to confirm. Drive out to Chateau Tourville today, two nights there and two days of talks on the Guadeloupe thing, then back to Paris."

"Right. You know anything about the place, Guadeloupe?"

"I don't. The ambassador said something about pineapples."

"Columbus is supposed to have discovered them there," Lake said, "like no one in the history of the world had seen the damn things before. That man gets a lot of credit for a lot of shit, if you ask me."

So not big on Italians, either, Hugo thought. The two men sat in silence as a waiter arrived with a silver coffee pot and two cups. The aroma of fresh coffee tempted Hugo into letting the waiter pour for him. He stirred in sugar, Lake took his neat.

"Anyway," Lake continued, "Guadeloupe is tucked in amongst islands most people have actually heard of. Barbados, Martinique, Saint Lucia. Closer to Venezuela than America, but closer to us than the French. The island is its own French ... what do they call it, department?"

"Department, yes."

"Right. Along with a couple other pieces of rock right next to it, called Marie-Galante, La Désirade, and the Îles des Saintes. They are included in Guadeloupe and together have always had a chip on their shoulder."

Lake spoke with authority and Hugo was surprised. The man knew an awful lot for an anti-French isolationist, even if he'd learned it rote from a textbook.

"A chip?" Hugo prodded.

"Long history of unhappiness with mother France, some of it recent. Hence the petition to tag along with us. Puerto Rico is nearby, I guess they like the look of that deal."

"And, if I may ask, what do you care?"

"Me?" He winked at Hugo and lowered his voice. "Personally, I don't give a rat's ass. Hell, maybe it's a nice place to vacation and I could always use more of those. But professionally, politically, I care. I mean, what better way to promote democracy around the world than to have the people of an island like Guadeloupe exercise their voting power and become American?" He leaned forward. "And if we stick it to the French at the same time, even better."

"I guess I'm just surprised that people care enough to have meetings and dinners and, frankly, for you to come all the way over."

"Yeah, best I can tell it's a matter of timing. The world stage is pretty quiet, in terms of actual events grabbing headlines, but at the same time tensions are high in North America and Europe thanks to the crappy economy. Plus, as you learn early in politics, the squeaky wheel gets the grease."

"And Guadeloupe is squeaking right now."

"Like a mouse with its balls in a vise."

"Well," Hugo said, "with that image in mind, shall we head out? You can ride with me, Rousek and Ruby can follow."

"Sure thing." Lake stood. "Think they'll serve snails down there? For some reason, I've always wanted to try them. Probably just the garlic butter and bread, but still."

Hugo smiled. "I'll make a call. If they're not on the menu, I can't imagine it'd take long to catch a couple for you."

Lake chuckled and slapped Hugo on the back. "Gonna take a leak before we go." He beckoned to special agent Rousek. "Come on, Charlie, walk me to the head."

CHAPTER FOUR

The professor approached the house at dusk, following the stone path that looped from the front of the minichateau to the back, where wide green lawns fell away into darkness to the right. It was, in the way of many old French houses, a burglar's delight. Windows sat loosely in their frames and the doors were heavy but rarely locked. Owners, such as the Bassin family here, relied on remoteness and a history of safety to stave away any fear of thieves.

Too bad for them but good for me, the professor thought. Country boots, heavy but quiet, allowed a silent approach and therefore a close look into the house: a few lights on here and there but no one home, as expected. Watching a house like this wasn't easy, but a routine had quickly established itself: on Friday nights the Bassin family would pile into their Renault and take the E54 out of the countryside and into nearby Troyes for dinner. The drive was twenty-five minutes one way and the meal no doubt two hours or more, which meant more than enough time to find the object that was the sole purpose of this trip.

The professor stood on the patio, a dark shadow beside the supporting beam of a pergola carrying crisscross strands of wisteria that in May would drape purple, sweet flowers over the worn stones of the terrace. Inside the house, the drawing room was unlit but lumpy shapes of furniture were visible, silhouetted by a glow that emanated from a room deeper inside the house.

A deep breath and then a hand on the latticed glass doors that led inside, pressure downward on the handle but no movement, no give: locked. Adrenaline flushed into frustration, but there were other doors on this side of the house and, if necessary, windows. This was supposed to be a quick and easy heist and, if all went to plan, one that might go unnoticed for days or even weeks, but if a rock had to fly through a window, so be it. Too much was at stake.

The next door brought relief, an unlocked side door that led into a mudroom. It smelled damp in there, and rows of boots and shoes sat on their low wooden racks beneath pegs laden with coats. Half a dozen umbrellas poked out of a ceramic planter at the far end, mostly black, but one was half-sized and pink for the young lady of the house. Two steps led into a tiled hallway that looked to split the house—this wing of it, anyway.

The professor ventured down the passageway, confidence growing, but froze as a voice called out from the drawing room, where the lights were now on.

Why wasn't she at dinner?

Panic fought with anger, both quelled by a moment of stillness and deep breaths.

"Allo? Il y a quelqu'un?"

Retreat, thought the professor, *I can come back another time, next week or the week after.*

"Allo? Monsieur, whoever you are, I saw you outside and I'm calling the police."

Which meant no retreat. How to explain the car tucked behind a hedgerow, a blatant if weak attempt to be surreptitious, let alone the nighttime entry?

One chance, perhaps: bluff.

"C'est moi," the professor said, stepping into the large room, hands extended to the side and a smile to show no threat. "It's just me."

"Who are you?" Collette Bassin seemed more puzzled than afraid, but she held a cell phone in her hand. "Why are you in my house?"

"You don't remember me?"

"No." The woman's eyes flickered down. "Why are you wearing gloves?"

"It's cold outside. I get cold easily." *And I'm losing control of the situation.* Calmly, the gloves came off, tucked into a back pocket, a gesture of friendliness and trust.

But the old woman shook her head. *"Non,* it's not cold at all." Her eyes moved back up to the intruder and she began to raise the phone.

"Non, please, you don't need to call the police!" The professor started forward. "I was here a month or two ago, we talked about your family, don't you remember?"

"I talked to a young lady, not to you. About my family, she was asking questions."

"Oui, c'est vrai, but she's ... Madam, I was here too, in the other room talking to your daughter, and we *did* meet."

They were four feet apart now and the professor could see the suspicion, the disbelief on the old woman's face and the fear that lingered in her eyes.

"I don't remember that, I don't remember you." She looked at the phone and pressed a button to bring it to life. "The police. When they come we can settle this."

"No!" The professor stepped forward and reached for the phone, intending just to diffuse the immediate danger, take away the phone and talk, but the old woman let out a cry and stepped back. She stumbled and twisted her body to stop herself from falling.

"Don't hurt me, please." She fumbled with the phone, crabbing sideways between tables and over-stuffed chairs, legs weakened with fear taking her away, but too slowly, from the thief in her home. The intruder's own fear kaleidoscoped, splintering into flashes of frustration, desperation, and anger, all coalescing in the time it took to grab hold of a thin vase in a teeth-gritting resolve to finish the job, to break away from the transfixing glow of the phone and the danger it represented. Reputation, honor, profession, all flickered within that rectangle of light, and all would disappear if this old woman called for help.

The vase swung down, aimed at the phone but catching the woman on the wrist and the room echoed with a loud crack that came from more than just the china breaking. The phone dropped to the floor and the old woman grabbed her arm and turned deathly pale. She began to wail, fear and pain combining into a high-pitched sound that wouldn't stop, even when she sank to her knees.

"I'm sorry, please, be quiet, I'm sorry." But the line had been crossed and no clever invention or story would undo this, and the horror of the future that was itself shattering elevated one emotion above all others, and the fear that burned through veins like acid suddenly froze into a cold and sharp drive for self-preservation.

The cushion was blue and rough, a rectangle half the size of a pillow, and it fit over the woman's face as though it had been designed for this purpose. Thin arms flailed as Madam Bassin's brain screamed for air and began to shut down, the professor's weight more than a match for her struggles and the soft cushion that starved her of life also muffled the sounds of her killer's voice, a whispered and mildly regretful chant of, "You weren't supposed to be here, you weren't supposed to be here . . ."

Ninety years old and weak, weak enough that it didn't take long before she bucked twice and was still. So quick that, much later, the professor would find comfort in the idea that there was no premeditation, that it was a reflex action just to hush the old lady and that death came because of her age and frailty, not because of murder.

The small chest was where Collette Bassin had said it would be, a throwaway story told months ago, tucked into the back of a huge wardrobe in the old lady's bedroom. Seeing it was like a charge of electricity and the professor pulled it out carefully, kneeling beside the strongbox to admire it. Made from walnut, it was square and no more than two feet every which way. Solid, though, made by a true craftsman and held together with hinges and handles made of brass, as were the inlaid strips and swirls that decorated it. The metal was dark with age and this chest had been harshly treated at some point, but an experienced eye could recognize it as a more ornate piece than the plain sailor's chests of old.

Getting it down the stairs was a slow but simple task and it was halfway down that the professor stopped and swore.

"*Merde, les gants.*"

They were still tucked deep in a back pocket but, once they were back on, a dish towel grabbed from the kitchen sufficed to wipe down the wardrobe, and then the area around the body. The heavy boots took care of the vase, crushing it into pieces too small to render evidence.

A quick time check, and a pang of guilt; theft and death had taken longer than planned so the professor retreated back out through the mud room and, the chest weighing more with each step, a stumbling run down the gravel driveway to the car, pathetically camouflaged and suspicious-looking rather than hidden. Especially after what had just happened.

CHAPTER FIVE

Hugo drove and Senator Lake rode in the front seat beside him. "I'm an egalitarian, don't expect me to sit in the back."

Hugo smiled. "You do that in taxis, too?"

"Tried it a few times, actually." Lake shook his head and laughed. "Just scared the driver, turns out they're not used to it. Plus, no offense, but a lot of cabbies smell a little funky, with their pots of weird food next to them." He saw Hugo shoot him a look. "Oh, I get it, you think I'm a racist. God forbid I don't like the smell of Indian food."

"I didn't say that, not at all."

"Look, Hugo, I'm a regular Joe who happens to be a senator. That's *why* I'm a senator, because people are sick of electing the same family name decade after decade. They want one of them, a blue-collar guy with no pretensions." He laughed gently. "No pretensions, but I can get defensive, sorry. The lecture's over."

They headed west out of the city center, swaying in and out of the busy traffic with an identical black vehicle close behind them, two agents glad of a break, Hugo thought. They crossed over the Boulevard Périphérique, the road that marked the boundary between the city center and the suburbs, and one of the busiest thoroughfares in Europe. Hugo didn't drive often in Paris, there was no need, but when he did he hated this road with its endless loop of fume-spitting traffic, the four lanes bordered by concrete rather than shoulders so that the inevitable accidents always tied up traffic for hours.

They stayed on it for less than two miles before peeling onto a quieter road toward their final destination a hundred kilometers away, Chateau Tourville. Lake was quiet, watching out of his window as villages rose out of the countryside and disappeared as fast, low stone houses connected by one or two winding streets that led out into the flat fields of northern France. Overhead, gray clouds gathered and filtered the sunlight into an eerie yellow.

After a while, Lake grunted. "Pretty countryside isn't it?"

"Absolutely."

"I do like these old stone buildings, amazing how long they've stood. Hundreds of years, I'd bet, through use, war, and the weather." He sounded almost wistful and Hugo was surprised to hear him express such appreciation. It didn't last long, as if Lake had surprised himself. "Be prettier if the weather wasn't so bad. Rains pretty much all year, I'm told."

"A slight exaggeration," Hugo said. He felt Lake watching him now.

"Look. I know what people say about me, the whole isolationist thing. And I play that up to some degree because a lot of people in my district like it, they believe in that. And I do, too, but for slightly different reasons. I'm not a xenophobe, Hugo. I don't hate the French or the Germans."

"The English?"

"Nor them. The royalty thing disgusts me, but that's another subject. The point I'm trying to make is this: I'm an American. I even have native blood, or so my grandmother told me, but it's not just about that. I love America and I'm sick of policing the rest of the world, saving Europe from the Nazis, Iraq from a lunatic. What is it now, Iran? North Korea? I'm just saying, enough is enough. We do all that and what thanks do we get?"

"Not my bailiwick, so I wouldn't know."

"None, Hugo. Instead we get scorn. And we get fleeced because it's our troops who get sent in first. So all I'm saying, let's just make the most of being American and let the rest of the damn world fend for itself for once. Let them have inbred Royal families and eat snails. Go for it. Just keep it to themselves."

"And your constituents, you have this discussion with them?"

"Like I said, most are more anti-Europe than I am. And not just anti-Europe, but anti-privilege, and I'm one hundred percent on board there." Out of the corner of his eye, Hugo could see the man was annoyed. "And this discussion is between you and me. The people who support me, with votes and money, are perfectly happy to malign Europe, and since our interests are one and the same, the nuances of my position are irrelevant. And potentially damaging. Do I make myself clear?"

"Just between us," Hugo said mildly. "But when you say, 'people who support me,' do you mean the big donors or the small ones?"

Lake smiled. "Here's how it works. The big ones follow the lead of the small ones. I piss off my blue-collar base, the heavy wallets leave, too. Double whammy, you might say. Ugly game, isn't it?"

"Sounds like it," Hugo said. "Glad I'm not playing."

"Right." Lake took a breath, as if to calm himself. "So you're former FBI, right? Into all that profiling business?"

"I did some of that, yes."

"Interesting. You have some pretty high-tech surveillance equipment, too, for that antiterrorist work."

"We do."

"Got my hands on some, it's amazing."

Hugo glanced over. "Why would a senator need surveillance equipment, if I may ask?"

Lake chortled. "Are you kidding? Some is because I like playing with it, some to make sure no one stabs me in the back."

"I don't follow."

"People come into my office and we talk. Then they leave my office and misquote me, misrepresent my position." He shrugged. "I got sick of that happening."

"You bug your own office?"

"Heavens no. I just record the conversations I have with people, to protect myself."

"Phones, too?"

"Of course. I'm not stupid, I know there are people out there trying to trip me up. The closer you get to the top, the more that happens, believe me." He looked out of the window. "This way I'm covered. Safe."

They drove in silence for a moment, then Lake turned to Hugo. "So, did you profile the people meeting us for dinner? Any psychos?"

Hugo raised an eyebrow. "A few politicians, if that answers your question."

"Funny guy, Hugo, but yeah, it does. Seriously, I don't know much about the people there, do you?"

"Not really." Hugo tried to recall the brief that his secretary Emma had given him. It was tucked in his overnight bag, but Emma had included insight as well as facts, which meant it was for Hugo's eyes only. He recited the bits he could remember, the facts anyway. "The chateau is owned by Henri Tourville, been in his family for years. Centuries probably. He's high up in the MAEE, roughly translated as the Ministry of Foreign and European Affairs."

"That guy I know. Spoke to him on the phone when I took Jonty Railton's place, asked whether I preferred brandy or port. Felt it was like some kind of test."

"It probably was."

"You think?" Lake grimaced. "Anyway, he said his drinking buddy would be there, Felix or Victor someone."

"Felix Vibert. I don't have my ministers and undersecretaries straight, but I gather he's the brains behind the political power Tourville wields. They met while teaching at the Sorbonne—Tourville is a history buff and Vibert was a bigwig in international relations." Hugo glanced across. "No offense, but shouldn't you know who you're dealing with?"

"On the one hand, you'd think so. On the other hand, it's a dinner party with, what, twenty people? Maybe thirty? And we're talking about a pile of rocks in the Caribbean that you, as a member of the voting public, don't seem to care about. I'm pretty good with people,

Hugo, despite what you may have heard about me, and as far as personalities go, I'm confident I can wing it a little." He paused and his tone changed. "Although I have heard a little about Tourville's sister."

"Ah yes." said Hugo. "Although I imagine she's been misrepresented." Emma had briefed him on the sister, too, in a way that tiptoed the line between informing and gossiping. She knew that Hugo disdained the latter, believing that salacious tattle, particularly among the upper echelons of society, was usually exaggerated if not completely wrong. And if factually correct, it was no one's business anyway.

"Turned her life around, do you think?" Lake said—a little sarcastically, Hugo thought.

"You can ask her when we get there."

"Oh, come on, Hugo. In a room full of stuffed shirts, myself included, she could be the most interesting person there. She off limits to your intelligence briefing? Since you're there to protect me, I doubt it."

Babysit, thought Hugo. "My brief relates to security, I think, not so much sexual trysts."

"More's the pity."

And not entirely true. Hugo had wanted to know the background of everyone there and Emma hadn't been able to resist some of the more scandalous details, delivered with a knowing smile and entirely designed to provoke Hugo into self-righteousness.

The sister, Alexandra Catherine de Beaumont Tourville, or Alexie to her friends, had long been the black sheep of the Tourville family. Booted from several boarding schools for her antics, she managed to make her way to university where she found her niche, using her high intelligence to breeze through several degree programs and develop her liberal instincts.

When she'd finally racked up enough diplomas, she used them and her father's money to try numerous careers, skating between the entertainment world and the political. Hugo suspected, from what he'd read and heard, that she may have some minor mental or emotional issues, becoming focused on a project or person to the exclusion of pretty much everything else. Greenpeace, saving the whales, the death penalty in America, and legalizing LSD and marijuana were the ones Hugo could remember. If Emma was right, she'd used up pretty much all of her inheritance chasing world peace and harmony, and a few magical dragons to boot. An internationally successful blog, mostly kept up by one or two people close to her, kept her name in the news whenever she upset a political apple cart or blew into an awards ceremony.

Two years ago, the gallivanting around the globe had come to an end in a blaze of humiliating publicity. She'd returned to France to live full time, reformed her blog to discuss the more serious issues of the day, and eschewed the party circuit. She then launched a serious and expensive campaign to win a seat in the National Assembly, France's lower house of Parliament, using her family's name and reputation at every turn and relying heavily on the electorate's short memory, libertine instincts, and forgiving nature.

Her reliance had been misplaced. A sex scandal too rich even for the French had undone her credibility and sent her financial backers scattering for cover. Lake was obviously recalling the details and pondering her fate, too.

"You know, I'm surprised she'll be there. I'd heard she was off at a convent or something."

"Like I said," Hugo said mildly, "you can ask her over dinner."

Dinner was at eight but everyone gathered for drinks soon after six, when two waitresses carried around trays of champagne, hors d'oeuvres, and then more champagne. The drawing room was as elegant as it was large, and Hugo suspected that most of the furniture had been there longer than he'd been alive; it was the kind of house where antiques and art settled into place, where their beauty and value was appreciated as a whole such that occasional additions or removals by chateau's owners went all but unnoticed by family members and staff, unless a table had been swapped for a vase when someone wanted to put down his cognac. The living room was bright, though, the antiques polished, and its two sets of French doors and several large windows let in the low evening light, while the wall sconces added their sparkle and glow.

There were about two dozen guests, all approved by Ruby and Rousek, but only half of them were of interest to Hugo because only half of them would spend the following day talking international politics. The others, well-dressed and no doubt well-heeled, were Tourville's fillers brought in to make sure the main players had people to talk to, drink with, and didn't rattle around the old chateau unamused.

Hugo tucked himself in the corner, wedged between a bookcase and a curtained window, watching the evening unfold with interest because it had been a while since he'd attended a function like this, wary political opponents playing nice as they slowly got drunk. The Guadeloupe Islands were on the agenda for tomorrow, this was just the ice-breaker, but Hugo suspected that the important people in this room had been too long in the game to not play some of their cards tonight, so he watched their interactions closely.

Henri Tourville was the easiest to spot and didn't look unlike his American guest. Taller and heavier, though, with the kind of figure you'd expect from a wealthy man who enjoyed throwing dinner parties and whose only exercise came from wandering his estate with a shotgun in the crook of his arm. His size seemed to be magnified by a large and very bald head. He smiled a lot and was an expert host, moving around the room like a ship broken from its moorings, bumping elbows with this couple for a minute or two before drifting past a chintz-covered sofa to find himself nestled into a different couple for a few minutes more.

Also there, as expected, was Felix Vibert, who was a little shorter than his friend Tourville and considerably paler, but with the same soft figure. Hugo had the impression that the unlit pipe in his hand, the moustache, and the eyeglasses were welcome barriers to strangers, and it was clear that Vibert became more comfortable the closer he found himself to his friend and host. His interactions with others, as best Hugo could tell, consisted of listening rather than talking, his face set in an unreadable mask. Occasionally, he'd eye the crowd, keeping track of his and his friend's personal secretaries, elegant middle-aged women who could take shorthand or serve drinks as required.

Lake's interest, unsurprisingly, was in Alexandra. In many ways, she was the exact opposite of her brother. She had his height, not too far from six feet tall, but was slender and wore a slightly closed look on her face, though that could have resulted from Lake's attentions. She had thick brown hair pulled into a broad ponytail held with a glittering clip. Elegant in a burgundy-colored dress, she seemed to attract a lot of glances from the men in the room, though Hugo had the sense she wasn't trying to.

Hugo turned as a figure appeared at his elbow: a woman in her late twenties, a sharp nose and even sharper brown eyes. He'd seen her at Alexandra's side earlier, the less glamorous assistant—but up close she had a certain confidence of her own, which always appealed to Hugo. Her dress was black, neither sexy nor dowdy, and her short brown hair was loose and sported a streak of pink that should have been too young for her, but wasn't.

"*Bonsoir*, monsieur. I'm Natalia Khlapina."

"*Bonsoir*." Hugo extended a hand and they shook. "Hugo Marston."

She switched to English, her accent light. "Can I get you a drink?"

"Maybe in a little bit, for now I'm fine just—"

"People watching?"

"Yes."

"Paris has always been good for that." She eyed the people in the room, too, then looked up at him. "If you change your mind, let me know."

She started to move off and Hugo suddenly thought he'd been rude. Or maybe he just wanted to talk. "You're Russian?"

"From Saint Petersburg. Ever been there?"

"Once. I'd like to go back."

She laughed gently. "As I tell people, it's a great place to visit, but I wouldn't want to live there."

"No?"

"No. Too dark, too cold, and the politics are to die for. Literally. And look around, look where I live now, why would I want to go back?"

"For the snow and vodka?"

She shook her head. "I prefer champagne and sunshine. And working with Alexie, I get plenty of both."

"What exactly does she do? What do you do?"

Natalia watched him for a moment, appraising. "You know about her history?"

"I know what people have told me. I don't know how much is true."

"It doesn't matter at this point. What's done is done and what people say, well, no one can control what stories go around or what people choose to believe."

"That's true."

"We met at the university in Saint Petersburg. She was a guest lecturer, I was a PhD student in history. She ended up staying the whole semester, partly laying low, and we worked together on a couple of papers. When it was time for her to leave she asked me to come with her."

"I see."

She smiled, almost a tease. "You are wondering if we were lovers?"

"Not really, no," Hugo said. "None of my business."

"You think that stops people asking?" She looked away and frowned. "Men, mostly."

"We are pigs, no doubt. So are you working now?"

"Yes. We have started a small business doing genealogical research. Family trees. We just got back from America, where people are obsessed with where their ancestors came from."

"I've noticed."

"Yes? I don't understand it. It's as if people don't have an identity of their own, or as if it's not enough. I've been there several times and whenever I meet someone they inevitably tell me they are English, or Irish, or German, even though they, their parents, and their grandparents were born in the United States. Even your senator, his website says he's part Native American. Why does all that matter to people so much?"

"America is a land of immigrants, I think it's natural to wonder where your family originated from."

"What about you? Where's your family from?"

Hugo smiled. "Texas. Austin, Texas, if you want to get specific. As far back as I know."

"And how far back is that?"

"My great-grandparents."

"For a few hundred Euros I can take you further back than that."

Hugo still couldn't tell if she was flirting with him, he'd been too long out of the game. "Thanks. If I feel the need, I'll call you."

"You should." From nowhere she produced a business card and pressed it into his hand. "My number's on there. You might find it interesting."

They stood in silence, watching the gentle ebb and flow of the room, everyone in there experienced at the art of small talk and momentary seduction. Glasses clinked and the hum of chatter never rose too high, apart from the occasional peal of laughter. With the yellow light and gold drapes, with the classic furniture and formal attire, Hugo thought of old-time movies, and this one he watched with his companion from the anonymity of their corner, a front row seat.

Right now, they were both watching Charles Lake deep in conversation with Alexandra Tourville. He could tell from Lake's body language that he was enjoying himself, but his companion was harder to read.

"Does she need rescuing?" Hugo asked quietly.

"I doubt it. She's pretty good at taking care of herself."

There was a note of . . . *something* in her voice that made Hugo wonder. But it could have been admiration, envy, or even bitterness, so he didn't ask.

"Time for that glass of champagne," Hugo said. "And maybe you can introduce me to your boss, whether she needs an intervention or not."

CHAPTER SIX

Senator Lake raised a glass as Hugo and Natalia approached. "Here come our invaluable assistants. Hugo, have you met Alexandra Tourville?"

They shook hands, and once again Hugo had the feeling of being appraised. Peas in a pod, this woman and her Russian aide.

"Please, call me Alexie. Everyone does."

"Thank you, I'm Hugo, nice to meet you."

She nodded and clinked glasses with him. "Welcome to my home, or should I say my brother's home? I don't get it until he shoots himself or gets savaged by a wild boar."

Natalia touched her arm and smiled. "Seriously, you need to stop saying that, someone will think you mean it."

"Don't be silly. I'm told it's very hard to shoot yourself with a shotgun, and I believe wild boars are vegetarian."

"Actually, I think they are omnivores," Hugo said. "But I'm pretty sure they'd leave your brother well alone, he'd be a little too much of a feast."

"You're a hunter?"

"He hunts bad guys," Lake said. "Or used to. FBI—for how long, Hugo?"

"A long time," Hugo smiled. "Now life's a little more sedate."

"No longer collect scalps?" Alexie asked.

"Not sure I ever did. But no, nowadays if I collect anything, it's books."

She turned toward him, more interested now. "Oh really? Like what? Which authors do you like?"

"I have focused on French authors, actually," Hugo said. "I have some first editions of Camus, Sartre, and the pride of my collection is a signed first edition of *Le Petit Prince.*"

"Signed by Saint-Exupéry?" Lake asked. "How does a public servant afford that? I'm guessing it cost a pretty penny."

"Yep, it's a 1943 true first edition, with his signature. But don't worry senator, your tax money is safe, I didn't pay for it. It was a gift from a friend with far greater resources than mine." From Claudia, actually, to mark her gratitude at the conclusion of the bouquiniste investigation. Not only had he saved her life, but he'd done her father's name and reputation a great deal of good. The book had come from his collection, and Hugo had been deeply moved when she presented it to him, Claudia herself giving in to a few tears. It had been a wonderful moment between them, each trying to express their thanks while waving away the other's. As so often between them, seriousness had turned into laughter and pretty soon they'd shed their clothes and were competing to express their gratitude in other ways.

"Who else do you like?" Alexie asked.

"Well, he's not French, but he died in Paris."

"Oscar Wilde?" Lake said.

"Two out of two, Senator, I'm impressed," Hugo smiled.

"Don't be, my first job was teaching high school English. Did that while getting my masters so I could teach political science at college level."

"I like Wilde, too," Alexie said. "Not just his wit, but can you imagine being jailed for being homosexual? Poor man, and such a waste of his talent. How old was he when he died?"

"Forty-six, I think," said Hugo. "And I agree, a terrible waste of talent."

The specter of a reputation ruined by sexual indiscretion flitted amongst them, taking shape as Alexie held Hugo's eye and said, "'A kiss may ruin a human life.'"

"What's that mean?" Lake said, looking from one to the other as if he didn't like to be left out.

"It's a quotation from a Wilde play," said Hugo. "*A Woman of No Importance*. Said by Mrs. Arbuthnot, a respectable woman with a secret past."

"I see," Lake said, and Hugo thought he colored a little at the obvious parallel.

But confronting the specter had driven it away, though not too far, because there was a shadow to Alexie's voice as she said, "Perhaps one day you will have a signed first edition of my book. I'm writing a mystery novel."

"You are?" Hugo asked. "Do tell."

"It's part mystery and part magic realism. A lowbrow mix of Fred Vargas and Garcia-Marquez."

Natalia rolled her eyes. "It's not lowbrow at all. Sexy and smart, I'd say. It's wonderful. Really wonderful."

"Can we read it?" Lake asked.

"Not yet. Not until it's finished, and maybe not even then." She held up a finger to silence Natalia. "And despite what my wonderful assistant was about to say, it's not there yet."

"They say there's a novel in everyone," Lake chimed in. "Not me. I prefer to live in the real world."

Alexie cocked her head. "Meaning?"

"No offense," Lake said, "but novelists, artists, tend to be a little wrapped up in their own heads. Which is fine, I'm not saying otherwise. I just prefer to get things done in the real world."

"So, as a politician you wouldn't support the arts with public money?" Hugo asked, genuinely curious.

"God, no. I'd let rich people like the Tourvilles do it." It was meant as a joke, but no one in their little group was smiling. His tone changed, defensive now. "Look, I'm struggling with how to say this. I've lived an interesting life, and not an easy one. I've worked hard to get where I am and I have never had the time to sit in my garret and craft pretty prose."

"Whereas I," Alexie said, "had everything handed to me on a plate and so can sit in my garret all I like."

Lake tried to be garrulous again. "We've all led different lives and had different opportunities. You've been luckier than most, there's nothing wrong with that." He shrugged. "I guess I don't like the idea that writers shed some sort of revealing light on humanity because as far as I know, none of them have experienced what I have."

"You have nothing to learn from them?" Alexie said. "Even assuming what you say is true, that they can't show you anything about yourself, maybe you can learn something about the mass of humanity that isn't you."

"I doubt it. I have town hall meetings, office visits, and elections for that. What the hell can some stuck-up author in a tweed jacket and pipe tell me that my constituents can't?"

"Well," Alexie said with a smile, "that assumes you listen to them, of course."

Lake bristled. "In America, a politician would do well to listen to the people who elected him. I'm well aware of your aristocratic ways here, your history of kings and earls and whatnot. And I'm well aware that you good people fared well in that system. But I prefer ours, where a man like me can work his way up from the middle of nowhere and the edge of nothing, and be a member of congress. That's a system that deserves respect."

Hugo and Natalie exchanged amused looks but the tension was rising.

"So a man is only worthy if he comes from nothing and works his way up?" Alexie asked.

"I didn't say that. I'm saying a system that rewards hard work and merit, rather than hand-me-downs and patronage is a better, fairer system of government."

"And that's how you got your position?" Alexie pressed. "Through hard work and merit, not through a few rich people deciding you were electable and throwing money your way?"

Lake lifted his hands, a partial surrender. "I'm not saying our system is perfect. Far from it. Perhaps there's too much money in the hands of too few people, but what's the alternative? Socialism?"

"What if those few people, your rich friends, suddenly decided they didn't like you any more, Monsieur Lake?" Alexie asked. "What would happen if they decided to take away their financial support?"

"Why would they suddenly not like me?" He looked wary now and Hugo felt the ghost of Alexie's past sweep around them again. She knew what it was like to be respected and appreciated, and then abandoned.

"Who knows?" She smiled suddenly, as if that would dispel the ghost. "I can promise you that people are far more invested in their own reputation than they are yours, and they are quick to believe the very worst. What's true, or what's right and what's wrong, well, they play a very secondary role. I've seen that myself, haven't I?"

Lake shifted uncomfortably but was saved from responding when movement from the far end of the room indicated a shift toward the dining room.

"Good," said Lake, "I'm famished."

They shuffled into the large room that was served by a fireplace at each end and was dominated by a long, teak table that flowered with crystal and colorful china. Hugo was supposed to sit between Felix Vibert and Natalia, with Lake on the other side of the Russian woman. Hugo delayed sitting down, though, knowing that French meals could be drawn-out affairs that would make his legs twitchy. He spent a moment admiring two antiques on the side table behind his seat. One was a Chinese porcelain moon vase, depicting a battle between grinning warriors, the effect enhanced by the pinks and yellows that adorned those fighting on the outside of the vase.

Felix Vibert joined him as he was running his fingers over the second piece.

"An old sailor's chest," Vibert said.

"I was wondering." It was slightly smaller than a case of wine, its wood burled and shining, the smell of polish faint but distinctive.

"Lots of them around, very fashionable a hundred years ago. Two hundred, maybe." Vibert was tipsy, his words just starting to run into each other. "Sailors had sturdy ones, but those who could afford it had them specially made."

"Why? It's just a box."

Vibert guffawed. "Just a box. I suppose some might have been, but many weren't. They were specially made with secret compartments so that wandering fingers didn't take the sailor's valuables. When the middle classes and then the upper classes got wind of these ingenious little boxes, they designed their own or had craftsmen do it. They'd show them off to their friends, secret bottoms and hollow tops, hidden latches and levers." Vibert waved a hand. "Although once you've shown off how clever yours is, it's not much use for hiding things."

"I suppose not. Is this one old?"

"Looks to be," Vibert said, "but I couldn't really say. I'm no antiques expert and I've not seen this one here before. I can also ask my assistant, Katrina, she knows more about that sort of thing."

Hugo felt a hand on his elbow and turned. Alexie pressed a glass of champagne into his hand and smiled. "Sit, but take this with you. I gave one to the senator, you may need them." She drifted away and took her place at the far end of the table from her brother.

Hugo took his seat and Lake leaned back, behind Natalia. "I see you got more champagne, too. She said Henri Tourville sometimes likes to make speeches before dinner." He rolled his eyes, then nodded at the place setting in front of him. "Maybe I should ask her to bring us a couple more."

It was halfway through the meal when Hugo noticed Natalia shift her chair back a little and toward him. Hugo shot her a quick glance and she indicated with her head, a subtle nod toward the senator.

His face was red and his eyes glassy, a sheen of sweat on his forehead. Hugo checked and saw that both glasses of champagne had been taken away, which no doubt meant he'd emptied them. A full glass of red wine sat in front of him but Hugo had been to these dinners before and had never seen a glass remain empty for more than three or four seconds.

Hugo looked around for the two secret service agents, then

remembered he'd excused them himself. It was evening and he was, after all, the babysitter. The senator was making conversation with an elderly woman to his right who, by the looks of it, was one sheet to the wind beyond even Lake. Their heads lolled as they talked and Hugo half expected a crack of foreheads.

"I hate flying too," Lake was saying. "Now the old ships, they're the ones. The *QE2*, even the *Titanic*. Very romantic, and so much safer than being in a tin can thousands of feet in the air. That has to be the definition of insanity."

"But what—" the woman hiccupped and giggled, "but what if the boat sinks?"

"A watery grave is itself very romantic. Better than many endings people have, including a fiery plane crash."

The pair nodded wildly at each other, and Hugo returned his attentions to Natalia. After a few moments of polite conversation with her, he noticed Lake sit straight up in his chair and stare down at his plate. The senator turned to Hugo and said, "I don't feel so great. Think it's something I ate, maybe the food's too rich."

"Maybe," Hugo said. Or maybe a long flight and too much silky champagne. "Can you make it through dessert?"

"Depends on how many courses until we get there."

Hugo checked the rows of silverware left in front of him. "Two at least. Something and then cheese. Then dessert."

The senator paled. "Then no. I think I need a bathroom."

Natalia pretended to be listening to the conversation across the table as Hugo stood and beckoned for Lake to follow him. They moved quickly to Henri Tourville, who looked up in surprise. The chatter around them lurched for just a moment but picked up again, politeness trumping curiosity. For now, anyway.

"*Ça va?*" Tourville asked.

"A long flight and maybe a glass too many," Hugo said quietly. No shame there, not in France.

"The food," Lake mumbled behind him, "too rich, something didn't agree . . ."

"*Bien sûr,*" Tourville nodded, concern on his face, "I will have someone bring tea, that should help."

"Thank you," said Hugo, "I'll see the senator to his room and be back in a few minutes. Excuse us."

Hugo held the senator's elbow and steered him to the first set of stairs.

"Why did you tell him I was drunk?" he muttered. "I'm not, it was the food."

"In France, you get points for consuming your host's wine but lose them rapidly if you insult his food. I thought we could use the points."

"I had three glasses of champagne and didn't touch the wine," Lake insisted. "Maybe four glasses."

His words were slurring together and Hugo didn't plan to start a debate. "OK, we'll get you to your room, see how you feel. You want a doctor?"

"I'm sick, not dying. I just want to lie down."

A few minutes later Senator Lake was sitting on his bed, head between his knees. Hugo roused him and helped him undress to his underwear, then steered him into the bathroom and waited until he returned, taking a wobbly line back to the bed. He slid his bulk between the sheets with a sigh of deep pleasure. As his eyes closed, Hugo discreetly checked his pulse: slow, but still pumping.

He let himself out of the room and saw a maid walking toward them with a mug of tea on a tray.

"*Merci, mademoiselle,* but he's sleeping. He won't need that. Perhaps in the morning."

"*Oui, monsieur, d'accord.*" She did an about-turn and started back down the hallway.

Hugo considered his options, tempted by a few quiet moments on his bed, a book in his hand . . . Then he gathered himself. His charge may be out cold, but Hugo was still on the clock, which meant another hour or two of small talk but maybe, just maybe, a good glass of his favorite wine of all: port.

CHAPTER SEVEN

A loud banging on his door woke Hugo at seven the next morning. He fell out of bed and went to the door. He opened it to find Lake standing there, wrapped in a dark blue robe, his feet bare. His hair was mussed and his eyes were blood-shot.

"We need to talk," the senator said.

"Sure." Hugo opened the door and stood to one side. "How are you feeling?"

"Fine. Well, a little shaky but I slept it off." He looked at Hugo. "I don't remember going to bed, which sometimes means I made an ass of myself. That happen?"

"No, sir. Jet lag followed by a glass or too more than you should have, but your exit was moderately surreptitious and reasonably graceful."

"Good. Did you come check on me in the night?"

"No," said Hugo. "You were fine when I left you and once we finished downstairs I pretty much crashed myself."

"I see." He hesitated, then said, "Look, don't think I'm crazy but . . . I think someone was in my room last night."

Hugo looked at him but said nothing.

"I'm serious. I'll be honest, Hugo, I think I was drugged, not drunk, and someone came into my room."

"OK, but why would someone . . ."

"To look through my stuff. Papers. Maybe get a head start on the negotiations. Look, I didn't drink all that much, and I can hold my liquor when I do." He sank into an armchair by the window. "And I'm telling you, whether I was drugged or drunk, someone was in my room."

"Could you see who? Man, woman, young . . ."

"No. It's not even like I saw the person clearly." He ran a hand over his face. "It wasn't a dream. I know what you're thinking, but it was like . . ."

"A dream."

"Kind of." Lake sank back and stared at Hugo. "Yes, but no. I mean that. It wasn't a dream."

"Could it have been a maid?"

"Whoever it was, I felt them leaning over me, touching my face."

"I'm guessing it was a maid, one of the staff checking on you. Perhaps Tourville sent a doctor up." *Although he'd not seemed worried, Hugo thought, making jokes at Lake's expense for the remainder of the evening.*

"They should have locks on these doors."

Hugo laughed gently. "They probably did at one point. Keys go missing over a hundred years or so."

Lake grunted. "I'm not happy about this, Hugo."

"Were any of your bags opened? Anything tampered with?"

"Not that I could tell, but that doesn't mean anything. If they're smart enough to knock me out they're smart enough to crack a stupid lock on a briefcase."

"That might qualify as a breach of security, yes. I'll talk to Tourville, see if he sent someone upstairs to check on you. That's my bet."

"And if he didn't?"

"Then we'll take it from there," Hugo said. "If you want to shower up and head to breakfast, I'll meet you downstairs."

Lake pushed himself out of the armchair and shuffled to the door. "Talk to him as soon as you can, if you don't mind. I'll try not to touch anything except my clothes in case we need to dust the room for prints."

Or swab it for DNA, maybe get bloodhounds in, Hugo thought. But he was relieved Lake was letting him take the lead because on the morning of potentially delicate negotiations, one side didn't need to be hurling accusations of malfeasance at the other before the pencils were sharpened.

Hugo caught Henri Tourville in the main hall as he was heading out of the door with two black Labradors tugging at their leashes, and therefore him.

"*Bonjour*, Monsieur Tourville, do you have a moment?"

"*Bonjour*. That depends on these two, I would say a little less than a minute."

"Then I'll walk with you, if that's OK."

"Of course. I normally let them have the run of the house, but since we have so many esteemed guests I thought I'd take them out to the field and let them blow off steam."

The two men walked down the steps in front of the chateau and angled left, across the gravel driveway and the lawn to a wooden fence, beyond which a dozen cows grazed, heads down and paying no mind to their approach. Hugo wondered whether that would change once the dogs joined them. A large drop of rain hit the end of Hugo's nose and he looked up to see heavy gray clouds filling the sky.

"It's supposed to come and go all day." Tourville unclipped the leashes and the dogs slid under the fence and sprinted away into the field. "How is Monsieur Lake, have you seen him this morning?"

"I have, that's what I wanted to talk to you about."

Tourville held up a hand. "If you plan to apologize, please don't. A long trip from America, wine, heavy food . . . It could happen to anyone."

"You are kind, thank you." Hugo paused. "Tell me, did you have anyone check on him during the night?"

"Check on him?"

"Yes. Did you have anyone go to his room? Make sure he was alright."

Hugo tried to keep his voice casual but Tourville was looking at him with a frown on his face.

"No. Are you saying I should have?"

"*Non,* monsieur, not at all."

"Then why the question?"

"I'm sure it's nothing, but Monsieur Lake told me this morning he thought maybe someone had come into his room during the night."

When Tourville just stared at him, Hugo continued. "I told him it was probably a dream, he imagined it somehow."

"In his state, that seems almost certain."

"Agreed, absolutely. It's just that, he's insisting someone was in there, leaning over him."

Both men turned as the sound of footsteps on gravel reached them. They watched in silence as Lake strode toward them.

"You told him?" Lake asked Hugo, approaching at full steam.

"We were discussing the matter, yes," said Hugo.

"There is nothing to discuss," said Tourville, his tone clipped. "No one in my household would enter the room of a guest at night, it's out of the question."

"I don't mean to accuse anyone," Lake said, "or insult you. But unless you stood guard at my door all night, you can't possibly give me that assurance. And," he turned to Hugo, "I was wrong about my things. Last night my briefcase was propped between the bed and the side table. This morning it was lying flat on the floor."

Tourville snorted. "Senator Lake, given that you . . . how you were feeling last night, I don't see how you can be sure exactly where your case was."

"I put it there before dinner. I remember that, and I'm guessing that I got into the bed from the other side last night."

"Guessing?" Tourville looked as though laughter might take over from outrage, and Hugo suspected that would be even worse.

"Actually, that's right," Hugo said. "I helped you into bed from the other side because that's where the bathroom is. Still, it's entirely possible you somehow knocked or . . . I don't know. Things fall, it doesn't seem like definitive evidence of anything untoward."

Lake spoke through clenched teeth. "I remember someone coming in and leaning over me. And my briefcase has been disturbed. I call that evidence, Mr. Marston. You yourself said that if an intruder had been in my room, that would be a security breach. Did you not?"

"I did suggest that it might be, yes."

"Right. Precisely. Which means I expect you to investigate this and bring me some answers. This may not seem like a big deal to you, and if it turns out that some wandering maid came to feel my forehead, then fine. But I won't have you acting like it's nothing at all when you have no clue who was in there, or why." He pointed a finger at Hugo's chest. "You will investigate, Hugo, because I see this as a personal violation and I appreciate neither the intrusion nor your collaboration in pretending nothing happened."

Lake straightened, looked past both men for a brief moment, then turned on his heel and marched back toward the house.

Hugo and Henri Tourville watched him go. When he was out of earshot, the Frenchman said, "Why is he here, anyway?"

"What do you mean?"

"I know that he replaced the man we intended to speak with. I was not told why, other than some sort of family emergency."

Hugo nodded. He'd wondered about the official story on that.

"Everyone knows he doesn't like foreigners, especially us," Tourville went on. "Why did they send him, of all people? And why did he agree to come?"

Hugo laughed. "How would I know that? I'm just keeping him company."

"I'm serious, you are an intelligent man, I'm guessing you keep up with the news, with politics. Tell me what you think, because from where I'm standing he's an odd replacement for Senator Railton."

"I agree, they are quite different." Hugo paused. "Between us, Monsieur Tourville, Senator Railton was threatened. He was scared off, that's why he didn't come. And that made finding the perfect replacement hard, I'm sure."

"Why didn't they tell us? Surely they didn't think—"

"No, no," Hugo said hurriedly. "Some local crackpot, nothing to do with you. But, I'm guessing it made finding a replacement hard. As Railton's second-in-command, it made sense for Lake to fill in." Hugo thought for a moment. "And If I had to guess, I'd say that he's come here to prove himself. To show the people who are giving him money that he can come here and be a tough negotiator, but also to show his opponents that he's able to strike a deal with foreign counterparts.

Potentially it's a win–win for him. And if it all goes wrong, well, with all due respect, Monsieur Tourville, not too many people in America will dwell on the fate of the Guadeloupe Islands."

"Meaning there's nothing for him to screw up too badly."

"Right."

"Is he the man we've read about, or is there more to him? Our press has been quite unkind."

"You know," said Hugo, "I think he's a conflicted man, I really do."

"Conflicted or paranoid?"

Hugo raised an eyebrow. "No comment. But I don't think he's as isolationist as he acts, I think a lot of it is just hot air. Now, his major backers, the people who put him in office, I can't speak to them. I know a couple of the places he gets his money and I'm sure they are less than excited about him being here."

"Do you like him?"

"I wasn't expecting to, that's for sure," Hugo said. "I don't think I know him well enough to say. I'm not sure we'd ever be best friends but then again, I'm also pretty sure he's a lot nicer than he lets on."

Tourville grunted. "The paranoia aside."

"Well," Hugo smiled, "we all have our issues."

"We do, and mine is resurrecting these talks. Do you have any suggestions?"

"I'm afraid I'm not a politician, Monsieur Tourville, I'm just keeping him company." This was, indeed, a problem for the politicians to handle, but still. Not taking Lake's allegations seriously could mean the end of his participation, certainly in the short term, and Hugo had a strong feeling that brushing off the senator's concerns might just make a minor dispute that much worse.

They turned back toward the fields and leant on the fence in silence. The grass was now bathed in sunlight as overhead the bulky rain clouds had fragmented, showing thick ribbons of blue sky that twisted amongst them. A breeze pushed across the open land bringing with it the soft and musty smell of wet and fertile farmland.

"Is he serious about an investigation?" Tourville finally asked.

"It seems like it," Hugo said.

"I was afraid of that. I can't allow it, I'm afraid. I won't allow it, such a thing is unthinkable here." He shook his head. "This is ridiculous. What if he's playing some kind of idiotic game? I mean, think how this looks; an American officer investigating on French soil, in my house. And because of what? No, no, I don't think so."

"I understand completely. But I also know you want to get these talks moving." An idea was forming in Hugo's mind, and after a moment he turned to Tourville and said, "You know, I may have a way to satisfy the senator and safeguard your home and reputation."

"You do?" He gave a tired smile. "You know, Ambassador Taylor is a friend of mine and he's told me good things about you. That you can be trusted. So please, tell me."

Hugo dialed and the phone rang twice before being answered.

"*Allo?* Hugo, is that you?"

"*Bonjour, mon ami*," Hugo said. "How are you?"

"Always better for hearing from you. But since you ask, very busy."

"Are you too busy for a wild idea and a trip to the countryside?"

"I don't have time for much of anything these days, as my wife will testify. Especially one of your adventures."

Capitaine Raul Garcia sounded tired, Hugo thought, but there was still humor in his voice. Hugo had once compared the policeman to a cactus, prickly on the outside but sweet inside. Their friendship had begun with Garcia extending a few, and grudging, professional courtesies during Hugo's hunt for his bouquiniste friend Max. They'd worked well together on that case, learned to trust each other, and soon become friends as well as colleagues. And now more than ever, Hugo needed a friend in a policeman's uniform.

"This is less an adventure and more a matter of dry international politics."

"Sounds tedious. But safe, at least. What could international politics possibly want from me?"

Hugo explained the situation, trying to be tactful and even-handed in describing Senator Lake's allegations and Tourville's concerns for his reputation.

Garcia listened attentively, then asked, "Even if someone was in his room, why is it such a big deal?"

"He thinks it's a breach of security, which makes it a big deal to him."

"And that makes it a big deal to everyone, I suppose. But suppose he's right, how can it be proven and what can be done about it?"

"I think the point is that we try."

"We?"

"I need it done discreetly. If I tell Monsieur Tourville that we are friends and I tell Lake that you've helped me solve cases in the past, then we can take care of this quickly and the politicians can get back to work."

"And stop acting like babies."

Hugo chuckled. "Well, they'll still be politicians, so let's not expect miracles. What do you think?"

Garcia sighed. "I don't know, Hugo. I really am swamped here and I wasn't kidding about my wife, things have been . . . difficult lately."

"I'm sorry, Raul, I wouldn't ask if I had another solution. And I would very much like to see you again, maybe Madam Garcia can come with you for some country air. Be good for you both to get away."

"Nice idea, but we're not . . . *Alors*, I can come down tomorrow, is that soon enough?"

"It's perfect. I'll ship the senator back to Paris, seal off the room, and when you can get here you can dust the place for prints and talk to a few people."

Garcia sighed again. "It'll be good to see you, too, Hugo. Friendly faces in this business can be few and far between sometimes." His voice perked up. "And it's been a year or two since I've taken prints at a crime scene, it'll be a good refresher for me."

"Excellent, thanks Raul. And so you know, the chef is wonderful here and they serve very good wine. Very good indeed."

"Well then," Garcia said, "I really do have something to look forward to. I'll bring cigars."

CHAPTER EIGHT

Senator Lake was happy to go back to Paris. He packed his bags while still bristling at the outrage of the night before, although he'd been somewhat mollified by the impending investigation and was grateful to Hugo for taking charge of it. Lake shook hands with Henri Tourville on the chateau's steps, both a little cool, but they agreed that in a couple of days talks could resume, here or elsewhere, perhaps depending on what the Paris policeman discovered.

Ambassador Taylor was less thrilled at the prospect of entertaining his compatriot for forty-eight hours but impressed by Hugo's solution.

"And it leaves me," Hugo told the ambassador, "with a few days to enjoy the fresh air and find a book or two to read."

"The place probably has a library, right?"

"I'm in it right now. Quite small but comfortable and well-stocked enough for me to have spent the morning in here. I read about hunting dogs favored by the rich and famous and a little bit about the demise of King Louis XVI and his lovely wife. Anyway, it looks like the sun's coming out, so I'll probably go for a walk in a little bit."

"Don't rub it in, Marston," Taylor grumped. "And wrap things up as soon as you can, we do have an international crisis to resolve remember."

"We? Oh no, not me Mr. Ambassador, I'm just the—"

"Yes, yes, I know what you are. But you might want to remember that I can easily promote you. Note taker, perhaps. Or sandwich bearer."

59

Hugo rang off with a laugh, then looked at the phone in his hand. He pulled himself out of his armchair and wandered out of the library into the main hall, headed for the main doors. Outside, he followed the gravel pathway around to the back of the house and found a quiet spot at the rear of the garden, a wooden bench protected from the sun, and to some degree the rain, by a trellis laced with brown vines of some creeping plant he couldn't recognize.

He sat quietly for a moment, his mind turning to Claudia, and he wondered if a phone call would bug her, interrupt her at work—he'd no idea what she might be doing—but he dialed anyway.

"What a nice surprise!" Her voice sounded bright, and he knew she was smiling.

"How's my favorite newspaper reporter?"

"You charmer." Claudia laughed, the gentlest of sounds. "But how many reporters do you know?"

"Millions," he lied.

"I'm glad to hear it. And glad to hear from you. I'm fine, keeping busy. They have me covering that Archambault case."

"I saw the headline, and your name, but didn't read it."

"Horrible business. A suicide and then some. Monsieur Archambault was a fairly prominent banker, he had a nice house and a pretty wife. But he was working long hours, was stressed, and for some reason he thought his wife was cheating on him. He checked her internet history, her emails, and found some from a man he didn't know that seemed to be in a code of sorts. He was convinced she was going to leave him so instead of talking to her, getting an explanation, he strangled her and hung himself. She lived, thank God, but he died."

"She wasn't having an affair?"

"No, quite the opposite. She was arranging a trip for just the two of them and the cryptic emails were from a travel agent trying to keep the secret. The poor husband got an idea in his head and for whatever reason he couldn't shake it. Especially sad because they had two kids."

"Like you say, a horrible tragedy," said Hugo. "Sometimes the reality in our heads is more powerful than actual reality."

"For sure." Her voice brightened. "Other than that, I'm doing well. You?"

"Yep, fine. Out in the countryside for a few days. It's a work thing, but I have a day or so of down time."

"Lucky you." There was a slight catch in her voice and Hugo knew she was wondering whether he was about to invite her to join him. He wondered the same thing.

"Yep. I was actually hoping to see you again at some point."

"Oh Hugo, I can't get away for a few days." She laughed again. "Or maybe you didn't mean out there."

"Whatever works, my schedule's pretty flexible. I'll take a hurried lunch at this point."

"Yeah, me too." She paused. "It's been a while since we really talked."

"Well, here I am, something wrong?"

She sighed. "No, not really. I meant about us. Not that there is an *us* to speak of, it just seems like we sizzled for a while and then exploded into nothing."

"You make me sound like a fried egg."

She laughed again. "*Alors*, then we're both fried eggs. But you know what I mean, Hugo, and I don't like to play dating games or lead anyone the wrong way."

"That makes two of us. So what way are we going?"

"I don't know, everything is so . . . I'm just not sure I have time to devote to that side of my life right now."

"That's OK Claudia, I understand." He kept his voice light but a small hollow opened in his chest. Suddenly the bench felt too hard at his back and the brightness of the garden dimmed a fraction.

"Do you? You are OK with us being on hold for a while?" Her voice seemed small. "You're a great catch, Hugo, I will understand if some other lucky lady pounces on you."

He smiled. "If they've tried they must have missed, because I've not noticed any pouncing from anyone."

It was true, he'd not dated anyone since Claudia and not had any interest in doing so. He was wrapped up in work, yes, but she'd found and filled a little hole inside him. Not permanently, of course, but in a way that made him want to reserve his time for her and her alone. Being put on hold, despite being able to laugh about it, felt like a weight in his chest.

"It'll happen, trust me. Hey, before I forget, how is Tom these days?"

"He's fine. Still living with me off and on, though he's traveling a lot. I guess the CIA consulting picked back up once he stopped drinking; he's a pretty good employee when he's sober."

"And he's managed to stay off the booze?"

"As far as I know. We don't keep any in the apartment, and if we go out together I don't drink either. I'm sure it's difficult and I have no idea what he's like when I'm not around, but I think he's on top of it, I really do."

"You're a good friend, Hugo, you know that?"

"Well, it doesn't hurt for me to cut back myself. I've lost a few pounds in the bargain."

"Well," Claudia said, her voice quiet again, "maybe one of these days I'll get to see the sleeker Hugo." They both knew what she meant, and that *one of these days* probably didn't mean soon.

"I'd like that, I really would."

He sat back and looked up, the vines overhead rustling and shifting in the wind, showing glimpses of white clouds scudding across the sky. Downtime suddenly seemed like wasted time, the small pleasures of reading and walking in the fresh air tainted by Claudia's gentle, honest, yet surprisingly hurtful rejection. He'd been lucky in life, personally and professionally—he knew and appreciated that. He couldn't help but wonder about his love life, the emptiness that he ignored so much of the time and filled just occasionally with painful memories. Memories of his first wife, Ellie, who he'd loved so desperately and who'd died in a car accident, sucked from his life in an instant. Memories, too, of

Christine, his second wife who he'd thought he'd loved and who'd left him . . . why, exactly?

He shook his head and stood up. *Maybe that's part of what I need to figure out.*

He looked up at the sound of feet on gravel and his mood shifted immediately. A dapper man was walking gingerly across the lawn toward him, a little plumper than he'd been the last time they met but still impeccably dressed and sporting one of his many bow ties. Hugo started toward him and they shook hands warmly.

"Raul, you made it early. I'm so glad to see you."

"*Merci*, I'm pleased someone is."

"Problems at work?"

"Work, home." Capitaine Garcia wore those problems for all to see—for Hugo, anyway. Garcia's normally happy face looked gray and heavy, even the extra weight in his body looked to Hugo as if it came from stress and not pleasurable indulgence.

"Anything you want to talk about?"

"Maybe over a drink, later." Garcia nodded toward his feet. "This grass, it's like a carpet. My shoes are cleaner walking on their lawn than in my own home."

"I know, it's a lifestyle I could get used to."

"You?" Garcia snorted. "Not a chance, you are a man of action, you'd be bored here within days. Hours, probably."

"Possibly," mused Hugo, "but there are days when I'd sure like to give it a try."

"*Certainement.*" Garcia looked back at the house. "So what exactly is going on here?"

"I'm not sure there's anything going on. As I said on the phone, Senator Lake insists someone was in his room, and Henri Tourville insists not."

"Somehow I'm supposed to get to the bottom of this? How is that possible unless they have cameras in the hallways?"

"They don't have cameras, and your job is much harder than solving that little mystery."

Garcia cocked an eyebrow. "Oh?"

"Your job, and mine, is to investigate and keep both sides happy. Seriously, I can't imagine you'd find anything, any prints will belong to family members or staff, all of whom have a right to be in there. Lake emptied his briefcase and left it behind, so I think the plan is for you to make a good show of it so I can report that you interviewed everyone here and dusted for prints."

"Right, well, I should get started. Everything I need is in the car." He gave Hugo a wry smile. "I do have real police work to do, you know."

Hugo clapped a hand on his friend's shoulder and they began to walk toward the chateau. "Not today, my friend, not today."

CHAPTER NINE

C apitaine Raul Garcia watched as Hugo peeled away the masking tape that he'd used to seal Lake's bedroom immediately after the senator had packed and vacated it. Garcia stood behind him making a note in a small pad that, according to the witness, Hugo Marston, the tape had not been broken and therefore no one had entered the room since it was closed up. Once the door was open, Hugo stepped aside and left Garcia to his work.

Standing in the bedroom, Garcia took a few deep breaths and looked around. He could feel the age of the room, with its worn rug and oaken floor that a thousand feet had polished to a shine. To his right a table flanked the inside wall of the room; behind it from where he stood was a wing-backed chair and ottoman in cracked brown leather. A reading lamp, the most modern thing in the room, sat in the corner behind the chair. The right hand wall was dominated by an armoire that was seven feet tall and six wide. The four-poster bed was in front of him, up against the left-hand wall, and behind it Garcia could see another door—to the bathroom, he assumed.

He stooped over his bag, a black box with a carrying handle like attorneys used to lug around their papers and books. He pulled on a pair of latex gloves and flexed his fingers as he surveyed the room again, this time planning his incremental assault.

He didn't mind that it was, for all intents and purposes, a waste of his time. To have a couple of hours to get back to basics, to remind himself how to do the fundamentals of his job in peace and quiet, those moments were always to be welcomed. And at an alleged crime scene where no one expected you to find evidence, well, that was the kind of pressure he could live with.

He'd considered dusting the door knob, but Hugo assured him that he himself, the senator, and heaven-knew-who-else had touched it recently, so he began with the table to his right. He knelt down to inspect the highly-polished wood, seeing several possible prints. He dusted them with gentle strokes and carefully laid his tape over the dust, pulling it back up swiftly and smoothly before transferring the tape to a backing pad, laying the print on the glossy side of the pad before documenting where he'd found the print on the back. He worked slowly, methodically, enjoying the occasional creak of the floor under his feet and the muffled sounds of the house beyond the bedroom, settling into a rhythm that was as pleasant as it was efficient.

He paid special attention to the tables beside the bed and to the bedpost nearest the door. If someone had come in and leaned over the senator, those would be the places he'd most likely have touched. Finally, he turned to Senator Lake's briefcase, and sat on the bed as he worked, hunched over the case as though it held the solution to a heinous murder.

After ninety minutes he had a stack of cards, dozens of prints, and a sore back. As he stretched himself, he checked the room for other evidence, but, having no real idea what he might be looking for, that didn't take long. Nothing looked broken or out of place, no strange stains or scratch marks. Just an old bedroom with the kind of furniture money couldn't buy any more.

Garcia texted Hugo when he'd finished, wanting to get started on interviewing people who were at the chateau that night. After a few seconds, Hugo texted back and directed him to the library. Garcia hefted his case down the broad staircase and found the library door wide open, his friend and Henri Tourville sitting inside, the latter looking slightly impatient.

Tourville stood and shook Garcia's hand. "Capitaine Garcia, thank you for doing this. Something of a charade, I'm afraid."

"*Bien*, you are welcome. Not too much of one, I hope, the police don't like to play parlor games while on the clock." He smiled but hoped that his tone made it clear that he wasn't entirely kidding.

"Of course. You have everything you need?"

"I just need to talk to whoever was here that night and get prints to compare against the ones I found."

"Prints?" Tourville's brow creased and he looked back and forth between Hugo and Garcia. "*Mais non*, you're not taking prints from anyone here, absolutely not."

"If I don't do that, Monsieur Tourville, then how do I know whose prints I lifted?" he gestured to his bag.

"You run them through whatever databases you have and see if a random stranger shows up, that's what you do. I'm certainly not having my family and staff printed like they were common criminals. You can talk to a couple of staff members but forget interviewing my family. It's an insult to even suggest they might be involved." He turned to Hugo. "I trust, Monsieur Marston, that you're not going to suggest lie detector tests or interrogations for my sister or myself?"

"No, not at all. I think all the capitaine is saying is that if he can compare the prints he found in the room against those who are normally allowed in there, others might stand out. Give him something to investigate. And you'd discard their prints immediately after that, right Raul?"

"Certainly. We never keep the fingerprints of witnesses on file, only those people actually convicted of a crime."

Tourville was unmoved. "You both talk as if there is something to investigate. A stranger didn't come into the house that night, and no one here went into that man's room." He stiffened. "As I've already said, you may talk to whichever staff members were here, and that's it. Type up your nonsense report and make the senator happy." He softened his tone a fraction. "I apologize if this has been a waste of your time, Capitaine, and I suspect it has. But I never wanted to bring you down here in the first place."

Garcia shrugged. "It's your house, monsieur. I'll do those interviews and be on my way."

"Thank you. But for wasting your time today I insist you stay for dinner, do that for me, please. And I can have a room made up for you, no trouble at all."

Garcia glanced at Hugo. "Well, I've heard your chef is most gifted."

"*Bien!*" Tourville nodded and said, "My wine is as fine as my chef, so I'll have a bedroom prepared. Can't have the police drinking and driving, can we?"

"No, I suppose we can't," Garcia said. His wife would be unhappy at his delayed return, work intruding on their marriage yet again. That, however, was a problem for tomorrow.

The next morning, Hugo stood with Garcia by the policeman's car.

"So," Hugo smiled, "a couple of pointless interviews and a stack of useless fingerprints."

"On the plus side, I won't have to painstakingly analyze each card to eliminate members of the household."

"You'd have done that yourself?"

"If we're trying to be discreet here, I think so. Plus, I like detailed work sometimes, it has a calming effect on me."

"So is that it? Investigation done?" Hugo looked around in frustration. "I suppose it is, but I hope Lake will be happy with it. He needs to get on with the Guadeloupe Islands talks."

"One charade after another, eh?" Garcia's eyes twinkled.

"Maybe. Anyway, thanks for coming down, and please tell Madam Garcia that I am to blame, not you."

They'd talked last night, not for long but long enough for Hugo to get the gist. Raul's mother-in-law had moved in with them six months ago, a woman neither he nor his wife particularly liked. Garcia had an advantage over his wife, however, in that he had a job that provided an escape from the endless inane chatter and demands for attention. It wasn't just that he'd started working longer hours, though he had, rather it was that his wife resented his not being there to help, to be a buffer between two strong women who were related but so very different.

For Garcia's part, he wasn't proud of abandoning his wife in this way, but then again, his suggestions to relocate the mother-in-law to her own apartment or rest home were summarily dismissed as disloyal and unloving. Exhaustion and frustration had settled over the house like a fog, and no one inside could see their way to safe harbor.

Garcia shook Hugo's hand and sighed. "Life does test us at times, but we will prevail. What other choice do we have?"

"None, you're right. You'll let me know when there's a report or something I can share with the senator?"

"*Bien sur.* I will probably run the prints through FAED, just to be thorough. It'll pad the report as well as make your senator feel better; I can't imagine it will kick anything back."

"Good idea," Hugo said. "But let's hope it doesn't. Finding a criminal's prints in that house would open a very unpleasant can of worms."

Garcia opened his car door and climbed in. He looked up and Hugo and smiled. "Is there any other kind?"

"True enough. What's your time estimate on all this?"

"I'm writing the report today and the forensics work will only take a few hours once I get it all scanned and uploaded. Should get the all-clear this afternoon, you can let Lake and Tourville know and they can get back to work."

"Assuming it's all clear."

"Aren't we?"

Hugo watched his friend leave and was about to head inside when a black Mercedes cruised down the driveway and came to a stop in front of the chateau. Alexandra Tourville smiled as she got out of the driver's side.

"*Bonjour,*" Hugo said. "I didn't realize you'd left."

"*Bonjour,* Monsieur Marston." She smiled, coquettish, unconcerned. "Wasn't I allowed to?" She wore tight jeans tucked into riding boots and a white cashmere sweater. Elegantly simple and quite sexy.

"No, it's fine. The police are finished here anyway."

"The police?" She retrieved a handbag from the front seat and walked toward him. "What exactly do you think happened here?"

"No clue, that's why we called in the professionals."

"My understanding is that the police aren't called unless something happened."

"The police are called all the time, for all kinds of reasons. The only thing that matters is whether they find anything."

"I see." He held the front door as they entered. "Will our American guest be coming back?"

"Now that's beyond my expertise, you'll have to ask the politicians. Your brother, for example."

"I will." They walked together down the main hall, the smell of fresh coffee luring them all the way into the enormous kitchen. "Join me?" she asked. Hugo nodded and she poured him a cup, then they sat at the long pine table that dominated the center of the room. "I almost became one, you know."

"A politician?"

"Yes. One of the many things on my resumé." There was a moment of silence, the first awkward one because they both knew why she was no longer in politics. She smiled, the lines around her eyes and at the corners of her mouth making her look her age. "It's OK, I know almost everyone who meets me is thinking it, if not thinking *about* it."

Hugo took a sip to avoid having to say anything.

"You're different, is that right?" she added.

Hugo wasn't sure if she was teasing him or testing him. "It's none of my business."

"I've led an interesting life, you know. Most of it in the public eye because of my family, and some because of my own doings. Don't you think it's funny that a sex scandal should be my undoing?"

Undoing was putting it politely. Alexie had been secretly taped enjoying the close attentions of two young American men and the

French girlfriend of one of them. Such revelations might have been manageable in the old days but since this one made the rounds through live moving pictures, her candidacy was no longer taken seriously. Worse, the camera had captured a German shepherd roaming around in the background, generating grist for the rumor mill and provoking jokes about everything from sexual positions to Franco–American–German relations and her penchant for leashes and muzzles.

Her camp had cried protestations of outrage at the invasion of privacy and launched a few libel lawsuits, but within weeks her coffers were empty and her camp consisted of herself, a couple of old friends, and her brother Henri, the nobleman who became even more noble for standing by his disgraced sister. Her humiliation was complete when *Paris Match* cited, without necessarily making relevant, the French proverb, *Qui se couche avec les chiens se lève avec des puces*, which the American press gleefully (and correctly) translated as, "If you lie down with dogs you get up with fleas." Even the *New York Times*, in a short article in the foreign section, reported that she'd withdrawn her candidacy after being "dogged by indiscretions."

"I admit," said Hugo, choosing his next words carefully, "that the demise of a politician's career because of romantic activities does seem rather un-French."

Alexie gave a half smile. "I'm not sure 'romantic' is the right word, but you are kind. And you misunderstand what it really means to be French. If you are a man you can do as you please, no matter your position in the world. The farmer, the politician, the businessman, it doesn't matter. If you are caught with your pants down, then the women sigh and the men wink or pat you on the back."

"A double standard?"

"Yes, but not the same as the one you have, which is worse. In America, any woman seen to be enjoying sex is a slut. Here, if you are an actress, a writer, a painter, or maybe even a housewife then your sex life is your own business and a reputation for . . . sexual expertise and experimentation can be excused, understood. But try being a woman in business or politics." She shook her head and tutted. "No, no, then you

must be celibate or single and monogamous. Most certainly vanilla."
There was something in her voice that Hugo couldn't pinpoint, a mix
of wistfulness and bitterness perhaps.

"I didn't realize it worked like that."

She stared at her coffee mug, her mouth tight. "People think I
withdrew through shame." She raised her head and held Hugo's eye.
"Not so. I did it out of anger, and I knew that I could only make things
worse for myself, for my family. No one likes or respects an angry
woman trying to defend herself." She laughed bitterly. "There's another
emotion men are allowed but women are not: outrage."

"But you like what you're doing now?"

"I like it well enough, it's not all digging in libraries and government records. With the Internet and advances in DNA, you'd be
amazed how far back you can go."

"And people pay well for that kind of research?"

"No, they pay as little as possible. For now I'm still dependent on
my brother," a small smile, "at least if I want to maintain this lifestyle.
A teaching job here and there, some freelance work on genealogical
projects, I don't have it all figured out just yet. I can tell you that some
American clients pay very well."

"I'm glad to hear that, for your sake." Hugo was pleased to be on
safer ground. His view on sex and privacy were in line with Alexie Tourville's, but his comfort level when it came to discussing those topics was
more old-fashioned.

Alexie stood and picked up her coffee cup. "*Alors*, nice to chat with
you, Monsieur Marston, but all this talk reminds me I have work to do."

Hugo stood, too, then went to the cavernous sink to put down his
empty cup. He looked out of the window for a check of the weather
and was secretly pleased to see dark clouds gathering above the waving
branches of the estates trees, almost bare from the season and the
blustering wind which promised rain—if not now, then very soon.
Impending rain meant he could refill his coffee cup and take refuge in
the library for a few hours.

At eight that evening, Hugo trotted down the stairs on his way to dinner, luxuriant aromas of meat and garlic greeting him in the main hallway. He felt his phone vibrate in his pocket and, when he pulled it out, saw Garcia's name on the display.

"Raul, what news?"

"*Salut*, Hugo." There was a pause, then Garcia's voice, hesitant but clear. "My friend, I am afraid I have some bad news."

Hugo stopped in his tracks. "Bad news? Explain that."

"Of course. First, I did everything I said, ran the prints through FAED. It checked criminal records all across Europe."

"Don't tell me you got a hit. Everyone in this house is clean, Tourville assured us of that."

"No, I'm afraid it's worse. Quite a lot worse."

"Worse than someone here having a criminal record?"

"Yes." Garcia cleared his throat. "Believe it or not, it seems possible that someone there committed murder."

CHAPTER TEN

H ugo kept going through the main hallway and out of the front doors. He needed to be alone for this conversation.

"Murder? What do you mean?"

He heard Garcia take a breath. "*Bien*, so once the FAED results came back with nothing it struck me there was one more thing I could do. You know, to be thorough."

He explained that he'd used the French version of ViCAP, the FBI's data information system that collects and analyzes information about homicides, sexual assaults, missing persons, and unidentified human remains. Users could input case information hoping to identify related incidents, where new leads might be lurking. "Hugo, one of the prints connected to an unsolved murder east of Paris, not far from Troyes. I pulled the report of the crime, and it looks like a burglary gone wrong at an old country home. Some jewelry stolen, but not much else."

Hugo sat on the lowest of the front steps, trying to absorb this information. "This changes things, Raul, you know that, right?"

"Yes, of course. I haven't told the police handling the murder yet, figured we should work it from this end first to know what we have."

"Which isn't much, because we have no idea whose print it is," Hugo said. "You want me to talk to Tourville?"

"I don't know, Hugo. I've thought about it and I'm torn, because at this point we have to treat everyone in that house as a suspect."

"Including Tourville himself? I understand the theory, Raul, but that's a stretch. The guy has more blue blood than the Queen of England and is hardly in need of other people's trinkets."

"True enough, but I'm not really in the business of doing French aristocrats favors."

"I appreciate that, I do. But it's not so much a favor as being realistic. Not only is he extremely unlikely to be a murderer, but if we alienate him now it could hamper the investigation."

"*My* investigation," Garcia said, "which means that if you're wrong it's my head that rolls."

Hugo chuckled. "A fine French tradition, head-rolling. I think you'll be OK, though, I'll make sure you get political asylum in the States if I see them polishing the guillotine."

"You better."

"So let me talk to Tourville, maybe we can start by taking prints from his staff if he's not willing to do more, I can't imagine he'd mind that. If we don't get anything from them, we can look to the family and guests."

"*Bien*, let's go with that. And tell him I'll come back there and print his people myself, try to keep this discreet for as long as possible."

"Tonight?"

It was Garcia's turn to laugh. "No, not a chance. Americans are workaholics, not Frenchmen. I'll be down in the morning. Midmorning; you know I like my breakfast."

When they hung up, Hugo started to head back inside but stopped at the top of the stairs. He put a quick call into the ambassador, passing on Garcia's new information.

"Jeez, Hugo, this isn't what we need, not right now," Taylor said. "If Lake finds out he's been sleeping in the shadow of a murderer he'll go ballistic."

"Sounds like a board game, doesn't it? The murder of a senator in the library with the candlestick."

"Not funny, Hugo."

"No?" Hugo's tone was light. "Of course, it's always possible the fingerprint in question is the senator's, which makes him the murderer not the murdered."

"Still not funny."

"Well then, keep the info to yourself for now. I'll call tomorrow with an update."

"Thanks. And Hugo? Call me with good news one of these days. Would you try that sometime?"

Hugo headed into the chateau, pausing when he saw Henri Tourville having a drink in the sitting room with Felix Vibert. The two men stood with their backs to an oversized painting of a peasant girl in a garden looking wistfully upward with one arm extended. It was oddly familiar to Hugo, though he couldn't begin to place why.

"Monsieur Tourville," he said, "I'm sorry to interrupt, but can I have a word?"

"Certainly, you can speak freely in front of Felix."

Hugo tilted his head, an apology. "Actually, on this matter I'm afraid I can't."

"*Pas de problem*," Vibert said. "I will leave you gentlemen to it, but please don't keep us waiting for long, dinner smells wonderful."

They watched him leave the room and Hugo indicated the painting behind them. "Why do I recognize that?"

"Ah, it's something of a knock-off. The version you may recollect is in a New York museum, and the young lady is Joan of Arc at the moment she is spoken to by God. Getting her marching orders, you might say. The famous one is by Jules Bastien-Lepage, but about the time that one was painted a lot more were produced of her, sculptures too. I'm told this one was also by Jules Bastien-Lepage, but it's not signed and an art dealer told me it might not even be finished." Tourville shrugged. "Like most of the stuff in here, I've no idea where it came from, what it's worth, if anything, and it's been in the family longer than anyone can remember, so there it hangs."

"Not a bad problem to have." Hugo turned back to Tourville. "Let's sit for a minute."

Tourville raised an eyebrow but acquiesced, moving to a pair of plump, faded-red armchairs. As they sat, Tourville said, "Things not going as planned?"

"Not exactly. And please, let me finish talking before you say anything."

Tourville nodded. "*D'accord*."

"*Merci*. First, I won't have answers to some of the questions you will ask because I have only a preliminary report from Garcia. He's coming down tomorrow and should have more for us, but I wanted to come to you as soon as possible. Like you, I want to get these talks back on track and you've been very gracious with your hospitality and this unusual situation."

Tourville nodded again, the corners of his mouth turned down in anticipation of whatever bad news was coming.

"Unfortunately, this situation just got a whole lot more unusual. One print from the senator's room matches a print found at a crime scene at a country home on the east side of Paris."

Tourville blinked. "How is that possible? What kind of crime scene?"

"To the first question, that's what we'd like to find out. To the second," Hugo hesitated, but guessed that he'd get more with honesty than obfuscation. "A robbery–murder scene."

"How can that be?" Tourville repeated, his voice a whisper.

"I haven't seen the file on that case yet, this really is early stages."

"But what can it mean?"

"Honestly, it can mean a lot of things, or even nothing. Right now, the most we can say is that the same person was at that house and this."

"What kind of house is it?"

Hugo though back to what Garcia had told him. "I'm not a hundred percent sure, but a very old country house, not as large as yours but several hundred years old."

"Then it's quite possible that someone passed through both there and here, someone unrelated to any crime at all."

"It's possible," Hugo said. "We want to check that possibility out, even if not for the sake of our little investigation here, then the police looking into the murder will want to follow up a lead like that. And you probably want us doing it, not them."

Tourville straightened in his chair. "I don't mean to be difficult, my friend, but I have a strong feeling I should talk to my lawyer about this. What is it you want to do?"

"Well, we'd like to take prints from everyone in your household, staff and guests at the dinner, maybe we can find out who was at the other house. Maybe there's an innocent explanation, but we need to know."

"Why can't you just ask if anyone knows that other house?"

"Because where murder is involved, we can't trust people to tell the truth. People lie, but fingerprints don't."

Tourville stared down into his drink and Hugo let him process the news. After a moment, Tourville looked up and slowly shook his head. "*Non*, I can't allow it, I'm very sorry. I don't like to stand in the way of a legitimate investigation, but I don't consider Senator Lake's claims to be legitimate and I most definitely can't let my family become suspects in a murder case."

"Then let us start with your staff, the people who work here and worked here the night of the dinner party."

"I don't know about that. Why should I allow them to become suspects and not my family? How does that look to them?"

"Monsieur Tourville, you know that the police can ask them for their prints whether you like it or not?" Hugo's tone was soft but he knew the frustration rang clear.

"Please. Let me call my lawyer and if he tells me I am wrong, then I will reconsider. You said Garcia is coming tomorrow?"

"Yes, he'll do the work himself to try and keep this under the radar."

"I am grateful for that consideration." Tourville rose. "And, of course, you are still my guest. Go in to dinner and I will join you once I've spoken to my attorney."

Hugo wandered into the dining room and joined those already seated. Felix Vibert was there, as was Natalia and Alexie Tourville. Four other people—couples, Hugo assumed—introduced themselves as friends of the family but didn't elaborate on where they'd come from or why they were there. It was an informal meal, much more to Hugo's liking than the stiff, multicourse marathon earlier that week. Two members of staff, who themselves seemed more at ease than the previous evening, brought in platters of braised beef and roasted vegetables that were left on the table for the guests to dig into and pass around. Wine bottles were placed at generous intervals, close to everyone so there'd be no need to reach too far or, heaven forbid, request one be passed.

Hugo was considering a second helping when Tourville appeared in the doorway and beckoned him over with a polite nod. Hugo excused himself and joined Tourville in the hallway, the pair moving away from the dining room to be out of earshot.

"We appear to be bringing each other bad news tonight," Tourville said grimly.

"I'm sorry to hear that. Your lawyer doesn't want you to cooperate?"

Tourville was gruff. "What he wants or doesn't want is irrelevant. He knows that and is very good at telling me where I stand legally. Once he has done that, I do what I think is best." He looked at Hugo and frowned. "I'm sorry, that sounded more harsh than I meant it to. What I'm trying to say is that according to him, the *code de procédure pénale* does not authorize the police to obtain any kind of warrant or court order requiring anyone here to give fingerprints."

"We were hoping for your cooperation, not warrants."

"I understand, but without legal authority our cooperation is entirely optional. As he explained it to me, and it was very much the same as you said, all anyone can say from this information is that the same person was at the same two locations sometime in the recent past. He assures me no judge will sign one based on so little." *Especially for my family* was unspoken, but Hugo caught the suggestion just the same.

Hugo nodded. "I'm sorry to hear this but I do understand. I'll let Capitaine Garcia know."

"And if this is all the capitaine managed to find from his expedition here, I will act under the assumption that any investigation into the senator's so-called intruder is now complete. Agreed?"

Hugo held Tourville's gaze, and said, "That will depend. Whoever is investigating the robbery–murder will be made aware of the connection, and even though I expect you are right about the warrant, I'll have no control over what they do, or try to do. It really would be better to clear as many people as possible so that—"

"*Non.*" Tourville held up a hand. "I'm sorry but as far as I'm concerned, as you Americans say, it's 'case closed.' Now, let us return to the table, I expect dessert is in there by now, and I'm not missing out on my Crêpes Suzette."

Tourville led the way, and as they walked Hugo's phone buzzed in his pocket. He took a peek to see who was calling, intending to remain polite and get back to them after the meal. He smiled to himself as the name Tom Green lit up the screen. Best friends through the FBI Academy—and ever since, really—Tom had been recruited by the CIA after several years. For years he'd rattled between anonymous missions for the Company and the whisky bottle, both taking a heavy toll. He'd kicked the latter, for now at least, but was still working on and off with the former.

And a call from Tom right now meant just one thing: this case was far from closed.

CHAPTER ELEVEN

Hugo heard the noise twice. He checked his watch and it showed two thirty in the morning. There it was again, a noise that could have been a door opening, closing, or maybe a footfall in the hallway.

He listened. The wooden floor and joists of the chateau creaked and muttered like those in any old house, but after several nights Hugo had picked up a familiarity to these sounds and he knew when something was amiss. His mind cast back to Lake's tale, but even if that was true, this couldn't be the same thing. No one would try to sneak into two people's rooms, Hugo couldn't believe that. He heard the noise again and slipped out of bed, moving to the doorway on silent feet. He listened for a moment but heard nothing. He opened the door and stepped halfway out to look up and down the long hallway.

Felix Vibert stood in pajamas and a blue robe standing at the top of the stairs that bisected the long hallway. He and Hugo looked at each other in surprise.

"Anything wrong?" Hugo asked.

"I don't . . . I thought I heard someone come into my room. And then out here." He sounded hesitant, but Hugo remembered what time it was and put the uncertainty in his voice down to tiredness, and maybe a little fright.

"Probably just the wind."

"Perhaps." Vibert didn't look persuaded but he waved a hand, took a last look down the stairs, and shuffled back to his room.

Once Vibert had closed his door, Hugo went to the top of the stairs and stood quietly, the dim light from the upstairs hall fading into the black well of downstairs. He heard nothing, saw no one, but that didn't stop his ears and an old house teaming up to play tricks on his mind. But after a minute he felt as sure as he could be that everyone was asleep, and went back to his room.

He closed the door and froze at the sound of a voice that came from the armchair opposite the bed. "Good evening, Monsieur Marston. *Comment ça va?*"

Hugo spun around and peered at the man, a dark shape sitting with one leg crossed over the other, relaxed. *Probably smiling*, Hugo thought, *knowing him*.

"Well, we know it can be done, anyway," the voice said.

Hugo flicked on the light. "Jesus, Tom, you scared the hell out of me. When are you going to grow up?"

"Not for a while. Come on, this was a scientific experiment to see how hard it is to sneak into someone's room at this place. And I'm here to tell you, it's pretty easy."

"You're CIA, Tom, of course it is."

"And you're FBI. Which, come to think of it, might tell us something about which agency is superior."

"Former FBI, and apparently out of practice." Hugo wagged a finger. "Though I still carry my gun, which means I could have shot you."

"No chance. When did you ever shoot a man without seeing his face?"

"Well, never." Hugo shook his head but couldn't help but smile. "Although I don't know why seeing your face would stop me pulling the trigger."

"You'd never destroy such a thing of beauty. Now, go back to sleep, I'm here to protect you from any intruders. Any *more* intruders."

Hugo sat on his bed, more than happy to oblige but a thought struck him. "Tom, did you go into every room in this hallway?"

"Of course, I had to."

"Had to?"

"Your names aren't on the door."

"Right. Good night, Tom. And please don't snore."

Hugo and Tom were eating breakfast when Henri Tourville entered the dining room. He stopped in surprise and Tom quickly rose to introduce himself.

"Tom Green, a friend and colleague of Hugo's. I arrived late last night, Hugo was kind enough to let me in and share his room."

Tourville shook his hand but his eyes were on Hugo, his look clear. *What's going on?*

"Tom used to work with me at the FBI," Hugo explained. "He still consults here and there. Seeing him was something of a surprise to me, too."

"A pleasant one, of course," Tom said. "Anyway, now that we're together it might be a good time to let you know precisely where at the murder scene that fingerprint was found."

Tourville moved to the large table that carried the food and drinks. He poured a cup of coffee and stirred in some sugar. When he spoke, his voice was level. "Some of us have no interest in any fingerprints, monsieur, and if you came into my house to try and persuade me otherwise, you may leave immediately."

"The print," Tom said casually, "was found inside the armoire where the jewelry was hidden. We believe it belongs to the person who broke in, stole from the old lady, and then killed her."

Tourville smiled. "Please, Monsieur Green, have some breakfast before you leave. And Monsieur Marston, I suspect since the Guadeloupe talks appear to have been indefinitely postponed, you will be leaving, too. Am I right?"

"Well," Hugo said, "if I can't change your mind, I suppose I might as well. But before I go, may I speak to everyone who is here?"

"I already have and no one wishes to have their prints taken, thank you very much."

"I'm sure you have, but I wouldn't be much of an investigator if I let a . . . well, technically a potential suspect, run my investigation. And you may refuse me, of course, but then I'll have to follow people as they leave the premises and catch them unawares. In the village, in public."

Tourville narrowed his eyes and shook his head. "Why are you doing this? You know that nobody here committed that crime. Is this some kind of political stunt?"

A new voice, from the doorway to the dining room. "If it were, Monsieur Tourville, I wouldn't be here, that's for sure," said Capitaine Raul Garcia.

Tourville turned on his heel and glared. "Fine," he said after a moment, "talk to whomever you want. Waste all the time you want. Then get out of my house."

They let Garcia run things. It was technically his investigation and he was their official liaison with the police handling the murder near Troyes. And the staff, if not the family members, would be more likely to talk to a Frenchman than an American. So Hugo and Tom hovered in the background, Tom's nervous energy making him pace the kitchen floor where the interviews were done. So keen was he to remain busy, he shook everyone's hand and offered a glass of water to each person who came in and sat down. But, without exception, they didn't sit for long. Each politely declined to provide fingerprints, most shaking their heads while not meeting the eyes of the capitaine, his treaties and endearments falling on deaf ears.

They were done in thirty minutes. Garcia and Tom went outside to enjoy a balmy day while Hugo headed upstairs to pack his bag. He sought out Tourville one last time, determined to leave on a positive, if not friendly, note.

"I'm very sorry things turned out this way, and you have my word that I will do everything I can to be discreet, assuming I am a part of any ongoing investigation."

Tourville shook his hand. "I know you will. I trust you, Hugo, and I am also sorry things have worked out this way. Perhaps you can quickly solve this other murder and we can resume our business." But he didn't sound hopeful.

"If I can, I'll let you know how things are going. And I'm sure Ambassador Taylor will be in touch, maybe even Senator Lake himself."

"Maybe. An interesting man, that Senator Lake. Do you really think he has a chance to be your president?"

"Anything's possible." Hugo shrugged and smiled. "After all, America is the land of opportunity, and pretty much anyone can try and become president."

"We're not quite that naïve, though, are we? We both know it's the money that counts as much as the person. Without the money, well, look at my sister. Potential for greatness, but once the people with the money decided she wasn't worth supporting, whether they were right or not, her career was over. We're just lucky she had other talents, other things she could do."

"True. And she seems to be doing fine."

Tourville was staring at the ground and he was silent for a moment, before looking up. "What? Ah yes, doing fine. That's the thing about people, you never really know, do you?"

Hugo thought of Tom, the alcoholic who'd apparently given up booze with a snap of his fingers. "Very true," he said, "you never really know for sure."

Tourville turned and headed back to the house, a tall man weighed down by the disappointments and frustrations of the past few days, Hugo thought. And of the possible embarrassments to come, if that fingerprint really did lead police back to the chateau.

Hugo's car had been driven back to Paris by Special Agent Emma Ruby when Senator Lake left, so he rode with Tom and Garcia. Tom, who'd taken a late-night taxi to the chateau, grumbled but put himself in the back seat of the Frenchman's Renault.

"There's a reason no other country in the entire world buys French cars," he said. "You want me to tell you what that reason is?"

"Be quiet, Tom," Garcia said. "One more complaint and I'll drop you at the train station. Maybe a couple of miles away from it, so you can appreciate the countryside a little."

Hugo smiled at the banter but his mind was on the staff interviews, such as they were. "Raul, how many statements did we get in the end? And by statements," he added, "I mean complete rejections."

"By my calculations, we spoke to four of the seven staff who were working that day, and only Tourville himself from the family. As far as I know, there were eighteen outside guests we'll still need to approach."

"No Vibert, Natalia, Alexandra?"

"Vibert wouldn't come out of the library, and the two women are in Paris for the day. At least, that's according to Tourville. The cook, whatever her name was, confirmed that—not that it matters much."

"So," Hugo said, "pretty much a complete waste of our time."

"Well," Tom said lightly, "I wouldn't go that far."

Hugo turned in his seat. He recognized that tone, the way a father recognizes the guilty tone of a mischievous son. "Tom, what did you do?"

Tom patted a duffel bag on the seat next to him. "You know, sometimes I feel like I just don't get the appreciation I deserve."

Hugo turned and looked forward again as they eased onto the main road. "Here we go. Fine, Tom, I'll play. Why don't you feel appreciated?"

"Oh, that reminds me," Tom said. "Can we stop somewhere and buy some packing materials?"

"Packing materials?" Garcia asked, with a worried look at Hugo. *Is he mad?*

"Yes, packing materials. For the glasses I borrowed from Tourville's kitchen."

"The . . . glasses?" Hugo turned around again. "What the hell are you talking about?"

"The water glasses," Tom said. "The ones carrying the fingerprints of four potential suspects." He patted the bag again. "Those glasses."

"Ah, I see." Hugo smiled. " But just four? I suppose it's a start."

"Like I said." Tom sniffed exaggeratedly and looked out of the side window. "I just don't get the appreciation I deserve."

As they headed east toward Paris, a silence fell over the car. Each man, Hugo knew, had a slightly different role in what had happened and what was to come. Hugo's next move would depend on whether the ambassador believed Lake had seen a ghost, a real intruder, or nothing at all. Garcia was going to be busy with the robbery–murder case no matter what. And Tom? Hard to know with him. He'd get involved in whatever was happening in Paris and beyond if asked—and likely if not asked.

It was Tom who broke the silence. "Oh, crap, I meant to tell you."

"Tell me what?" Hugo asked. Garcia pricked his ears, too.

"About our mild-mannered senator," Tom said. "I got curious and poked into his background. You know he's divorced, right?"

"So?"

"I think I know why, though the court paperwork didn't say anything. A few years back he was arrested for assaulting his dear wife."

"Lake?" Hugo asked. "Are you sure?"

"Yep. Happened before his political career took off, and it remained a secret because his lawyer got him into a deferred prosecution program."

"What does that mean?" asked Garcia.

"Most states use them for first-time offenders," Tom explained. "It's basically a short probation term, you have to take classes, get counseling, maybe do some community service. If you do everything you're supposed to, your criminal charge goes away. Thin air."

"And that means if anyone runs a criminal history check on him, nothing shows up," Hugo added. "But apparently he's not so mild-mannered after all. Good to know." Hugo's phone buzzed, and he pulled it from his pocket. The ambassador. "Good morning, sir. We just left the château, we'll in be in Paris for lunch."

"No lunch today, Hugo." The ambassador sounded tired.

"Meaning?"

"Meaning we have a potential disaster on our hands."

He explained in three short sentences and when he'd finished, Hugo said, "We'll get back as fast as we can, see you soon." He rang off, and looked over at Garcia. "Got lights and sirens on this thing?"

"Yes, but why would I need those?"

"Senator Lake has disappeared."

CHAPTER TWELVE

OUTSIDE PARIS, 1795

Four people stood beside the grave. On one side, the little boy's father and mother were silent with grief, staring down at the wooden box in its final resting place. On the other side were Jacques the old gardener and Olivier their groom, not much younger, the two servants entrusted with digging the little hole. They were men who were silent by nature, and they'd been given a year's wages to stay that way.

The wind swept off the open fields that surrounded this wooden copse, rattling the stand of trees that sat atop the only real hill on the property. The father had promised his wife that by laying him to rest here, their little boy would always be visible to them and therefore never be forgotten.

That word sat heavily with them both, *forgotten*. Earlier, at the house, the boy's mother had finally said what they both knew to be true, whispering her words through tears as she wrapped the body of their only child in the best sheets they owned.

"We have to forget him. If this is to work, then we have no choice." She'd looked up at her husband, pale with grief and thinner than she'd ever seen him. "I don't think I can do it any other way."

"*Oui*, I know," he said. "I know."

To deny their little boy's death meant denying themselves the balm of grief, those few and weak moments of relief that came from wailing and screaming at the sky. They knew this to be true: no parent can bury a son and then safely, unobtrusively, bury the agony that comes with living without him. She was right to say that their survival, not just of the plan they'd put in place, but the survival of themselves as living, breathing, human beings, depended on the total shutting down of this part of history. In effect, they'd agreed, they wouldn't just be denying his death and their own grief, but they would be denying their little boy's entire existence.

Now, leaves fell from the oak trees around them and cartwheeled along the ground past their ankles, golden and crisp and dead. They fell into the open grave and soon Jacques shifted, ready to get past this.

Of all those who worked on the estate, he'd been closest to the boy. He'd taught him the difference between a flower and a weed and then, when he was older, the difference between types of flowers, which ones loved the sun and which the shade.

"*Moi*, I'm more of a shade man, I think," he'd laughed.

"Not me," the boy had said, "I want the sunshine, like the roses."

On his tenth birthday, Jacques had taught him how to set a snare for the hares that loped across the bare fields, a simple yet strong apparatus of wire and sticks, and then how to skin one when he caught it. The boy had watched, wide-eyed the first time Jacques cleaned a dead animal, fascinated but also, Jacques thought, a little sad.

For today, Jacques had made a cross with wood from this very copse, but the mother and father had explained how it couldn't be there—not upright, anyway. And so Jacques had whittled the arms down until it fit flat on the coffin, and he wept as he reached into the pit and laid it down with soft hands, hands that lingered as if hoping the little boy would somehow notice this final gesture of love from a man too old to have children of his own, but who'd loved this one like a son.

When told his grave marker would have to be buried with the boy, Jacques had understood and felt a glimmer of happiness that something of his would be there to accompany the child. And he'd asked—no, begged—the boy's parents to let him build a garden for their son, a perfect circle made of roses right in front of the house, a garden that he would tend until the day he died. The circle would symbolize the family's unending love for their son, with soft grass cutting through it north to south and east and west, a cross, through the roses to give it meaning and to give them access to its center, a way into and through the rose patch from every direction. They had said yes.

Finally, the mother and father moved away, clutching each other with their heads close, bowed, as they made their way across the field back to the house.

With a momentous effort, Jacques and Olivier turned and picked up their shovels. They looked at each other, and with a small nod from the older man they began the rhythmic stab and tip of heavy soil into the grave. Both men flinched at those first hollow thumps as the wet mud landed on the wooden casket, but soon the fall of earth became muffled as the top and then the corners of the boy's coffin disappeared from view. The men's shovels became heavy with mud and they huffed with the effort, their breath steaming in the cooling air as they worked. They didn't speak until they were done, nor did they rest, pausing only to draw a rough sleeve over their eyes, wiping at the rivers of tears that wouldn't stop.

At the house, the mother and father let themselves into the guest room and stood hand-in-hand looking down at the bed. Another boy, the same age as theirs, lay asleep. His breathing was labored and his forehead shone with fever, but last night he'd turned a corner, moved away from the dark and jagged path that had led their son on his final walk.

The mother knelt beside the bed and took a wet cloth from a bowl, then dabbed gently at the boy to cool him down.

"He's better," she said. "He's doing so much better."

"*Bien*. We don't have much time, we have to travel soon. If anyone finds out, if Monsieur Pichon were somehow to find out what we're doing..."

"Hush," his wife said gently. "No one will find out. And by the time they do, we will be gone." She stood and dropped the cloth back into the bowl, then stooped over the boy and kissed his now-cool forehead. She stood next to her husband and took his hand. "He's ours now. We have to take care of him, especially on a trip such as this."

"I know. We can wait another few days, that should be enough time."

"He will be eating by then." She looked up at her husband and then back at the boy. "Our son. This is our son now."

"Yes," whispered her husband. "He's our son."

CHAPTER THIRTEEN

Capitaine Garcia dropped Hugo and Tom in front of the US Embassy and they went straight in to meet with the ambassador.

"Still no word," Taylor said. "We're still hoping he went sightseeing rather than . . . anything else."

"Well, Paris is a beautiful city, so it's entirely possible," Tom said cheerily.

"And as we all know," Hugo said, "if there's one thing we can expect Lake to do, it's appreciate Paris."

"Now, now, no need to be sarcastic," Tom said. "Paris can win over even the hardest of hearts."

"Guys, focus," Taylor interrupted. He looked at Hugo. "What's your best guess, does this have something to do with his phantom intruder at Chateau Tourville, or not?"

"I honestly don't know," Hugo said. "I can guarantee he's not out buying souvenirs, though. It's possible he needed to get out and clear his head but I'd be surprised at him going to the trouble of losing his security just to do that. Very surprised. And you said he didn't take his phone, which means he's either forgetful or he really doesn't want us tracking him." Hugo looked at the ambassador. "We're absolutely sure he slipped his guardians and someone didn't take him?"

"Correct. He sent them both on bullshit errands, which he's done before, so they both made sure his room door was locked before leaving him safe and secure inside."

"And surveillance?" Tom prompted.

"Yeah, it also crossed my mind that someone knocked on his door and tricked his way into Lake's rooms, but nope, he walked out himself less than a minute after Ruby and Rousek did and sailed straight out of the hotel."

"Which direction?" Hugo asked.

"Toward the river."

"And has anyone looked at his phone, or checked with the hotel to see if a call was made to his room at any point? A call from someone out of the ordinary."

"His phone has a code and we don't want to break into it unless we're sure there's a problem—you may have noticed he's a little temperamental. I can't imagine he'd leave it lying on his bedside table, which he did, by the way, if it contains some kind of incriminating evidence."

"Fair enough," Hugo said. "Any calls into his room?"

"In the two hours before he left the hotel, four. One from his brother in the United States, two from his staff there, and one from here in Paris." Taylor held up a hand. "And before you ask, no way to know from whom, or even the number. The Crillon is a hotel, not the CIA, as they politely reminded me."

"So a clue with a dead end, fucking marvelous," Tom said. "Now what's the plan?"

"Not sure, to be honest." Taylor looked chagrined. "I was kinda hoping you boys would come up with one."

"We did," Hugo said, winking. "Just wanted to make sure it didn't contradict yours. We talked on the way up, figured Tom would take lead here looking for Lake. He can get access to security and surveillance cameras via his CIA contacts and generally be more use than me up here. Whether this has something to do with the mysterious intruder and the Troyes murder I don't know, but both need looking into. And fast."

"Agreed," Taylor nodded.

"Garcia's briefing his boss right now, and if you give the go-ahead he and I will swing down to meet with the Troyes police, maybe go visit the crime scene or talk to the victim's family."

"You think there's a connection?"

"No idea," Hugo said, "but we'd be nuts not to look for one."

"Then get to it." He looked at Tom. "And you find Lake, Tom, whatever it takes. If you need something from me just ask, but I don't want to hit the panic button right now."

"Meaning?"

"Meaning I don't want a full alert with the Paris police. If he has gone out to clear his head and enjoy some anonymous time, then we can yell at him when he gets back. But if there's a chance in hell of getting these damn talks back on track, the fewer people who know about this little breach of security the better. On both sides of the Atlantic."

They took the A5 heading southeast away from Paris, Garcia driving his police Peugeot fast, weaving in and out of traffic as they left the city behind with rolling green fields opening up around them. Once clear of the city, Hugo called the police department handling the murder and talked to the detective in charge for the second time in twenty-four hours. The detective was unable to get away until the next day, but he'd arranged for the victim's son, Georges Bassin, to meet them there.

The drive took two hours and by the time they arrived Hugo was ready to stretch his legs, and his back. Garcia parked behind a white Landover, sparkling clean, and a tall, thin man in his late-fifties came out of a side door to meet them. He wore a heavy blue cardigan and baggy brown corduroys, and he walked with a slight stoop. His grip when he shook hands, though, was firm and his English was flawless.

"Gentlemen, thank you for coming."

They followed him inside, taking seats in a large drawing room that looked out over a patio and, beyond that, a wide and manicured lawn. "You have a beautiful home, Monsieur Bassin," Hugo said.

"Thank you. It's been in my family for almost three hundred years." He smiled. "And in some places, you can definitely tell. My mother wasn't eager to update or even repair, so I'll have the pleasure of doing that."

"She lived here alone?" Hugo asked.

"Yes and no. I have an apartment in the city, I spend most of my time there. But I come twice a month, sometimes more. My children grew up here but now one lives in Cannes and the other in Australia so yes, most of the time she was here alone."

"Did she have many friends, people who visited?"

"You want to know whether she was targeted or this was random," Bassin said. "It's OK, for a while I was in military intelligence. Twenty years ago. No, thirty now." He shook his head. "Time steals a march on us all, *n'est-ce pas?*"

"It does," Hugo agreed. "Then you'll also know that we'd like to hear about any tradesmen or repair people who come to the house."

"No, like I said, she didn't have much done here. Left it to me, and it's only now I'm getting to it. As for friends, a few close ones from the village but as far as I know none of them had any reprobate sons or nephews looking for drug money."

"Monsieur," Garcia said, "are you familiar with Henri Tourville?"

"Yes, of course." He frowned. "I'm not sure I could tell you what post he holds in government right now, but naturally I know the name."

"And that of his sister?" Garcia asked.

"If the newspapers are to be believed, which is doubtful, she is quite a handful and while I have no problem with her personal life, I'm not sure I want my politicians engaging in such . . . indiscretions."

"Not the female ones, anyway." Hugo muttered, unable to help himself.

"Precisely," Bassin agreed. "Oh, I know it's a double standard, believe me. But if we're to get the respect of foreign countries then, until they become as progressive as we are, we have to appreciate that there are some things men can get away with that women cannot."

Garcia cleared his throat to get them back on track. "We're wondering whether you've ever visited Chateau Tourville, or if anyone in your family has. Likewise, if you've had members of the Tourville family stay here."

"No, I'm sure I'd know if we had."

"Is it possible you've hired people to work here that may have come from Chateau Tourville?"

"Definitely not. We have two men who work part-time on the gardens, my mother insisted on keeping those in perfect shape. And the farmland is leased out and has been for decades. We have cleaners, but they are from the village, the same family has done that for us for years. Decades, again." He chuckled. "When I listen to myself it's like we're stuck in history with no one new coming to the house this century. But, that's about the way it is."

"Do you think you would know of everyone who might have visited?" Garcia asked. "I mean, is there someone else we should ask about visitors or people connected to Tourville?"

"My sister, Marie, was here a few months ago. She has a home in Provence but comes to stay for a week or two when she has time. I believe she's in Italy right now. Or did she go on safari to Namibia?" He shrugged. "Well, I'll give you her phone number, you can track her down."

"Thank you. Anyone else?"

"I don't think anyone would know more than us, but you're welcome to talk with the two men who work in the garden. I'm sure they've been interviewed by the police, but they wouldn't mind talking to you. As for anyone else, I doubt it. My mother's memory was fading, she had lapses and frequently forgot things, even my visits. So, she wasn't good company for outsiders, and most of her old friends are either dead or not mobile enough to come out here." He paused and then looked between Hugo and Garcia. "Can I ask, what is the connection with Henri Tourville?"

Hugo said, "There was an incident at his house, nothing like what happened here, but a fingerprint lifted from his house matched one of those taken here. One of those taken from the armoire."

"It has to be one of his staff, surely?"

"That seems most likely."

"So why not just fingerprint them?"

"We've asked," Garcia said, "but they're not cooperating. Understandably, they don't want to be associated with what happened here. And there simply isn't a strong enough connection to require everyone who works there to give prints. Our lawyers tell me there has to be a definite link to the crime and some indication of a specific person. In other words, we can't just go around forcing people to give prints until we get lucky."

"And it being the Tourvilles, you have to be extra sure to persuade a judge, I'm betting," Bassin said. He held up a hand. "*Non, ça va,* the Bassin family has some standing here and I wouldn't object to a judge being sensitive to our name and reputation."

"I know you've been asked the same questions numerous times, but indulge me," Hugo said. "You know of no one who had a grudge against you or your mother?"

"No one at all."

"No money problems for her or business problems for you?"

"No, our family has always been very fortunate. Nothing like that at all."

"No business dealings with the Tourvilles?"

"As I said, I don't even know what ministry he works with right now." A thin smile. "Certainly, no interactions or dealings with his sister."

"Do you know Felix Vibert?" Hugo asked.

Bassin shook his head slowly. "The name seems familiar but . . . I can't place it. I can tell you for certain that I don't have direct dealings with anyone of that name."

"Thank you." Hugo thought for a moment. "The police reports says that the only thing stolen was jewelry."

"That's right."

"And forgive me for asking, but you're absolutely sure nothing else was missing?"

"Yes, absolutely. You are thinking there was some other motive?"

"Wondering, anyway," Hugo said. "The obvious choices would be sexual assault, and there was no evidence of that at all, and robbery. But it's possible there was another reason, it just seems like an out-of-the-way place to rob for a few earrings and necklaces."

"I agree," Bassin said. "Now, I believe some of it was quite valuable but I couldn't say which pieces with any certainty. I think my sister provided the list to the police and the insurance people; she knows better than I do what my mother had."

"Do you have a copy of the list?"

"In the study, yes."

"I'd like to get a copy, if you don't mind. But can we see where the jewelry was kept?" Hugo asked.

"Of course. Please, follow me."

They followed single file into the hallway, past the open door to the study, and up a flight of stairs. At the top they followed Bassin to the left and he led them to the closed door of his late mother's bedroom. He seemed to hesitate for a moment, gather himself maybe, then he opened the door and let Garcia and Hugo pass through first.

"I don't think it's been touched since the police were here. I've not let the cleaners come in, even." His voice dropped. "Not yet, anyway."

"I understand," Garcia said, "and I'm sorry for the intrusion like this."

"*Non*, it's necessary. My sister and I, we won't rest easily here until whoever did this is caught." He took a breath and then straightened up, pointing at a large armoire. "She kept blankets, sheets, and towels in there. And the jewelry, you'll see an empty space but . . . that's all there is to see, I think."

Hugo went over and opened the doors to the armoire, which reminded him of the ones he'd seen in the bedrooms at Chateau Tourville. Not surprising, they were *de rigeur* before the built-in closets of today. As Bassin had said, bed linens and towels took up most of the inside space, leaving a gap at waist height where Madam Bassin had stored, with no concern for security apparently, those items that mattered most.

"Thank you," said Hugo. A germ had planted itself in his head and he was ready to move downstairs. "Can I see that list of stolen items now?"

"Of course." He gestured weakly at the armoire as Hugo closed it. "No clues?"

"One thought occurs to me, but . . . that list might help."

It did. Garcia looked over Hugo's shoulder at the type-written inventory, twenty-eight items that included bracelets, broaches, necklaces, rings, and earrings. Brief descriptions of each were included, but no estimated values because Madam Bassin hadn't acquired any of them recently. Some pieces were treasures from her youth and early married years, but more than half had filtered through to her from previous generations.

"Twenty-eight," Hugo said.

"Yes." Bassin said. "That means something?"

"Well, it's a lot to carry for one person and the police reported no indication of a second intruder." Hugo looked at Bassin. "I'm wondering how he managed to carry it away. Too much for pockets, so either he brought a bag with him or . . . what was the jewelry kept in?"

"An old box," Bassin said.

"All of it in one jewelry box?"

"Not really a jewelry box, more of a chest. It had been in the family for almost as long as the house."

"How long is that?" Garcia asked.

"Four hundred years. Not my direct line, there are family stories of feuds and the house moving from one branch of the family to another."

Hugo barely heard the response, impatient to get back on track. "The chest, you were saying . . ."

"A sailor's chest, *maman* called it."

Hugo's chest tightened. "Can you describe it?"

"*Bien sur.*" Bassin furrowed his brow in thought. "Made of wood, probably walnut because it was burled but you couldn't really see that because it was so old. The fittings were brass, ornamental in a way, but again the hinges and decoration were darker than you'd think because of its age." He smiled at a memory, and said, "You know, now that I think of it my mother had sort of a special affection for that chest, she used to say it contained all kinds of family treasures." He shrugged. "But that's the tragedy of burglaries like this, *n'est-ce pas*? The thief takes items that may prove valuable or worthless to him, but without question contain priceless memories and sentiments. I'm sorry, I didn't think to list the chest as it's not really worth anything. Is it?"

"To someone," said Hugo, "I suspect it is."

Garcia put a hand on Hugo's arm. "What is it? I've seen that look before and it means you've discovered something, an answer . . . What this time?"

Hugo turned to Bassin. "Is there any chance you have a photo of the chest?"

"Not that I know of."

"But you'd recognize it if you saw it again?"

"Yes, I think so. I mean, there can't be too many like it, can there?"

"Precisely what I was thinking," Hugo said. "I think we have all we need, Monsieur Bassin. Raul, we should go." He winked at his friend. "I think you'd call this a clue. And one that takes us right back to Chateau Tourville."

CHAPTER FOURTEEN

Ambassador Taylor was emphatic. Hugo had finished his progress report, having already called Bassin's sister and gone straight to voicemail. He'd left her a message and immediately called the ambassador.

"Tonight, Hugo," Taylor said. "He's not back and I'm about to call the cavalry but before I do . . ."

"I honestly don't think it'll make any difference. I'm not going to see anything in his room that Tom or anyone else missed."

"Maybe, but you're only an hour away and you pretty much have to go through Paris to get home."

"Well, that's true." He glanced at Garcia, both hands gripping the wheel and eyes on the road. "The capitaine will want to get home, too, I imagine." A twitch at the corner of Garcia's mouth said *thank you.* "I was just hoping for a beer and some down time."

That was close to the truth, though an incomplete version. He'd hoped to entice Claudia for a drink, maybe dinner. Days filled with theft, murder, and mistrust had pushed him into wanting a moment of peace with someone who could make him feel utterly comfortable. Taylor's request that he comb the still-missing senator's room for clues pulled in the opposite direction from the plan he'd imagined ever since shaking hands with Georges Bassin and wishing him good-bye.

"Missing senators don't allow for much down time, sorry."

"I know," Hugo sighed. "Someone can meet me there and let me in?"

"The Crillon staff know you're coming. They're being great about this whole thing, discreet and very cooperative."

"You get what you pay for, I guess."

"True enough. Call me when you get there, OK?"

Hugo hung up and stared out of the window. Dusk was settling over the countryside, an orange sun spilling across the horizon to their left. On either side of the highway lay fields that, little more than a month ago, had rippled with healthy rows of golden wheat and barley. Now they lay ragged and bare, cut to stubble that had been browned by the autumn rains and torn by the wheels of tractors. Clusters of still-yellow bales, as large and solid as boulders, gathered at seemingly random intervals, awaiting transport to the barns where they would carpet the floors for the dairy and beef cattle spending the winter inside.

Hugo let his eyes wander the countryside while he pondered the disappearance of Senator Lake, but through tiredness or . . . something, he couldn't concentrate. When his phone buzzed, he was glad for the excuse to stop trying and surprised to feel a jangle in his blood when he saw her name on the screen.

"Claudia, how are you?"

"Fine, I got your message." A smile in her voice. "Obviously."

"It's good to hear you."

"Is everything OK?"

"Yes. A little tired, maybe."

"So I don't think I can do drinks tonight, I'm sorry. A work thing, someone retiring and I said I'd go."

"That's OK, I—"

"Ah. Something happened between you calling me and me calling you back?"

"Yeah, pretty much."

"Well, that works out then." She sounded amused rather than annoyed, but somehow that didn't help. "Anything a reporter should know about?"

"Yes. Absolutely. Kind of a huge scoop, when I think about it."

"Which means you won't tell me. What a tease."

"Sorry, can't."

"Can't and won't are equally unhelpful from where I'm sitting."

"Not to me," Hugo sighed, "honestly, I'd love to spill my guts, and preferably over a bottle of wine."

"Oh, Hugo, you do sound tired."

"Told you."

"Maybe we can get together this weekend, are you free?"

"That depends on how tonight and tomorrow go. Can I call you when I know?"

"Only if you're allowed to." She was teasing him now—the first time in a while, and he felt himself grinning like a teenager.

"I'll sneak out and call if I have to."

"Do that."

Garcia looked over as Hugo put his phone away. "What's the plan?"

"If you don't mind, drop me at the Crillon and then your evening is your own."

"You want some help there?"

"No, thanks. It'll take me a minute or two and there's no point both of us wasting our time, especially since you have someone at home waiting for you."

"With open arms and a three-course dinner," Garcia said, his flat tone disguising either sarcasm or longing. "So what's with you and the lovely Claudia?"

Hugo shrugged. "Nothing, literally. Best described as off-again, off-again."

"Is that how you want it?"

"Sometimes. Mostly not, to be honest."

"I don't blame you, she's a special lady."

"She is. I like being around her, Raul, she's smart and funny and we have a good time." He pictured her, laughing in his apartment in tank top and jeans. "Sexy as hell, too."

"Can't argue with any of that. So, she's not wanting more?"

"I'm assuming not. Ever since that business with Max and her father, she's been distant. Friendly, always, but she's hard to read as far as wanting more."

Garcia smiled. "Ever thought about asking her?"

"Nope. Maybe this weekend if I see her."

"*Bonne idée*. But I suppose you have to find your senator first."

A serious young man in a gray suit came to the front desk when Hugo gave his name at reception. He introduced himself as Anthony, the head of hotel security. He looked too young to be the head of anything, but his smooth ebony skin probably knocked a few years off his real age and his intelligent eyes and firm handshake were reassuring. He talked, his English flawless, as they moved to the elevators. Two middle-aged women preserved by makeup and plastic surgery drifted up behind them and put down their shopping bags with conspiratorial sighs of exhaustion.

Anthony lowered his voice. "Your friend was staying in one of our deluxe suites. We show him leaving the hotel at ten this morning, heading toward the river. Since then, his two secret service agents and someone else, a Mr. Green working for your embassy, have been in the room. No one else."

"What time was Mr. Green here?"

"Around one." A small smile. "Mr. Green, sounds like he's a Quentin Tarantino character."

"Funny you should say that." The elevator gave a soft ding and Hugo stood aside to let the women enter. "He's very much a Tarantino character, though it's his real name."

"As far as we know, right?" Anthony winked. Hugo liked this young man very much.

Anthony unlocked the door with a swipe of his key card and bade the American enter Senator Lake's suite. Hugo stood just inside the doorway and looked around, getting the lay of the room, a separate lounge area, before moving to its center. It was just as he'd imagined, beautifully furnished in classic *grand-siècle* style, a warm red and cream rug on an already soft carpet floor, painted paneled walls, a marble fireplace, and the kind of plush yet elegant chairs that might have been plucked straight from the Palace of Versailles.

"A question." Hugo turned to Anthony. "Did the maid come into the room today, specifically after Senator Lake walked out but before his detail realized he was gone?"

"No, sir."

"You sound sure."

"I am. When he first got here, the senator phoned down and canceled all maid and cleaning services for his whole stay."

"Really?"

"Yes, sir."

"Is that common, for a guest to do that?"

"No, not really. I mean, this isn't the first time but I definitely wouldn't say it's common."

"I assume he didn't give a reason?"

"No, and the staff wouldn't have asked for one. You pretty much have things your way when you stay here."

"Especially when you're a senator."

Anthony shrugged. "When you're anyone. The people who stay here are accustomed to having things the way they like, and one of the reasons they come here is because we like to accommodate them."

Hugo started moving slowly around the room, compartmentalizing it and analyzing each section for what should or shouldn't be there. Small signs might tell him if the senator's absence was intentional or not, whether sudden or planned, or intended to be brief or extended. He spent a few minutes at the desk, which held an empty note pad, a pocket map of Paris, and some other papers that told Hugo nothing.

When he'd circled the room he moved into the bedroom, furnished in the same elegant style with a king bed taking up much of the room. The covers had been pulled up but the bed wasn't made, and Hugo found no evidence of a second person having slept in it, no makeup on pillows or long hairs laying in the sheets.

Hugo saw that Anthony had followed him from one doorway to the next, watching with interest but quiet, letting Hugo do his job.

"Let me know if you see anything amiss," Hugo said.

Anthony straightened, surprised. "Me? How would I know?"

"These are your rooms. I know you guys furnish them individually, but maybe they all have the same ashtray and it's missing. Perhaps a lamp should be in one corner but it's been moved to another. Something like that."

The security man's eyes narrowed as he looked at the room in a new light, as somewhere he was now relevant, potentially helpful. "I don't think so, nothing jumps out at me. I'll look in the lounge."

The bathroom was as unyielding as the other rooms. No signs of a struggle, no obvious indicators that told Hugo where the senator had gone or why he'd left. Lake hadn't taken his toothbrush or other toiletries, and Tom had already checked that all the senator's bags were present and accounted for, so they were still assuming he'd planned a short absence.

The oddity was Lake's phone. A man as connected and politically important, Hugo knew, very rarely went anywhere without his phone these days. It was more than just a phone, too, Lake could have used it to text, connect to the Internet, or guide himself around Paris.

"We need to have another look at the surveillance video," he said when Anthony returned. "See anything?"

"No. Why the surveillance tapes again?"

"He left here with someone. Either he met them in the hotel or close by. It's possible whoever that person was, he or she showed up and met him in the lobby, persuaded him to ditch his phone and his security and go out."

"He or she? You're thinking a lady friend?"

"This is Paris, and he's a politician. It's not impossible. What we do know is that he left here without his phone or his map, and having never been to Paris before, you can bet it's not because he knows his way around."

"So he's with someone who does know Paris."

"That's my bet."

Both men froze as the door into the suite opened. Hugo gestured for Anthony to move into the corner of the bedroom, out of sight from the lounge area, while he moved quietly toward the doorway. His hand hovered near his jacket, though he couldn't imagine using his weapon here in the hotel. Hugo heard someone moving steadily through the lounge, either carefree or in a hurry, and he took a deep breath and moved into sight.

CHAPTER FIFTEEN

Hugo took a moment to register.

"What the hell are you doing in my room?" Senator Lake demanded. He looked pale and tired, his clothes were rumpled and one of his shoelaces was undone.

"Trying to find you, as it happens."

Lake went to the drinks cabinet and poured himself a brandy, then slumped onto the sofa. "You found me, Hugo, you can go now."

Hugo turned and spoke to Anthony. "He's back. Thanks for all your help, I'll take it from here." Anthony nodded and walked into the lounge, where he nodded a respectful *bonjour* to the senator and kept going out of the suite into the hallway, closing the door gently behind him.

"Backup?" If it was an attempt at sarcasm it fell short, coming out as no more than a weary question.

"In law enforcement terminology," Hugo said, "he's what we call the key-holder."

"Well, you can call off the hounds, I'm home safe and sound."

"Mind telling me where you were?"

"Yes, I do."

"I thought so, but there are a lot of people who're going to be asking you that question."

Lake looked up, a flash of anger in his eyes. "It's Paris. When people are in Paris they explore, is that so fucking unusual?"

Hugo eased into a chair opposite the senator, keeping his tone mild. "It's a little unusual when the person is a senator who slips his security detail and wanders about without his phone or a map."

"I like to be alone sometimes." He sounded like a recalcitrant child and he dipped his nose into his glass to avoid looking at Hugo.

"We all do." Hugo let the silence draw out. "Senator, is everything all right?"

"Yes. Everything's fine, I'm just tired. You think everyone could just leave me alone until tomorrow morning? I'll be fresh as a daisy and we can get back to work." At last, he looked up. "But tonight, I would like to be left in peace so I can sleep."

"Sure. I'll let your detail know you're here and not to bother you. I can't promise that Ambassador Taylor won't phone, but I'll pass on your request. One thing, though."

"What?"

"You said 'get back to work.' You meant the Guadeloupe negotiations?"

"Yes."

"Then I'm not sure I understand. You're ready to go back to Chateau Tourville?"

"That's right. I think . . . I was wrong about seeing someone in my room, that's clear to me now."

"I imagine Henri Tourville will be pleased to hear that."

"I'm sure. I'll apologize when I see him and you can put an end to whatever little investigation you had going."

"I can certainly terminate that end of it, yes."

"What do you mean, 'that end of it'?" His tone was sharp.

"I don't know what the ambassador told you but the house is linked to another crime, a murder east of Paris."

"What the hell does that have to do with me? Or you, for that matter?"

"Nothing, I'm sure. I'm just letting you know that there is an active investigation that tangentially involves the chateau."

Lake put his glass down. "And how does Tourville feel about that?"

"As you'd imagine. Not happy at all."

"I should think not. Look, Hugo, I may have gone off the deep end a little for a day or so, but we need these talks back on track. I'm serious. You and the French police can't be poking around the hallways and bedrooms while we're discussing international law and the future of people's lives."

"I'm sure the police will be discreet, but if you think it's going to be disruptive, we can move the talks elsewhere. Here in Paris, at the embassy perhaps."

"No! Dammit, the whole point of going out there was to keep it low-key and friendly. If we'd wanted a media circus we'd have held talks at the embassy or somewhere else people could pester us. What the hell are we going to tell the press? This may not be the biggest story in the world but you can bet your ass it'll become one if you go around linking the Tourvilles to some random murder on the other side of the country." He stood up and began pacing. "No, Hugo. This has to get back on track, and you and the police need to sit tight for a few days until our work is done. You hear me?"

Hugo rose, also. "Loud and clear, senator. You're now telling me no one came into your room and you made the whole thing up."

"Imagined it." Lake pointed a finger at Hugo. "Not made it up, I was mistaken. So that part of the investigation goes away and the Tourvilles are left alone." He sat down again and ran a hand through his hair. "Look, I'm sorry, Hugo. I don't mean to be the yelling politician who wants to get his own way *just because*. This negotiation, it's important to my career and to the people who live on those islands, of course. Sometimes my imagination can . . . It's a little problem I've been dealing with my whole life. Nothing serious, really, I promise, but I can get an idea in my head and convince myself it's true. It can take a day strolling the banks of the Seine to clear my mind and get back to what matters." A tired smile. "Am I making any sense, here?"

"Yes sir. And if we're to get back on track, I should let you get some rest." Hugo moved to the door and opened it. He turned back and said, "I'll deal with the ambassador tonight, let him know all's well. He or

I will be in touch in the morning, maybe I can drive you back to the chateau myself tomorrow."

"Thanks, Hugo, I appreciate that. Tell Taylor I'll call him when I'm up, I don't feel like enduring another inquisition."

"I understand, have a good night." Hugo closed the door behind him and started down the hall. *The inquisition, Senator, has only just begun.*

Taylor picked up on the second ring. "Hugo, find anything?"

"Yes, as a matter of fact I did."

"Great, care to fill me in?"

"Sure. I found Senator Lake. A long complicated search, with clues leading me hither and thither, but I'll spare you the details. He's back in his suite, tired, grumpy, and wanting to be left alone."

"What? Are you serious?"

"Yep. He walked in the door while I was in there. Said he'd been wandering the banks of the Seine to clear his head."

"Bullshit."

"Yeah, that's what I thought but I didn't say so."

"What the hell's going on with him? Is he mentally unstable or something?"

Hugo chuckled. "People keep asking me that. No, I don't think he disappeared in a fog of mental or emotional confusion. I think he met someone."

"Who?"

"If I knew that, boss, I'd have mentioned it by now. No clue."

"A girl?"

"Possible, it's the city of love, after all."

"Jesus. Someone from the chateau? Must be, he's not been there long enough for anything else."

"Maybe, but these days it's easy to arrange something like that via the Internet. He could have planned this for weeks and we'd never know."

Taylor sighed. "When in France, do as the French do."

"Yeah, but I don't think that's it."

"Why not?"

"Why wouldn't he take his phone? He doesn't know whether we can track him or not, and so what if we do? Everyone looking after him here is used to political indiscretions, no one's tipping off the press or making a fuss. He's single, for heaven's sake, he can meet who he likes."

"Maybe it's a dude."

"I hadn't thought about that," Hugo conceded. "But he left with no phone, no map, and he came back all flustered and angry."

"Maybe he thought it was a woman and it turned out to be a dude."

Hugo laughed. "You sound like Tom, Mr. Ambassador."

"God forbid. Seriously, Hugo, what do you think's going on?"

"I have no idea. The other thing is, he insisted we stop the investigation into the mysterious intruder in his room. Says he imagined it all, he's now convinced no one was in there."

"That's an about-face."

"Agreed. And he knows it, too. He told me he wants the talks back on track, they're important to his career and the islanders, he said. Which is true but . . ."

"But you don't buy it."

"He's a mercurial man, so maybe my spidey sense is tingling for no reason, but it doesn't usually do that. I can't help wondering why, when everyone at the chateau seemed so squeaky clean, he was scared and angry at the thought of an intruder but now, when he knows someone at the house could be a suspect in a real murder, he's all about heading straight back into the lion's den."

"Good point." The ambassador cleared his throat. "Best I can figure, there's only one way to find out. Tomorrow, you can head back into the lion's den with him."

CHAPTER SIXTEEN

Henri Tourville welcomed Senator Lake like an old friend, the two men exchanging warm handshakes and clapping each other on the shoulder, but they barely made eye contact and as Hugo trailed them toward the dining room, he could see the tension in their stiff movements and hear it in the forced amity of their voices.

The original ten participants of the talks had been hastily summoned for an informal brunch, one that had required clearing the village bakery of every pastry and sandwich on its shelves. The coffee was home brewed, though, and a welcome and reassuring aroma filled the dining room.

Hugo stayed in the background, watching the ice crack but not melt, aware that he was probably the only one in the room who was glad to be there. And the only one with a simple, definable, and hopefully achievable mission: find the sailor's chest.

It was here somewhere, he knew, and other than the shared fingerprint it was the only potential link between the chateau and the murder in Troyes. Not a link yet, of course, more of a wild theory because Chateau Tourville was precisely the kind of place one would expect to find an antique like that. Even so, he planned to find it and photograph it for Garcia, who could then show it to Georges Bassin to see if it was the same one. Surreptitiously, of course, because recently-smoothed feathers didn't need to be ruffled by an overly nosy babysitter.

As the politicians piled croissants and mille-feuilles onto plates,

Hugo circled the dining room. The chest had been on a side table right behind his seat at the dinner, a table that was adorned with the same vase, now brimming with yellow and white flowers. But no chest. He looked around the rest of the room but didn't see it, and he realized he couldn't even picture it clearly in his mind.

He drifted into the hallway and then to the large living room where he found Felix Vibert in an armchair, papers on his lap and on the ottoman in front of him. He looked up when Hugo entered.

"Monsieur Marston, *bonjour*. I heard the commotion and assumed you and the senator had arrived."

"Yes, just in time for brunch. And then maybe some progress. Aren't you part of the French delegation?"

"I've been part of delegations, monsieur, and there is no such thing here. A silly squabble that will blow over no matter what we say or do." He smiled to show he was only half joking. "In my humble opinion, this is little more than a chance for politicians to be seen to be working when they are, in fact, eating, drinking, and making merry."

"Good work when you can get it."

"Indeed." He waved a sheaf of papers. "My assistant and I have already been working on a draft of the agreement, and the talks haven't begun. That tells you all you need to know."

"I'm sure they will be grateful."

"No, they won't. They will complain and thump the table for a day and *then* they will be grateful." He cocked his head. "And in the meantime, what will you do here? Look for more invisible intruders?"

"No, no," Hugo said. "The senator says that was all a mistake, he's even apologized personally to Monsieur Tourville. Case closed, you might say."

Hugo turned at a voice behind him.

"I heard my name." Henri Tourville smiled, but his eyes were wary.

"Explaining that I'm back to babysitting, and no longer hunting room-invaders," Hugo said.

Tourville nodded. "Nicely put, Monsieur Marston. And I'm very glad that's the case; as you said, the senator was gracious in his apology.

Case closed indeed." He paused for a moment, then said, "Even so, am I right in thinking that there is an outstanding allegation against someone in my household?"

"No allegations," Hugo said. "Just an undefined connection with another crime scene. But yes, a connection that the police would like to clear up."

"Is that why you're here? The senator has two capable secret service agents to drive him around, so I'm not clear why you returned with him."

"That was entirely his choice," Hugo said. True, too, though Hugo would have found a way to accompany the senator regardless.

"I see. While you are here, are you planning to work on that other matter?"

"My only job here is to make sure the senator is taken care of."

"You dodge the question, so let me ask it another way. Are you a part of the Troyes investigation?"

Hugo nodded. "I'm helping the lead detective when I can, yes. As you know, Capitaine Garcia and I are friends and he occasionally requests my help on serious cases, as I do his."

"That's what I thought, and it means we must have an accord of our own, you and I. While you are in my home, Hugo, I want your word that you will not go behind my back and interview any of my family, guests, or staff. If you are here only to accompany the senator, that should be a simple promise to keep."

Dammit. "I think I can agree to that," Hugo said.

"And I also want your promise that you will not go around lifting finger prints from wine glasses or anywhere else. My home is not a crime scene and I won't have it treated like one, do I make myself clear?"

"You do, abundantly clear."

"And so I have your agreement on this? No interviews, finger-printing, or other crime scene analysis." He held Hugo's eye. "I want your word."

Hugo hesitated but knew he had no choice. If he refused, or even equivocated, he would be asked to leave, and that would be bad every which way.

"You have my word," Hugo said.

"Thank you." Tourville turned to Vibert. "Felix, will you be joining us?"

"Once the chit-chat stops and the talks begin, maybe." He held up the papers again. "But I'm working, don't worry."

"Good." Tourville nodded at Hugo. "I should get back. I'm glad we understand each other, Hugo. Thank you."

"Very welcome," Hugo said. He watched Tourville leave and then drifted over to the large windows overlooking the lawn. He stared out at the green grass, soft and even as a carpet, and he wondered how much money someone like Tourville had to spend on gardeners and servants, how much money it took to be so divorced from regular society that you could demand an end, even a delay, to a murder investigation and fully expect that demand to be met. Hugo had given his word, and he would keep it. But he would abide by the letter of their agreement, and if the spirit flitted away, free to roam at will, then so be it.

He turned to Vibert. "May I interrupt you for a moment?"

Vibert looked up. "Of course, what is it?"

"Do you remember at dinner the other night, there was an antique right behind where we were sitting? You told me it was a sailor's chest, I think."

"A sailor's chest." He furrowed his brow. "I don't think I remember that. What did it look like?"

"A wooden chest, it was on the table behind us in the dining room. You said something about secret compartments."

"*Alors*, I'm sorry, I really am." He peeled off his glasses and gave Hugo a small smile. "If I remember rightly, there was a lot of champagne flowing that night. That stuff goes straight to my head, so it's entirely possible we had that conversation, I don't doubt you." He shrugged. "But I'm sorry, I don't remember it at all. Why do you ask?"

"I was just curious, I have an interest in antiques. Books, furniture, things like that." Hugo grinned. "I guess it's being an American, we don't have anything much older than a couple hundred years back home."

"Yes, I suppose that makes sense."

"And that piece," Hugo continued, "what you said about the secret compartments intrigued me, I wish I'd looked at it that night but it might have seemed rude. Have you seen anything like it around here?"

"It's not in the dining room still?"

"No, I just looked."

"*Non*, I'm sorry, I haven't." He put his glasses back on and looked down at his notes, but sharp eyes flicked up at Hugo for a second. *Careful, Hugo.*

"No matter. I'll leave you to your work."

He strolled out of the living room, but that look from Vibert had set him on edge. Was the man lying about forgetting their conversation? Or did he suspect Hugo's motive for asking about the chest? *No telling*, Hugo thought, trying to put it out of his mind. His best bet was to find the damn thing as soon as possible.

He headed for the library, breathing a sigh of relief that it was empty and closing the door softly behind him. The room was lined with bookcases and contained only enough furniture to enhance the space as a reading room. A small writing desk sat near one corner, but Hugo quickly realized the chest wasn't here. Other than the kitchen, he'd run out of public rooms to check. Tourville had a private study somewhere in the back of the house, but Hugo couldn't risk getting caught snooping, not just yet. Maybe one of the bedrooms, but that presented the same problem.

He turned to the door but stopped when it swung open. Alexandra Tourville walked in, her surprised look turning into a friendly smile.

"Monsieur Marston, *bonjour*."

"*Bonjour*, how are you?"

"Fine. Did I disturb you?"

"No, I'm just killing time. Anything to keep out of those meetings." He smiled. "I didn't know you were here. At the house, I mean."

"Why wouldn't I be, I live here, remember?"

"Of course. Silly of me."

"You are borrowing a book?"

"Just browsing. I have one in my bag, but if these talks drag out I might need one."

"Well, help yourself. Mostly the books in here just gather dust."
She breezed past him to the writing desk and opened a drawer. "*Merde,
rien ici*," she muttered, then turned to Hugo to explain. "We used to
have stationary with the house's address and family coat of arms on it,
I thought there was a stack of paper and envelopes in here but it looks
like I'll have to raid my brother's study."

"I'm sure he won't mind."

"I'm sure he won't know," she smiled, and again Hugo caught a
look that might have been flirtatious.

"While you're here, I have sort of an odd question," he said.

She wagged a finger. "Henri told us all you weren't to be asking any
of those."

"Oh no," Hugo said, "nothing like that. As I told you the other
evening, I have an interest in old books, antique furniture, that sort
of thing. Last time I was here, I saw an old sailor's chest in the dining
room but I didn't get a chance to have a closer look. Felix Vibert was
telling me how clever the construction is, how they sometimes have
secret compartments in them."

Her face was blank, unreadable. "It's not there anymore?"

"Gone, I'm afraid. Do you know the chest I'm talking about?"

"No, sorry. If it's been in the family years I may not even know it's
here, and pieces get moved around occasionally if one of us, or even one
of the staff, suddenly decides it'd look better elsewhere."

"I see. I have no clue whether it was a newly purchased piece or had
been here for decades."

"Ask Henri?"

Not a chance. "When he's not so busy, maybe I will. It's not a big
deal, I was just curious."

She gave a delicate shrug as she left the library, leaving Hugo to
ponder his next move. His first thought was to go to the seat of all knowledge in a place like this, the place where secrets and gossip unfurled like
spring flowers: the staff. More specifically the kitchen, which Hugo knew
would act as the fulcrum for the people who worked inside and outside
at the chateau. His hesitation was the promise he'd made to Tourville.

If Alexandra and Vibert mentioned to Henri that he'd been looking for something in the house, it would be no big deal. But pestering the staff was an entirely different matter, he could hardly claim to have accidentally wandered into the kitchen and made polite chitchat with the maid or groom about a Tourville antique. And it wasn't just a matter of getting away with this line of questioning. Hugo didn't like being coerced into a promise not to investigate, but once he'd given his word, he didn't want to go back on it any more than he had to.

The alternative wasn't much more appealing. Two days, maybe even three or four, wasting away at the house while the talks dragged on and he passed his time walking circles on the estate or plowing through books here in the library. Wonderful options for a long weekend, but frustrating in the extreme when there was work to be done in Paris.

He pulled out his phone and called Capitaine Garcia. "Any progress?" Hugo asked after brief pleasantries.

"*Non, pas encore.* Right now, I'm concentrating on the jewelry. Some of it is pretty distinctive and so we're contacting as many places as possible here in Paris to see if they're reselling it. The burglary unit here has good contacts, they do this sort of thing a lot."

"You think whoever stole that stuff would just show up at a used jewelry store and peddle it?" Hugo was doubtful.

"I'll be honest, Hugo, yes. For one thing, there aren't a lot of options for really old, recognizable pieces. Some of the stuff that was taken can probably be resold pretty easily but a lot of it, well, for the thief to get anywhere close to what it's worth he'd have limited choices." Garcia chuckled. "When I say limited, of course, I mean dozens in Paris, but you get the point."

Hugo had never been involved with art and antique theft or even regular burglaries, so he was happy to take Garcia's lead. One thing bothered him, though. "Tell me this, Raul. If you know where the bad guys sell the fancy jewelry, isn't it easy to track back and figure out who's selling to them?"

"No. I mean, if we set up cameras outside all their stores, maybe, but then they'd do business in the local bar. These are the people who recognize quality merchandise but happen to be totally blind when it comes to recognizing the people they're buying from."

"Intentionally blind."

"Absolutely. They don't issue receipts or have mailing lists. They do business with some of the same people but are happy to look at whatever walks in the door. And the people who buy from them are the same way, which means an item can disappear from someone's home and be two buyers deep in a matter of days."

"And wherever the police show up in the chain, no one knows who they bought from or where the object originated."

"Correct."

"Then is this jewelry angle even worth pursuing?"

"Sometimes it can be. Usually not. But we have an advantage in this instance, a little twist that might loosen a tongue or two in that chain."

Hugo thought for a moment. "The threat of a murder charge."

"*Exactement*. For a foreigner you are very intelligent, Hugo."

"Thanks, I say the same about you on occasion. Anyway, let's hope you're right and the specter of murder makes a difference. If you're going to get any hits, when do you expect that to be?"

"Within the next twelve to twenty-four hours. The unit's been hammering hard at their known dealers and we only need one lead to get moving."

"Good. In that case, I'm headed back to Paris. If we get something, I want to come with you."

"Fine by me, but what about your senator?"

"He can do without his minder for a day, he's in his element right now. Probably won't even notice I'm gone."

"And if he does?" There was mischief in Garcia's voice.

"If he does, *mon ami*, then I won't be here to incur his wrath, will I?"

CHAPTER SEVENTEEN

The call came through at a roadside café outside Mantes-la-Jolie, as Hugo held the door for a young couple holding hands and blissfully unaware of the gesture. When his phone buzzed, hope flashed that it was Claudia but the name on the screen was Garcia's.

"Hurry," Garcia said when Hugo answered. "Are you close to Paris?"

"Forty-five minutes to an hour, depending on traffic. Have something?"

"Yeah, a piece of jewelry from the Troyes murder. A shop in Butte-aux-Cailles. Since you're on your way, you might as well meet me there."

"OK, text me the name of the place and an address," Hugo said.

"One hour?"

"I'll be there. Don't go in without me, I'll never forgive you."

Hugo drove carefully; he always did when he was going somewhere that mattered. He could have sped, probably, as he was in an unmarked police car, but he'd learned that the cops who patrolled major highways were not always as obliging with their brethren as they might be. Once, he'd been running late for the funeral of a colleague who'd retired and soon after died in a car accident in North Carolina, one of the agents who'd taken Hugo under his wing at Quantico. Hugo had been high-tailing it along I-40 near Raleigh when he was pulled over by a state trooper. Pale-faced and military-smart, the trooper had been robotic behind mirrored sunglasses as he ignored Hugo's explanation for cresting fifteen miles per hour above the speed limit. Trooper

Anderson—Hugo could forever picture the sun glinting off his name-plate—took his sweet time with Hugo's license and then requested his FBI credentials, studying them the way a toddler stares at an ant hefting an entire leaf; part amazement, part amusement, and no hurry to do much of anything. Hugo had arrived at the funeral late, embarrassed, frustrated, and a living example of the haste-makes-waste motto.

Of course, diplomatic immunity was his current get-out-of-jail-free card, but the ambassador frowned on traffic-related abuses and expected those working for him to abide by speed limits and pay any tickets incurred when they failed to do so.

The midday traffic was light enough on the way into Paris, though, and he pulled into a parking spot in Rue Samson twenty minutes before his rendezvous with Garcia. He checked his watch and decided to walk a little, physical movement welcome after an hour and some in the car. He'd not visited this part of Paris, though he knew of it. In the southeast of the city, it was a lively hub in the otherwise fairly ordinary Thirteenth Arrondissement. With cobbled streets and more than its fair share of bars, cafés, and restaurants, it was a destination for locals who knew it was there, and for those tourists who looked past the usual guidebooks and didn't mind venturing a fair few miles from the Eiffel Tower.

He headed for the neighborhood's best-known street, Rue de la Butte aux Cailles, a narrow and cobbled lane that rolled slowly uphill. The sidewalk was almost as wide as the road, which had its own lane designated for bicycles—a nod to modernity in a place that seemed to have otherwise lingered in time. The whitewashed shop fronts and old buildings huddled close together as if waiting for the age of glass and steel to pass by.

His phone rang and he checked the caller before answering: Tom.

"Hey, Tom. What's up?"

"Can't talk long. Just wanted to let you know we finished the comparison from the staff members we printed at Tourville's little place. The water glasses."

"Great. Get anything interesting?"

"Nope. No matches. Be sure and tell Raul, will you?"

Tom rang off without a good-bye and Hugo smiled to himself as he cut left, down a side street. He admired for a moment the spray-painted image of an eagle clutching a wine bottle, no words or indication as to meaning, just a flash of red on a wall of white, more art than vandalism. Hugo meandered, checking his watch now and again as he headed toward the store where he was to meet Garcia. Maybe it was his imagination, too, but the closer he got the narrower the streets seemed, with more store fronts shuttered up, blank eyes not caring who came or went or what people might be doing.

Garcia was parked two blocks from the store and hopped out of the car, a twin of the one Hugo drove, as soon as he saw the American in his rear mirror. Garcia leaned on the back of the car watching him approach. "Enjoying the neighborhood?"

"Never been here before," Hugo said. "I like it."

"I lived here many years ago. When I was first married, actually. Unlike the rest of Paris, it doesn't seem to have changed all that much, there's still not a single chain store here, as far as I can tell."

"Yeah, I noticed that. Always makes me like a place."

"Agreed." Garcia straightened. "You going to let me do the talking?"

"I think I have to, don't I?"

"Just wanted to be clear." They set off toward the store, and Garcia explained the layout as they walked. "It's a long, fairly thin main room that you walk into off the street. They sell antique furniture, estate jewelry, that kind of thing."

"Been in business how long?"

"Just over four years. They hit our radar a year ago, three pieces of stolen jewelry within three months that our detectives found for sale here. They, of course, claimed they had no idea the items were stolen. And by 'they,' I mean the owner and his son, André and Bruno Capron."

"Could be true, right?"

"Could be. Our detectives didn't think so, and they're particularly interested in the attitude of people who run places like this. Total innocence usually results in the object being returned to us without a fuss, and the name of the seller being turned over."

"They didn't do that?"

"No. Not on any of the occasions."

"Red flag. indeed," Hugo said.

They waited on the corner for three bicyclists to breeze slowly by. "Anyway, the layout. There's the main sales area and just a small office and bathroom at the back, where a fire door leads into the alley where the trash cans are kept. The sales counter is on the right, a glass cabinet that contains smaller and more expensive pieces. That's where our detective saw the necklace. He'd seen it online and went by to make sure it was still here. The Caprons, by the way, are selling it for two thousand Euros."

"That's what it's worth?"

"No idea. But it's evidence in a murder investigation so if he paid anything like that to the seller, he's not going to be happy about us taking it."

"Do you have a warrant or anything to compel him to cooperate?" Hugo asked.

"No, I didn't have time. I don't need one to take the necklace, and I'm going to rely on my charm for the name and address of the seller." He gave Hugo a wry smile. "Very funny. I know what you're thinking, so there's no need to say it."

"I wouldn't dream of it."

"I'm glad to hear that. And yes, someone's putting a search warrant together right now in the bowels of the prefecture."

They reached the store and without pausing walked in, a bell jangling lightly as the door opened. Inside, the place was cluttered but neat, the wide-planked floors cut into narrow aisles by antique furniture and table-top displays of smaller items for sale. A bookcase filled with leather-bound volumes caught Hugo's eye, and he reminded himself he was there to investigate, not browse. Garcia started slowly down the aisle to the right, so Hugo took the one on the left, their eyes open for the proprietor.

They found old man Capron in his office, totally absorbed by whatever was playing on the screen of his laptop. He snapped it shut when

Garcia poked his head into the tiny room, his eyes alight with surprise at the intrusion. "*Oui*? Can I help you?"

Garcia and Hugo held up their credentials and Capron squinted to study them from eight feet away.

"You have something that doesn't belong to you," Garcia said. "Showed up on your online catalog and we need it back." He put his badge away and handed over a computer printout of the necklace.

Capron wrinkled his nose as he looked over the paper. "You people come in here claiming things are stolen. How do I know you are not stealing from me? Where is my compensation?"

Garcia bristled. "I imagine it's in the profit from the stolen items you manage to sell before we show up."

Hugo glanced at Garcia. It was unlike his friend to be so confrontational, especially from the word go, but this was the French detective's show, not Hugo's.

"I steal nothing, and if I sell stolen property I do so without knowing it." He rose and walked past them into the shop. "I want a receipt for this, my insurance company insists."

"You'll get your receipt. Where is the necklace?" Garcia asked.

Capron walked behind the sales counter and fished a bunch of keys from his pocket. He bent down and unlocked the sliding glass back of the case where his smaller and pricier items were on display. With a grunt he reached in and carefully scooped up the necklace, laying it gently on a velvet cloth.

Hugo looked back at where it had lain to see the price. "Two thousand Euros?" he asked.

"*Bien sûr*. This is entirely made by hand here in France, it's solid eighteen-karat gold. And look at these, seven of them I think, fine hand-crafted needlepoint flower sections, each one in a hand-made gold frame." He glanced up, as if he were talking to prospective buyers. "You can see, it has five strands of chain connecting each section, and the catch here has its original enamel trim."

"Distinctive," Garcia said to Hugo.

"Definitely," Hugo agreed. "How old?"

"I would think mid-eighteenth-century, something like that."

"Seems to me, it'd be a lot more expensive than just two thousand," Hugo said. "All that quality, its age."

"You're an expert, are you?" Capron said, not hiding a sneer.

"Should be pretty easy to check, and if you're selling it for half price, well, I'd think that's good evidence you know it's stolen."

The sneer dropped from Capron's face and his eyes darted between the two policemen. "I charge what the market will bear. If something is worth more, well, I mean . . . if people won't pay what it's really worth, what am I to do?"

"What indeed," said Garcia. "Now for the important question. Where did you get it?"

"I don't know." Capron straightened up and sighed. "You always ask me that and I never tell you. In this case, I don't know but my customers would not be my customers for long if I kept giving their names to the police."

"No, they'd be in jail," Garcia snapped. "And you really think we're just going to take 'I don't know' for an answer?"

"You're going to have to. My son brought this piece in and he didn't tell me who he bought it from."

"You must have paperwork showing that," Hugo said.

"Sometimes we do, sometimes we don't. It's not required by law, you know."

"Where is your son?" Garcia demanded.

"Out."

"Out where?"

"With a girl. Buying antiques. At the movies." Capron shrugged. "He is a grown man so when he goes out he doesn't ask my permission and doesn't tell me where."

"*Non*? Maybe we'll put a police car out front until he comes back. Could be inconvenient for any customers coming in, they'd all have to be questioned, asked for identification. How does that sound?"

"You do what you have to. And so will I."

The two Frenchmen were squaring off across the counter and

Hugo could see this going from unhelpful to disastrous. Whatever was eating at Garcia had devoured his objectivity, his professionalism, and if he kept this up it could easily derail the investigation.

"Look," Hugo said, "this necklace is more than just stolen property. The owner was murdered during the theft. Which means Capitaine Garcia is right, we can't take 'I don't know' for an answer. Whoever sold you this could have murdered an innocent woman. At the very least, your son is a link to that person."

Doubt flitted across Capron's face. "What murder? I don't know anything about that."

"I don't think you do," Hugo went on. "But this necklace cost a woman her life, and right now it's the only lead we have. So *I'll* ask you this time: Who sold it to you?"

Capron's face hardened. "And I'll tell you what I told him. I don't know because my son acquired it."

"Call him," Hugo said. "Or show us the paperwork."

"I will not call him because he's busy. And if you want to see the paperwork, you'll need a search warrant."

"No!" Garcia slammed his fist onto the counter. "You will show it to us now!" The capitaine's face was red with anger, his body taut as he leaned over the counter toward Capron. "Now, damn you, and if you don't I'll put handcuffs on you until the warrant gets here. And maybe forget to take them off after we've torn this shack apart."

Capron flinched at Garcia's anger, but it had the effect Hugo was afraid of: the store owner became more belligerent himself. "Get out of my store! You come in here and make accusations with no proof, you don't have the right to treat me like this."

Garcia was huffing mad and even Hugo was done being polite. If there was one thing that riled him up it was a crook acting indignant, and this old coot was playing the injured-businessman role to the max. Hugo scooted around the counter and took Capron's arm.

"Ow, you're hurting me!"

"Shut up," Hugo snapped. "We've been nice and polite, we even said 'please' a couple of times. So now you can sit down and keep quiet while my colleague gets his search warrant and we have fun taking this place apart."

Garcia closed his mouth, obviously trying to hide his surprise at Hugo's response to the old man. He pulled a pair of handcuffs from his belt and snapped them efficiently around the shocked Capron's wrists. As the jeweler sputtered with outrage, Garcia steered him to a chair and plopped him down, none too gently.

"You can't do this! Go get your damn warrant but leave me and my store alone until you have it. This is illegal, you can't hold me here like this, you have to go away until you have the authority to—"

"You'd like that, wouldn't you?" Hugo said. "But that's not how it works, you don't get time to hide or destroy evidence."

"What? No, I wouldn't—"

"*Ta gueule!*" Garcia snarled. *Shut the fuck up.* He turned to Hugo. "You OK to hang out with this idiot until I get back? If the warrant's drafted, which it should be, I'll find a friendly judge between here and the prefecture, I should be back within the hour."

"Sure."

"What if I need to pee?" Capron whined. "I can't sit here for an hour like that. *C'est pas juste.*"

Hugo looked around, then spotted the perfect solution. He grabbed it from a tabletop and put it between Capron's feet. "Porcelain, late nineteenth century. Not handmade because, well, they needed to mass produce these. Everyone had a chamber pot back in the day."

Garcia's eyes sparkled with delight and he clapped Hugo on the shoulder as he made for the door. He flipped the sign from Open to *Closed* as he went out, giving Hugo and André Capron a parting wave as he shut the door behind him, the tinkle of its little bell making Hugo smile again as the outraged old man shoved the chamber pot away from him with little pokes of his foot.

Hugo spent his time nosing around the store. He pretended to be browsing but he wondered if maybe he could recognize other valuable, and potentially stolen, items. His best bet, he thought, was with the used books, an area of antiquity in which he had some knowledge. He picked books from the shelves one by one, opening the front covers of those he recognized to see whether they were first editions before turning them over in his hands to check their condition. Most were battered, reprints, and moderately worthless, but a couple were worth the price Capron was charging. One was a copy of *Der Steppenwolf* by Herman Hesse, a first edition published by Berlag in 1927.

Hugo held it up so Capron could see it. "Original dust jacket?"

The old man nodded. "Good condition, too."

"Eight thousand Euros seems a little steep."

"So don't buy it."

Hugo flashed an evil grin. "I wonder. It's probably evidence, wouldn't you think?"

"Hey, don't you—"

"Stolen from some collection somewhere, I'd bet," Hugo interrupted. "Like this one." He slid another book from the shelf. *Where There's a Will* by Rex Stout, very much the sort of book Hugo would buy and read. "First edition, published by Farrar & Rinehart in 1940," he read aloud. "Love the Nero Wolfe mysteries, and I've not read this one."

"Take these cuffs off and leave, you can take the book with you. Compliments of the house."

"Two thousand Euros, you're asking?" Hugo looked up, mock surprise on his face. "Wait, are you trying to bribe me?"

"It's a book. Take it and go, leave me alone, will you?"

"I sure would love to own this book," Hugo mused. "Shall we see what else you have?"

"Take two books," Capron said, "three if you must." Hugo wondered at the note of hope in his voice, as if the question wasn't whether Hugo could be bribed, but how much it would take. If he'd had any doubts about Capron before, this wheedling attempt to buy his momentary freedom dispelled them. And because his freedom would likely be fleeting, Hugo was sure he wanted it to destroy evidence— specifically records of the purchase of that necklace.

Hugo was sliding the books back into place, watched by a rapidly deflating Capron, when the front door opened and a large, shaven-headed man stood there looking into the store, his bulk filling the doorway and small eyes blinking as they adjusted to the dim interior.

CHAPTER EIGHTEEN

"*C'est fermé*," Hugo said. "Come back tomorrow."

He chided himself for not locking the door. He'd assumed the sign would suffice, but before he'd finished speaking Hugo knew this man wasn't here to browse for antiques.

The man didn't move at first, then slowly stepped into the store. He stopped when he saw André Capron on the chair, hands pinned behind his back, but it was the old man who spoke first and as soon as Hugo saw what was happening he moved.

"*Allez, allez!*" Capron hissed, but the order to leave and Hugo's sudden movement confused the younger man, who froze, giving Hugo time to slide between him and the front door.

"Bruno, I assume?" Hugo said.

"Who . . . who the hell are you?" His voice was like gravel, rough and scratching. "What's going on? Papa, are you OK?"

"The police," Capron said. "An American policeman. The real ones are on their way with a search warrant."

Bruno's eyes narrowed, then moved left and right, and Hugo knew he was figuring his chances.

"Don't." Hugo kept his voice firm. "Your father's not going anywhere with those cuffs on, and it's generally a bad idea to assault members of law enforcement. Even if you win the fight, which you won't, the men in blue who back me up will be less than gentle when they catch up with you."

"Why are you here?"

"You're selling stolen property. Property from a murder scene, no less." The first comment didn't seem to faze Bruno, but the second did.

"Murder? We don't know anything..." His words tailed off and he looked at his father, as if for confirmation that they really didn't know anything about a murder. When he looked back at Hugo his eyes flickered with confusion and, Hugo thought, fear.

"Probably true. But when you buy stolen goods without asking too many questions, the chances are pretty good you're going to find yourself neck deep in a situation you didn't create."

"Monsieur," Capron senior said, "leave my son alone. He knows nothing about anything, just leave him alone."

Bruno drifted closer to his father, the look of confusion lingering, and Hugo moved with him.

"But that's not true, is it?" Hugo said. "You told us he's the one who brought the necklace here in the first place. Which means he knows something about that, wouldn't you say?"

"Necklace?" Bruno looked back and forth between them. "What necklace?"

"Be quiet, boy," Capron snapped, but the real message was in his eyes, or maybe in the tilt of his head, a message that Bruno picked up a split second before Hugo, a fraction of a moment that gave him a head start to the back door. Bruno took off like he'd been scalded, putting six feet between him and Hugo and getting lucky when his hip thumped a display table, shifting into Hugo's path and tipping half its contents onto the floor in front of him.

Hugo launched himself after Bruno and managed to turn sideways, avoiding the table that half blocked his way and hurdling the old school bell and the photo frames now littering the floor. He hit a patch of clear floor as he bore down on his quarry, but then Bruno side-stepped right, taking him around his father to the office, swinging himself through the doorway. When Hugo tried the same maneuver Capron kicked out, catching Hugo's left shin and sending them both crashing to the floor. The old man wailed like he'd been slashed with a knife, a disconcerting noise that combined with Capron's scissoring legs to hold Hugo back long enough for Bruno to disappear from view. The back door slammed and in desperation Hugo bucked to free himself of Capron, jabbing him in the chest with an elbow. He scrabbled to his feet, clear of the old man, who yelled obscenities at the top of his voice as he squirmed on the floor, but when Hugo finally made it out into the side street Bruno Capron was gone.

Hugo swore. They'd catch up to Bruno if they needed to, sooner or later, but Hugo's pride had taken a blow and no doubt both Garcia and Tom would have a thing or two to say about this. Although Garcia, at least, would try to be polite.

Hugo headed back into the store, checking his watch. Garcia had been gone for thirty minutes, and was hopefully on his way back. André Capron was lying on his side on the floor and Hugo stood over him, debating leaving him there for the duration. But it wouldn't look good, he knew, when Garcia and his men showed up to find old Capron writhing around amid his precious antiques, no doubt complaining about police brutality. That was a mess of paperwork Hugo could do without, so he hauled the man to his feet and picked up the chair. He plonked Capron back down onto the hard wooden seat, resisting the urge to wipe the smirk off his face.

"We'll get him, don't you worry about that. But you taught him well, scurrying off like a rat leaving a sinking ship."

"*Nique ta mere*," Capron muttered. *Fuck your mother.* He opened his mouth to say something else but obviously thought better of it. As he looked away from Hugo, defeated, the phone behind the counter startled them both, a shrill and insistent ring. Hugo let it go to voicemail but a minute later it rang again, then a third time. Hugo's own curiosity and a worried look in Capron's eye changed his mind. He reached over and pressed the speakerphone button.

"*Allo?*" Hugo said, his eyes on Capron whose Adam's apple bobbed nervously as he swallowed. Silence filled the store as the person on the other end said nothing.

Then a voice said, "I'd like to speak to Hugo Marston, *s'il vous plaît.*"

It could have been a man or woman, there was no way to tell. Whoever it was had used some sort of voice-changing device, handheld or, more likely, one of the half-dozen software programs that let you talk through a computer to disguise your voice.

"Who is this?" Hugo asked.

"If you want any information, you'll let me ask the questions."

The caller spoke in English, any accent obliterated, and that attempt to assert power over Hugo put a malicious smile on Capron's face. Hugo picked up the phone, which wiped the smirk away.

"I'm not good at that," Hugo said, "so I'll ask you again: Who is this?"

"Tell me something, monsieur, why are you there?"

"If you know I'm here, I suspect you know the answer to that."

A brief silence. "You are alone?"

"I'm with Monsieur Capron, but otherwise, yes."

"Capron?" The metallic sound of the voice couldn't disguise a note of concern.

"André Capron, yes."

"Ah, of course." *Was that relief?* "No other police are with you, or know you are there?"

"Just me." It was a lie, of course, but Hugo didn't need this person hanging up on him and if whoever it was wanted Hugo to be by himself, so be it.

"I see. Good."

"Who are you and why are you calling?" Hugo asked again.

"To help you. You want to know where the necklace came from, am I right?"

"I know exactly where it came from. What I want to know is who took it from the house. From a murder scene. You want to help me with that?"

"As a matter of fact, I do. I will tell you."

"I'm listening."

"No, not like this. I can't reveal my identity and I don't plan on being arrested, so I need a promise from you."

"What kind of promise?"

"If we meet, you will promise to hear me out before trying to arrest me and before getting anyone else involved."

"You want to meet me?" Hugo didn't bother to hide his surprise.

"Yes. Once I explain how the Caprons came into possession of the necklace I think you will have another avenue to chase down and you'll be happy to let me go. I want to help you, Monsieur Marston, is what I'm saying, but I cannot place myself into this investigation."

"Then why not just tell me now, over the phone?"

"My understanding of the law is limited, but I believe that the police may not base a search warrant or other intrusion on the basis of an uncorroborated and anonymous tip. Do I have that right?"

The truth was that Hugo didn't know. In Texas, yes, the caller would be absolutely right. But here? "Possibly, but if we meet and you want to stay anonymous, how does that change anything?"

"Because I have something to give you, something tangible that will help. I believe I'm right, and I'd think that would be especially true if that information went to the police from an anonymous source and through you, an American."

"Fine," he said. "But can we hurry this up?"

"I want that promise from you, that you'll hear me out before you do anything."

"Sure. I can promise that."

"I also want you to promise that you will come alone and not tell anyone. No one at all."

"Seems like that wouldn't be too smart on my part. Cops do that in books and movies, real police don't do that. It's stupid and dangerous."

"Not for a man who carries a gun."

"Not possible. This isn't my investigation, and I don't get to charge off by myself making secret meetings to get evidence. Or leads. Whatever the hell you say you're offering."

"That's a shame. I really want to help, but your promise to listen before acting doesn't mean much if ten policemen are waiting with their guns drawn and handcuffs at the ready. I need to believe that once you get this information, if you are satisfied with it, that I will be free to go." Another pause. "I also have a certain reputation to uphold, and the fewer people who know that I've come across details of a crime, the better. These are things you will understand when we talk."

"I already told you, I can't—"

"Enough." The ephemeral voice cut him off. "You have no choice. I will give you an address and you will meet me there in thirty minutes. If you are not there I will wait for five more, then your lead disappears. And if I see anyone else but you, I will disappear even quicker."

Hugo grabbed a piece of paper and scribbled the address down. "How will I recognize you?" he asked.

"That's easy, just find the pavilion and I will be right there," the caller said. "Not to mention, of course, we had dinner just a few days ago."

CHAPTER NINETEEN

Hugo had meant what he said, real cops didn't do this sort of thing alone and he'd been so intent on catching every word from the caller that he'd forgotten about Capron. If nothing else, Garcia would have to send someone to babysit him until the warrant arrived.

"You are leaving?" Capron asked, hope shining in his eyes.

"Yep. But not planning to take the cuffs off, if that's what you're thinking."

"You have to, you can't just leave me like this."

"I know." Hugo smiled and pulled Capron to his feet. He paused when he realized he didn't have Garcia's key for the cuffs, but he could spare his own for an hour or two. He dragged the grumbling Frenchman to a back corner where he'd seen an Aga for sale, an old coal-burning stove with two hot plates on top and a sturdy metal rail for hanging tea towels, or even clothes, for drying. "Don't make this stuff like they used to," Hugo said. "Solid, dependable."

"*Non*, monsieur, just let me be, this isn't right."

"Right? It's perfect." Hugo hooked one cuff to the chain connecting Capron's wrists and secured the other cuff to the Aga's rail. "You can stand, sit, hell if you can find some coal you can make a cup of tea while you wait." He patted Capron's cheek. "See? Cooperation is always much more convenient for everyone. Think about that for next time."

Hugo turned and walked out of the store, ignoring Capron's outraged protestations. Outside, he pulled his phone from his pocket and dialed. "Raul, where are you?"

"Sorry, my first choice of judge wasn't available. I should be there in twenty minutes."

"Change of plan." Hugo was striding and knew his breathing must sound ragged.

"Everything OK?"

"Yes. The phone rang while I was waiting, someone claiming to have information about the necklace."

"*Vraiment?* Who?"

"Someone I know, apparently. He used a voice-changer, I couldn't tell."

"Or she, then."

"Right. Anyway, he or she wants to meet me to hand over some evidence in person."

"I'll meet you there, give me the address."

"That might be a problem. Whoever it was insisted I come alone. Thinks I'm the only one who knows about Capron, is my guess, and wants to stay out of the investigation."

"Alone isn't good, Hugo. Alone is never good. Or smart."

"I know." Hugo grinned. "I wasn't planning on it. But just you, OK? If a horde of uniforms show up we may well lose this lead, and unless you can shake something loose from Capron, I think I'm right in saying this about our only one right now."

"Very true. I'll have another detective serve and execute the warrant, she knows a little about the case."

"OK." Hugo hesitated. "She's good? The Caprons are old school, she needs to be prepared for that."

Garcia's chuckle came through loud and clear. "She's tough, all right. Came up from Bordeaux about a year ago after shutting down their gang problem almost single-handedly. One or two stragglers came after her, *mon ami*, at her home while she was planting roses. The word in the office is that she disarmed and beat them both with a pair of shears and a rake." He lowered his voice and Hugo could detect both humor and truth in his next words. "Even I am a little intimidated by her."

"You, *mon ami*?"

"Yes. She's not just physically tough. I don't know how to put this, except to say her journey from patrol officer to detective has been far from easy."

"It's easy for anyone?"

"*Non*. But Lieutenant Camille Lerens began her career with the Bordeaux police as Officer Christophe Lerens."

"Wait, what?"

"You heard me. Christophe became Camille, and the street cop became a damn good investigator. Just imagine what she had to put up with on the way up."

"Wow, I don't know what to say about that." Hugo knew little about transgender issues, just what he'd read in the news or seen on television. He knew a great deal, however, about the male-centric nature, often misogynistic, attitudes that lived deep inside law enforcement agencies, especially in days gone by. And that meant he could well imagine the veiled hostility and likely outright prejudice a man would encounter during his transition to womanhood. That Lerens had not only made that transition but been promoted to lieutenant may have spoken to the open-mindedness of her superiors, but unquestionably reinforced Garcia's opinion of her as a tough and capable police officer.

"You know what, Raul, she sounds perfect," Hugo said, rounding the corner onto on Rue Samson. "And tell her to bring those shears along. If she waves them around just right, she might get those boys to spill everything."

"*D'accord*, and if the gender thing doesn't bother you I think you'll like her," Garcia said. "She's a lot like Tom in many ways. Although she doesn't swear or drink as much, and I think she goes to church sometimes."

"So nothing like Tom, then."

"She gets results, is what I mean. Just wait until you meet her, you'll see what I mean."

"Yeah, now I'm curious. So, back to business." Hugo gave Garcia the address. "They said they'd be in the pavilion. I checked on my phone, it looks like it's near an entrance to Parc Montsouris, which is only five minutes from here. If that."

"*Bien*, I'm on the E5 autoroute, I'm probably closer than you are."

"Good but just lay low, OK? If our anonymous friend sees you, they might split." Hugo started to pull away but the car dragged and lurched, pulling him into the curb. "*Merde*, Raul, I think I have a problem."

"What is it?"

Hugo jammed the car into a side street, wrestling with the steering wheel one-handed. He jumped out of the car and went to the passenger's side to confirm his fear.

"Dammit, flat tire." He knelt and saw a gash in the wall of the tire. "Looks like someone took a knife to it."

"*Ach, non*. Hippies and antigovernment people all over that neighborhood, they recognize an unmarked police car when they see one."

"And apparently do more than recognize them." His mind flitted to Bruno Capron, but it seemed unlikely that he'd done anything other than run as far and fast as possible. Like Garcia said, someone had probably been walking down this quiet street and decided it'd be funny to puncture a cop's tire. *Hilarious*, Hugo thought.

"Want me to go instead?" Garcia said.

"Whoever it is, they're expecting me, it's almost certainly someone from Chateau Tourville."

"How do you know?"

"They said we had dinner recently. Narrows it down to twenty or twenty-five people."

"If they're telling the truth."

"Fair point." Hugo checked his watch. "I'm supposed to be there in fifteen minutes, twenty at the outside, or they said the meeting was off. If I stop chit-chatting with you I can get this tire changed and still make it, so let's stick to the plan."

"If you're sure. I don't mind—"

"Gotta go, Raul, I'll call you if there's a problem." He rang off and dropped his phone into a pocket. He found the latch to the trunk, took a deep breath, and went to work. It had been a long time, a decade or more, since he'd changed a tire, but he managed to figure out the jack and find a place where it would have good purchase. It took him two minutes to lift the side of the car a creaking eight inches off the ground, and once it was up he set about removing the lug nuts only to find the wheel kept spinning with every turn of the wrench. Which is when he remembered: *loosen the nuts while the tire's on the ground, then use the jack.*

He contemplated fighting with the spinning wheel, hating to backtrack, but decided to cut his losses. He lowered the car and quickly loosened the wheel before jacking it back up. He'd spent ten minutes and a surge of anxiety hit his stomach like acid. As he was fitting the small spare he flinched as a shadow fell over him, the lip of a dark cloud closing over the sun and suggesting that if Hugo didn't hurry, he might get wet.

The spare tire looked weak and delicate, but Hugo double-checked the tightness of the nuts and heaved the flat into the trunk, slamming the lid closed as he checked his watch again. He had five minutes to make a five-minute drive, ten if the caller kept their word to stay put. He backed quickly out of the side street and headed to Rue Martin Bernard and onto Rue de Tolbiac. He cursed the red light at Avenue Reille, but the car's clock told him he might make it.

A final left onto Rue Gazan, which bordered the park, and Hugo gripped the wheel as he scanned for a street number. He caught one, then another, and knew he was close. Looking ahead he saw that his destination was a gap in the sidewalk, a narrow turning into what looked like a tiny parking lot, which likely gave access to the park.

As he slowed, the sound of sirens reached him. He checked his mirror and saw two police cars racing down Rue Gazan behind him. His skin tingled and he gripped the wheel a little tighter as he pulled to the side of the road to let them pass, but up ahead another police car appeared from behind a delivery truck, all three heading right for the park. As soon as the cars had rounded him, Hugo stamped on the gas and accelerated the last hundred yards to his destination, the road now blocked by one of the white police cars. He leapt out of the car and scanned the side of the street for Garcia's blue Renault, cursing when he didn't see it.

More sirens sang from across the rooftops to his left, an avalanche of noise heading his way, and fear seeped into Hugo's mind and body, chilling his veins and making him feel sick. That many police cars meant one thing, in his experience, and one thing only: an officer down.

He rounded the front of his car toward the uniformed officer blocking the street, but the man waved him to the side as an ambulance edged past them and turned right into the parking lot. Hugo's view was blocked and as he tried to get closer, the policeman put a hand in his chest.

"Police," Hugo said, gesturing to the unmarked car.

The *flic's* eyes narrowed, unsure. "Identification? This is a crime scene, I need to know everyone who comes in and out for the log."

Hugo fumbled for his embassy credentials, desperately hoping the young officer would give them the same weight he'd give to his own detective's identification. The officer looked back and forth between the photo and Hugo before handing it back.

"I'm not sure," he said. "You can go in, but my commanding officer is in there. Please show your identification to her."

Hugo nodded and blew straight past, striding the final twenty yards toward the entrance to the parking lot. When he reached it, his knees buckled. He grabbed at the stone wall for support and he heard a voice, his own voice, whispering a desperate plea, "No, no, no."

His friend's car sat neatly in a parking space not ten yards away, the driver's window shattered, glass littering the ground. The two *flics* assigned to preserve the crime scene weren't looking, distracted by a growing crowd in the park itself. As if in a trance, Hugo circled the front of the car, stopping only when he stood a foot away from the motionless figure laying across the steering wheel. Raul Garcia's face was turned toward Hugo, spider-webbed by the blood that seeped from two crimson holes in the side of his head, his mouth gaping and his eyes staring sightlessly toward the gentle roll of Parc Montsouris.

CHAPTER TWENTY

Hugo tried to process what he was seeing, but he couldn't understand why the men in the ambulance just sat there. He moved toward them as if in a dream, his mouth working but no words coming out. His hands flailed, gesturing for them to do their job, to go help his friend, *to stop fucking sitting there like nothing was wrong*.

One of the paramedics saw him coming and shouted to a police-woman in plain clothes. The dark-skinned woman turned and gave an order to two uniforms who stood nearby, the men approaching Hugo with grim faces. He held out his credentials, which bought him enough time and space to get near the woman, who was clearly in charge.

"Why aren't they doing something?" he shouted. "They need to stop the bleeding, get him stabilized. Take him to a hospital, for fuck's sake."

She turned to him. "Monsieur—"

"Why are they just sitting there?" Hugo couldn't tear his eyes from the surreal scene before him, unable to fathom why no one else seemed to care. "Raul needs help, please, make them help him."

The woman detached herself from the men around her and moved toward him. She wore military-style pants, heavy boots, and a black leather jacket.

"*Vous êtes* Hugo Marston?" she asked.

"Yes." Hugo blinked, another surprise. "How did you ... Are you ..." His mind struggled for the name Raul Garcia had given him but it wasn't there. His mind was a fog that reason couldn't penetrate, a haze that quivered with an image of his friend's smiling face and then, looming behind it like some hideous mirage, the destroyed version of the man who lay lifeless in the car.

"Camille Lerens." She put a hand on his arm, a strong grip, and steered him backward. "Monsieur Marston, I'm sorry. I'm very sorry. But this is a crime scene, you shouldn't be here."

"But someone needs to—"

"I know." Her voice softened. "But I'm sorry, there's nothing anyone can do. He was shot in the head, twice. *Il est mort.*"

He's dead.

Dead.

Raul Garcia is dead.

There was no time or place for those words, no way in which they made any sense. They echoed in Hugo's mind, bouncing around inside as if the words themselves demanded that he listen, accept, and absorb them. But he couldn't.

Lerens steered him back onto the street and knelt as Hugo sat on the curb, half falling as his legs finally gave way.

"Do you know who did this?" she was saying, her voice calm but insistent. "You were with him today, do you know who did this?"

I was with him an hour ago. I talked to him ten minutes ago. "No. I mean, yes." He shook his head to clear away some of that thick fog. "I don't know who it was, but I spoke to them an hour ago. Less."

"Explain. Quickly please."

Hugo told her about the jewelry store and the phone call, his words stumbling out at first but lining up as his mind focused on the simple task of relaying a story that took him away from what he'd seen and into the safer, easier territory of what he'd done. Soon his words twisted together like the strands of a rope, strong enough to pull him back into a semblance of control and hold him together while he tried to help this woman catch a killer.

"The store owner, he's still there?" she asked.

"Yes. Cuffed to a stove, he'll still be there."

"Do you think he knew the caller?"

"If he bought the necklace from him, yes, but he claimed his son had bought it. Did I mention that?"

"Yes, you did. Thank you." She stood and for the first time he paid attention to her appearance. She was squarely-built, but like an athlete so not overweight, with light brown skin and black hair that was cut close to her head. She had a soft, almost sensuous mouth, and above prominent cheek bones her dark, hard eyes appraised him as they talked. "I'll send a couple of men over there to search the place, I was on my way with the warrant when . . ." She stopped and shook her head. "*Merde*. Please wait here, I may have more questions."

Hugo looked up as a slow beeping announced the reversing ambulance, lumbering backward out of the small parking lot before it roared forward past the police blockade and away down Rue Gazan, its lights no longer flashing and its siren quiet, growling through the streets of Paris until it could light up again, maybe this time to help, to arrive in time to fend off death's merciless and unpredictable hand.

Hugo sat on the curb with his head bowed, unable to think, aware only of warm and heavy rain drops hitting the back of his neck and spattering the sidewalk and road in front of him. He looked over and caught Camille Lerens watching him. He looked away, wondering whether she was as good as Garcia had said, and knowing that he didn't have the luxury of waiting to find out.

Those bullets, he knew, could have been meant for him. But even if Raul had somehow provoked the shooting, by being spotted or exchanging words with the killer, Hugo also knew that his actions had put his friend in the line of fire. The caller had told Hugo, *ordered* him, not to tell anyone and Hugo had disobeyed. Out of necessity, yes, but if he'd played it right and done as he was instructed, then the only downside would have been an empty pavilion and no meeting. The anger and sadness that wracked Hugo with almost-physical spasms were made all the more painful by the desperate wish that Hugo could take back that last phone call to Raul.

Hugo willed himself to abandon the recriminations—for now, at least. He had to find whoever killed Raul, and right now there was just one person who could set him on the path to knowing who pulled the trigger. A fury burned white-hot in his chest, and Hugo knew, without any shadow of a doubt, that the person who'd killed Raul Garcia had done nothing less than sign their own death warrant.

CHAPTER TWENTY-ONE

Hugo slipped away while Lieutenant Lerens wasn't watching. Sooner or later, maybe already, she'd have her men at Capron's store and that'd be the end of Hugo's investigation. The murder of a police officer, pretty much anywhere in the world, meant a deep, painstaking, and meticulous investigation, one that would shake every corner of Paris until the killer was caught. But meticulous was not fast, and Hugo had no plans to wait for the scrupulous machinery of the Paris police to warm up and start shredding the city for clues.

Hugo backed his vehicle carefully through the rows of police cars that had stacked up, a show of solidarity that Hugo had seen at each of the five officer shootings he'd been unlucky enough to attend, in the United States, England, and now here in France.

As he finished a three-point turn on Rue Gazan, his phone rang and he looked at the display with irritation, ready to ignore Lerens's order to return to the crime scene. But when he saw who it was, he pulled to the curb and answered.

"Tom, did you hear?"

His friend's voice was tight, desperation and hope clutching at his throat. "Tell me it's not true, fucking tell me that it's not true, Hugo."

"I'm sorry, Tom. I'm really sorry, but it is, it's true."

"Bullshit. Fucking bullshit until you see him. I mean it, Hugo, I'm not believing this until you tell me you've see him."

"I did, Tom. I saw him. No mistakes, no miscommunication. Raul's dead."

Tom's breathing was ragged. "Do you know who did this?"

"No. But I'm going to find out, you better believe that."

"I'm already on my way, you're on scene?"

"I'm leaving, got somewhere to go right now."

A flash of a pause as Tom's mind worked. "You have a lead?"

"Kind of, yeah. I'm going to turn it into one, anyway."

"I'm close, tell me where and I'll meet you."

Despite it all, Hugo smiled. He needed Tom right now, and he knew Tom needed him. They'd pretend it was about the lead—and they did truly work well together—but right now it was more than that. It was the way family and friends gravitate to each other for comfort in the wake of a tragedy, and while both men had seen more blood spilled, more grief and agony, than most, it was rare for death to envelop one of their own, someone so close and dear to both of them.

Hugo gave Tom the address, then hung up and pulled away from the curb with a wheel-spin that turned the heads of several officers drifting around the perimeter of the scene. He drove fast, every car in front an infuriating impediment. The stop light on Avenue Reille was an enemy that he triumphed over with the police lights on his unmarked car and a hand on the horn. He didn't bother with a surreptitious approach to the jewelry store. Old man Capron would either be there or not, the cops would either have swarmed the place or not, and he thumped the steering wheel with relief when he saw the place was still dark, the *Closed* sign still in place, and no police in sight.

He marched through the door and saw Bruno Capron standing over his father, a hacksaw driving back and forth over the handcuffs. Both men looked up, shocked when they saw Hugo standing there with a gun pointed at their faces.

"No more fucking games," Hugo said. "This just got serious."

Bruno's eyes darted toward the office, his former escape route.

"You run, you die," Hugo snapped. "The last time you scurried out of here a policeman was shot and killed, which means that every cop in this city will kiss me and buy me drinks for shooting you in the back the moment you take one step toward that door."

"You wouldn't . . ." Bruno Capron started, but his voice tailed off because it was evident he believed Hugo would.

"Get on your knees," Hugo said. "Now." Bruno complied, kneeling beside his father, the hacksaw forgotten in his hand. Hugo walked up to him and snatched it away. He held the gun to old man Capron's head and looked into Bruno's wide eyes. "Now you're going to tell me what I want to know, because if you don't your dear papa is going to be very upset with you."

The two men looked at each other, but André remained defiant. "I don't believe you would."

Anger boiled inside Hugo, that this worthless thief would fight to keep hidden the one link to Garcia's killer, to the killer of Collette Bassin. He bent down and put his face inches from the old man, and tore into him. "Listen to me, you two-bit piece of crap. That cop who was here with me? He's dead. Murdered. Some *putain* put a gun to the back of his head and blew his brains out and if you think for one fucking minute I'm leaving here without the name of the person who sold you that necklace, you are very, very wrong."

Capron recoiled but Hugo saw the fear in his eyes, fear that served only to heighten Hugo's anger and his resolve to get answers from one or both of these men.

"I told you, I don't—"

Hugo cut him off with a hand on his throat. "If either one of you tells me you don't fucking know," Hugo hissed, "I swear to God you'll regret it."

A sound at the door made Hugo turn, his hand still clutching the thin neck of the gasping Capron.

"What are you doing, man?" Tom asked in English. The words were casual but his tone was like steel and he walked toward them, his eyes taking in everything.

"These assholes bought a necklace from someone. Someone who killed Collette Bassin and then killed Raul."

"OK then." Tom nodded and switched to French. "But we don't do it this way, Hugo. Take your hands off him."

"What?" Hugo hadn't expected that. "Tom, we don't have much time."

"I'm well aware of that. Please let him go."

Hugo did, his eyes on his friend who had changed somehow. The funny, irreverent Tom was detached, formal to the point of being almost robotic. The only sign of emotion was a faint and infrequent twitch in his jaw.

Tom looked at Hugo. "Which of these gentlemen bought the necklace? Both?"

Hugo waved his gun at Bruno. "The old man says he did."

"*Bien.*" Tom looked at Bruno and his voice was soft when he spoke. "I will ask you once and you will tell me the answer. But you need to understand that I don't work for the police, I work for an agency of the American government that lets me kill people that I don't like. And because you are together, if I kill you I will then have to kill your father. After that, your bodies will disappear and no one will ever see any sign of you ever again. Do you understand what I just said?"

Bruno nodded, a small whimper escaping his lips. Hugo felt the fear and confusion shimmering from the young man and his father, and when he looked down he saw that they were holding hands.

"Good," Tom continued in French, his voice almost a whisper. "When I've asked my question, you will answer it fully. If you don't, my friend here will need ten or fifteen seconds to leave the building." He smiled, a wicked and lascivious smile that made even Hugo shiver. "Now. Give me the name of the person who sold you the necklace."

Bruno Capron's throat let out a gurgle as he tried to speak, maybe to plead, but Tom just straightened and pulled a gun from his shoulder holster. He reached over to Hugo with his other hand, never taking his eyes from Bruno, his fingers finding their way to his friend's shoulder and squeezing softly. "Time's up. Hugo, can you leave please?"

"*Non, non*, I'll tell you." Bruno's hands were now tented in prayer and the words spilled out. "I don't know a name, I promise, I would tell you. I didn't know the necklace was stolen, not ... not ... from someone who was murdered, no way I would have bought it then. I'm not, I wouldn't . . ." His words petered out and turned to tears, a large and soft man on his knees begging for his life.

"I didn't hear a name. What is his name?" Tom insisted.

Bruno looked up, a flicker of surprise crossing his eyes. "His name? *Non.* It was a woman."

Tom and Hugo exchanged glances. "Describe her," Hugo said.

"A woman," Bruno whined. "I don't know, not someone I know and nothing special about her."

"My friend said to describe her," Tom said, menace in his voice. "Please do so."

"She was . . . average. Average height and build, her hair . . . just normal." Relief flashed in his eyes as he remembered something. "Pink. She had a streak of pink in her hair."

"Pink?" Tom looked at Hugo. "Mean anything?"

Hugo nodded. "Natalia Khlapina. Alexandra Tourville's assistant." Hugo looked at Bruno. "She have an accent?"

"Foreign. Not heavy but definitely foreign. Maybe from Hungary or Russia or somewhere east."

"Russian," Hugo said. "She's Russian."

Tom reached down and patted Bruno on the head. "Good boy. The police will be here and you can tell them the same thing." He tucked his gun away and nodded to Hugo. "Let's go find our little Russkie."

"Wait, what about me?" André Capron rattled the cuffs that connected him to the immovable oven. "What about these?"

Hugo unlocked his cuffs and stowed them in a pouch on his belt. Capron held up his wrists, still shackled. "And these?"

Hugo was already moving toward the door, so Tom looked at the cuffs and shrugged. "French, I believe. Shame I don't have a key, but you can ask the cops to let you out. I'm sure if you're nice and helpful they will." He started to follow Hugo but turned back. "One more thing, *mes amis.*" His voice was hard, and he slowly opened his jacket to remind them what he was carrying. "We weren't here and you didn't tell us anything. Understand?"

Hugo could tell that father and son were so desperate to end their ordeal and get rid of the Americans, especially the ice-cold Tom, that they would have agreed to anything. Heads nodded ferociously. *"Oui, d'accord,"* they said in unison.

Outside, they paused to regroup. A wind had picked up, the same one that had brought the rain clouds to Paris an hour ago. The debris that dotted the city streets, even somewhere as well-tended as the Butte-aux-Cailles, had started to shift and scuttle from the sidewalks to the street.

They stood by Hugo's car and Tom spoke first. "You won't usually hear this from me, but we need to proceed with a little care."

"What do you mean?"

"We now have a definite link to the Tourville household. Make no mistake, Hugo, that guy is powerful and he'll do all he can to obstruct an investigation into the woman who works for his sister. He's always protected her, and this is no different."

"Meaning we operate under the radar as much as possible."

"Precisely." He gave Hugo a tired smile. "And that's where I come in."

Hugo rested a hand on his friend's arm. "You already came in, Tom. And I'm very glad. Raul would be, too."

In truth, Hugo was relieved that Tom was willing to take the lead. Suddenly tired—of death and of chasing through the streets on this damn case—he welcomed a chance to share the burden with his best friend. It didn't hurt that Tom was right, this really was what he did best. Several times in recent years Hugo had needed help or information and had no way, no legitimate way, to get it. Every time, he was able to turn to Tom for assistance and get what he needed through Tom's murky and frighteningly effective CIA contacts.

"So my plan is just to locate her, and if she's somewhere away from Chateau Tourville then you and I can pay her a visit."

"That's good." Hugo shook his head. "But I want to bring in that police lieutenant, Lerens. Raul talked to me about her this morning, said she's good."

"Lerens? I heard she used to be a dude."

"Yep. That a problem for you?"

"It's a little weird, but as long as I don't have to date her, I'm fine with it."

"Charming."

"Hugo, I really don't give a crap. I just want to find the fucker who . . ." He took a breath, unable to say the words just yet. "Raul said she's good?"

"He did. Very good."

Tom shrugged. "Then I suppose she is, and if you want to bring her in that's fine. I'll find Khlapina and we can let Lerens know. Maybe she'll bring us along for that chat."

"Maybe." But they both doubted it. A meticulousness and pains-taking investigation didn't usually allow for courtesies like that, but if they had to back out, so be it. Pride, a sense of ownership in the case, all of that could go by the wayside, sacrificed for the only goal that mat-tered: catching Raul Garcia's killer.

"Jesus," Hugo said. "I don't even know what day it is."

"Saturday." Tom checked his watch. "OK, I'm making some calls, get the ball rolling. I'll let you know when we find her and you can tell Lerens. Assuming those two chumps in there talk, then the frogs will be looking for her, too. We'll have her today or tomorrow, is my bet."

"Just because she sold the necklace, doesn't mean she was the shooter," Hugo said. "That fact and her connection to Tourville may buy her some time."

"And distance. I need to get to work, she could be on her way out of France already."

"Love those porous borders," Hugo said with a grimace. "Chasing fugitives in Europe these days is like catching rats with a lasso."

"Interpol." Tom said. "They ain't perfect, but they have a lot of lassos."

"Then get to it." Hugo watched as Tom walked to his car, pulling his phone from his pocket. He was talking by the time he slid behind the wheel and sat there, giving instructions and descriptions, his free hand gesturing like that of a conductor. Once he took a sip from a clear plastic bottle, catching Hugo's eye through the windshield. *Water*, he mouthed.

Hugo nodded and climbed behind the wheel of his own car. He'd fought for months to get Tom to stop drinking, but it had taken a bullet from a serial killer to make him quit. As distraught as he was about Garcia's death, Hugo couldn't help but detect the specter of Tom's nemesis and he hoped against hope that the bullet that almost killed Tom, but saved him from alcohol, wouldn't be undone by the ones fired by their friend's killer. Hugo had always been strong and capable, untouched in some ways, amid the violence and sorrow that was an inevitable shadow to his career. But Raul Garcia's death had shaken him to his core and as he started his car and looked at Tom in his rearview mirror, Hugo wondered, truly wondered, how he himself might cope if today's horror sent his best friend ricocheting back to the bottle.

CHAPTER TWENTY-TWO

Hugo woke in a panic, a dream-weight that had been pressing down on his chest taking moments of wakefulness to evaporate. As his head cleared, the relief that came with a disappearing nightmare was replaced by the memory of the previous day's tragedy. He rolled out of bed and padded in to the kitchen, where Tom was sitting at the breakfast bar, his hand curled around a mug of coffee and the morning's newspaper in front of him.

"You've been out already?" Hugo asked.

"Couldn't sleep. Went for a walk and picked up the paper. Made coffee, too, but it tastes like shit."

"I'll take some anyway." Hugo went into the kitchen and poured a cup, stirring in a spoonful of brown sugar. "They write much about it?"

"Front page. Light on the details, as you'd imagine." Tom sipped his coffee. "What kind of a moron do you have to be to kill a cop?"

"A desperate one," Hugo said. He walked to a nearby armchair and sank down. "I've been thinking about that, because every criminal in the world knows you don't kill a policeman. Ever. For one thing there's always one more to fill his shoes but, more importantly if you're the criminal, you bring every kind of heat imaginable to the case."

"Like you said, she must have been desperate."

"Yeah. Or not a criminal."

Tom glanced over. "I'm not following."

"That's OK, I'm not making sense. No word from any of your people?"

"Nothing to get the juices flowing. They have a couple of addresses for her that the cops have already visited. No sign. She may have left the country, of course, but that takes time to verify, even assuming she did it through somewhere that has border control." He put his hand on the newspaper, almost a caress. "No word about a funeral, either."

"He was Catholic," Hugo said. "Shit, Tom, this . . ."

"Yeah, it does. And not being able to do anything about it also sucks."

Hugo drained his coffee and dropped his cup in the kitchen sink before heading to his room to dress. "I'm going for a walk. Join me?"

Tom looked up. "I may not be a drunk any more, but let's not go crazy here."

"You used to run ten miles without breaking a sweat."

"Sweaty crotch, actually, but I managed to hide it pretty well."

"Thank heavens for that."

"Damn right. Actually, I have plans later that involve walking and I don't want to wear my delicate self out."

Hugo cocked his head. "Plans?"

"Yep. A date of sorts. I would describe it, if we're being technical, as none of your business."

"OK. Be mysterious, see if I care." But Hugo couldn't help but wonder, and if memory served this was the third week in a row Tom had gone out on a weekend evening. He'd been back by eleven o'clock each time, and stone cold sober as best Hugo could tell, but until now Tom hadn't made any mention of going out, he'd just put on his coat and left. At first Hugo had wondered if maybe he was attending some kind of meeting related to his drinking, but Tom didn't believe in twelve-step programs, and since he'd been gone about six hours each time an AA meeting didn't fit anyway.

Hugo dressed, opening his bedroom window to check the air temperature, and decided that he'd do what he'd done the previous two weeks, and as Tom had suggested: mind his own business.

Hugo and Tom talked some more before Hugo went out. They both wanted to make sure there was nothing to be done, no angle they'd missed. They talked, too, about Senator Lake and together called the ambassador to make sure he knew the latest and to get an update on the senator.

"That's all on hold," Ambassador Taylor said. "I've not told him about the Russian woman being involved but he's no dummy, he knows something is up."

"He's not heading back to the States?" Hugo asked.

"Wishful thinking? No, but he's taken to walking every morning and afternoon, says he's enjoying Paris now. I don't know, maybe he is, but he's sure as hell antsy. I'm not having to hold his hand, which is a relief, and he's not wandered off again, which I'm also grateful for."

Hugo detected a note in the ambassador's voice, a thought unsaid. "Spit it out, boss, what are you thinking?"

"I don't know. It crossed my mind that he's got himself a girlfriend. I know we talked about that before, but he's got to be going somewhere. His security detail aren't saying anything."

Tom chuckled. "Off with their own pieces of tail, if I know the Secret Service."

"Yeah, well, maybe they're being discreet but I'm pretty sure they'd have said something if he was tasting the local delights, so to speak. Ah well, like I say, everything's on hold and he's not bugging me too badly so I'm fine with it." He paused. "And I'm so sorry about Capitaine Garcia, I know you guys had gotten to know him well, and I know how much you appreciated him as a colleague and a friend. Let me know when the funeral is, I want to be there."

When they rang off, Tom went and stood by the window, looking out over Rue Jacob, silent. Anxious to be moving, Hugo let himself out of the apartment and made his way down the stairs and out into the street.

He comforted himself with the familiar, narrow streets of the sixth and seventh arrondissements, wandering aimlessly in the direction of the river that split Paris into north and south, left and right.

He'd come to know this part of the city intimately, with its myriad art galleries, furniture shops, and clothing boutiques, most the size of his bedroom and selling quality not quantity, their owners knowledgeable and in business to sell the items they loved, not just to make a buck. Sometimes he'd turn a corner and find a store had disappeared, been emptied of merchandise and filled with something totally different, wedding dresses to watercolors, as if a coup had taken place overnight. He'd feel a touch of sadness because familiarity can itself be comfort, but, as much as he walked, he soon got to know the new shapes and colors on display.

He angled his walk to stay away from the wind, which billowed down the narrower streets and wrapped itself around him, alternately holding him back and pushing him onwards. At one point he sought refuge in a café just off Rue de Grenelle and when he looked at his watch it was two in the afternoon. He ate a slow lunch, an omelet and a basket of bread, and tried not to think about Raul Garcia.

One mental distraction was Tom, the little brother in his life who seemed to have finally turned things around. A master at deception, Tom was hopeless when it came to lying to Hugo—most of the time he didn't bother. Which meant that if Tom was drinking again, Hugo felt confident he'd know. Confident but not positive, and so these weekly outings, which Tom was being evasive about, were a concern. The normal things people hide from their friends, hookers for example, were not things Tom felt the need to keep to himself. Quite the opposite. On at least one occasion Hugo had found a beautiful and half-naked courtesan wandering around his apartment and, with Claudia's help, he'd even paid the bill.

Claudia. He looked at his phone and thought about her. He'd called yesterday to break the news about Raul and she'd taken it hard. They'd had a connection, those two. Raul, the wise and dapper man who'd been married for decades, had an unashamed and utterly harmless crush on the beautiful Claudia. For her part, she'd reveled in making the Frenchman feel special, a fondness that was as genuine as Raul's affection for her.

Hugo had stayed on the phone as she tried not to cry, stayed on longer when she couldn't hold it back, and talked to her for almost an hour as she regained her composure. He'd wanted to be with her last night, a longing he'd not experienced in years, a desire far more powerful than merely physical. But she'd declined, keeping that distance between them she'd put in place over the previous months. Hugo hadn't pushed, partly out of pride but mostly because he'd never been one to chase, a belief that if someone was running away or just needed space then coercing them back with pleas and entreaties was shallow and manipulative, and would ultimately ruin any chance for a relationship. They'd both been sad when the call ended, to be left alone with their thoughts of Raul, but Hugo missed her voice for other reasons, too.

He left the café at three, making his way slowly back to the apartment, stopping to arrange for flowers to be sent to Garcia's wife. Hugo smiled at a memory, one only an FBI agent could dredge up and grace with a smile. They'd been in the village of Castet under the gun of a madman. Hugo had begged for Garcia's life and in the process invented two children. Raul and his wife didn't have any—Hugo didn't know if it was by choice or circumstance—but at that moment, in that remote village, just seconds away from almost certain death, Hugo had made his friend smile. No more than a twitch of his mouth and a brighter glint in his eye, but Garcia had found it funny and for a moment Hugo wondered if he'd told his wife about it. He wished Raul had so Hugo could sign the card to her and their children, maybe provoke another smile at a time when one was so desperately needed.

It was four o'clock when Hugo turned onto his street, Rue Jacob, and saw the police car sitting in front of his apartment building.

Lieutenant Camille Lerens climbed out of the passenger seat and shook his hand. He noticed her cornrows now, delicate black trails across her scalp, and his mind took what he knew about her and gauged her handshake, the size of her hand even. It registered nothing out of the ordinary.

"Everything all right?" Hugo asked. He didn't like her being there, an instinctual reaction from someone who knew that cops never showed up with good news.

"Yes. I need to talk to you."

"You want to come upstairs?"

"*Non*, we don't have time. This investigation . . ." She looked tired, her skin looked gray, and her eyes were bloodshot. Hugo guessed she'd not slept much last night, if at all.

"I understand."

"Your role in it is what I wanted to discuss."

Here it comes, Hugo thought. He'd walked away from the murder scene when she told him to stay, and he'd almost certainly pissed her off by interrogating the Caprons before she did.

"Look, Lieutenant," he began, "I know what you're going to say but I'm going to have to disappoint you. The fact is, I know more about this case than anyone and if you want it solved you're not helping anyone by bumping me aside." He held up a hand to silence her. "Excuse me, but I'm not done. Maybe ditching me would be by-the-book and maybe your bosses are telling you that I'm a witness as well as an investigator, I get that. But even if all that's true, and even if this case has pretty feeble links to the senator, it still has links and I intend to do whatever I can to connect them and find out who killed my friend. And I don't mean to come across like a cocky American jackass, but you'd do well to consider the benefits of having a former FBI agent and a former CIA agent on your team."

Lerens nodded slowly. "Thank you for that speech, are you finished?"

"I am."

"Good. First, thank you for wasting two minutes of my life. Second, we found Natalia Khlapina. Third, I came here to tell you to be available. I'm well aware of your abilities, and they are enhanced in my view by the trust Raul Garcia placed in you. He talked of you often and with the highest regard. You're right in that some at the prefecture may not want to share this investigation with Americans and if they knew, maybe they'd try and put a stop to your involvement." She gave a tired smile. "But if you know anything about me, Monsieur Marston, and from the way you study me when you think I'm not looking it's obvious you know my situation, then you may also understand that I'm more than accustomed to ignoring and evading the negativity of my superiors."

"Absolutely, I'm sure you have. I'm sorry, I assumed—"

"I know what you assumed but assumptions have never been good for me, and it helps that I'm not an idiot. As you said, you know the case better than anyone and have more training, experience, and skills than anyone else in this investigation, myself included. Why the hell would anyone wanting to find Raul's killer exclude you?"

Hugo held up a hand in apology. "Too many encounters with bureaucracy, I'm sorry."

"Apology accepted. Can we get to work?"

"Please. You said you found Natalia, is she talking?"

"*Ah, non. Pas de tout,*" Lerens said. *Not at all.* "But then I don't blame her, it's not so easy to talk when you are dead."

CHAPTER TWENTY-THREE

Hugo let out a breath. "How?"

"Shot. Once in the head."

"My God. Who found her, when, and where?"

"Last night, someone called police because they thought they'd heard a shot under the Pont de l'Alma. Officers responded but couldn't find anything. One of them went back this morning on his own initiative and found some blood. Looks like she was shot at the edge of the river and pushed in. We fished her out about two hours ago. Her body had jammed up against a barge roughly a mile downstream, giving the owner quite a fright. I'm assuming the water will have destroyed any good physical evidence."

"Probably, but there may be something under her fingernails if she fought before being shot." Unlikely, he thought, if she was shot in the back of the head. "Any defensive wounds?"

"A little hard to tell, she was probably bumped around a bit in the water, but the medical examiner on scene didn't think so. They're probably doing the autopsy right now, so maybe that'll reveal something more."

"Any idea if it's the same gun that was used on Raul?"

"Not yet. Can't tell from the wounds, but we have a ballistics guy on standby. As soon as we get the bullet from Khlapina he might be able to tell us."

Hugo's phone buzzed and he pulled it from his pocket and checked the display. "My boss, can I update him?"

"*Oui, bien sûr.*"

"Thanks." Hugo answered. "Ambassador, how're you?"

"Slightly less depressed and angry than yesterday, but not much."

"I get that. Listen, I'm with Lieutenant Camille Lerens, do you know her?"

"Just by reputation, supposed to be good. And I saw in the paper she's leading the charge."

"She is. She wants my help, so you OK if I focus on that for a bit?"

"Hell yes, of course." A pause. "Except for one thing."

"Which is?"

"Senator Lake. Just as I was extolling his new and welcome touristic bent he's made off again."

"Solo?"

"Same routine as before. Gave his agent the slip and walked away."

"Wait, you said 'agent,' singular?"

"Yeah, I gather he was downgraded somewhere in the administrative pipeline. He's a one-agent worry now, apparently."

"Apparently not." Hugo ran a hand through his hair in frustration. "Not good timing, Senator."

"No shit. I'm sorry, Hugo, but do you have any ideas?"

"When did he disappear?"

"Two hours ago. Agent Emma Ruby called me, I said to sit tight and wait for him to roll back in like last time. She feels bad, but it's not her fault. Sent her on some errand while he was still in his slippers, but he was gone when she got back."

"So definitely planned and, again, likely by him. Had his stuff ready to go."

"Right."

"Then screw it, I think just stick to your plan. Have Ruby wait at the hotel for him to come back. Then have him bounced back to the States, if you can."

"Works for me."

"Did he take his phone this time?"

"Nope."

Hugo shook his head, frustrated and irritated. "OK. If he wants to get lost or keep risking trouble by pulling these stunts then let him. We have bigger worries right now."

"Agreed. I just wanted you to be aware. If you have any bright ideas, let me know."

"A leash?"

The men chuckled, a welcome relief from the stress, and when Hugo rang off he told Lerens what was going on.

She waved a hand. "Millions of foreigners wander around Paris every day. He's just another one of them, but probably has a girlfriend stashed away. Or a boyfriend." A mischievous glint in her eye made Hugo laugh again.

"That'd explain a lot."

"Is he married?"

"No. Divorced, I think."

"Then ask his ex-wife," Lerens said. "From what I hear, they love dishing dirt on former hubbies."

"If I cared that much, I might."

"Understood." She checked her watch. "Well, I have an autopsy to attend, hopefully missed most of it. You're welcome to join me."

"That's fine, seen my share and don't need to see any more. If it's OK with you, I'll update Tom Green and then wait to hear from you on the results. Assuming Tom's help is also welcome."

"Absolutely. Also, would you mind typing up a statement for our records about your visit to Capron's store and the phone call? I don't think I've had the full version, but whatever it is I'll need it in writing so everyone on the team is on the same page."

"Sure, I'll do that now."

"Good. I have some officers rounding up the Caprons. With this new development we want them in for questioning. Given your earlier interaction with them, it might be useful to have you there."

"Happy to. Call me when you find them, I'll come straight to the prefecture."

"*Merci.*" They swapped cell phone numbers and shook hands. "I'll call if the autopsy shows anything or we get the Caprons or ballistics. Basically, if I learn anything." She wagged a finger, but playfully. "And if you get any more anonymous calls, please return the favor."

"I will. Which reminds me, are you trying to trace the call to the store?"

"We did. Pay phone and no cameras in the area to catch who made it. With technology these days, voice distorters aren't hard or expensive to come by and easy to carry in a pocket. Dead end, I'm afraid."

Hugo watched as Lieutenant Lerens drove away, then turned to walk into his building. The door swung open as he put his hand out, and Tom appeared on the top step.

"Promoted to door man?" Tom asked. "If so, you need a suit with tassels and shit."

"Not yet, still working on that. Having a nice chat with our new colleague, as it happens."

"Who's our new colleague?"

"Camille Lerens."

"Ah. Let me guess, she wants you, which is to say *us*, to keep our noses out of their investigation because it's out of our jurisdiction, because Raul was a friend and we're too close . . . How am I doing so far?"

"About as wrong as you could be."

"For real?"

"For real. She wants all the help she can get, and that includes us."

"Well, fuck me. I knew I liked her for some reason. Tell me more." He listened quietly while Hugo filled him in on the death of Natalia Khlapina, and the dead-end phone trace. "Not much for us to do except wait."

"About right," Hugo said. "And Senator Lake has gone out on his own again."

"Does anyone care?"

Hugo grinned. "The ambassador and maybe the agent he left behind, but otherwise I don't think so at this point."

"So let him wander off. Fuck it."

"That's what I said. And speaking of which, where are you off to?"

Tom glanced at the sky, then winked at Hugo. "As the good senator himself might say . . ."

"Yeah, I know. Mind my own business."

"Call me if something happens, news comes in, or any development at all. Can't promise I'll answer, but feel free to leave a message."

"Will do." Hugo headed into the apartment building, leaving Tom to his own devices, but halfway across the lobby he stopped. His choice was between paperwork for Lieutenant Lerens or a little legwork of his own. He went back to the main door and looked out. He knew he shouldn't, that Tom had every right to tootle about Paris on his own. But Tom's premature bristling when he thought Lieutenant Lerens was going to shut them out of the investigation came into Hugo's mind because it would have been an instruction that Tom, probably both of them, would have ignored. In other words, Hugo told himself, Tom had no grounds to complain at Hugo's own little investigation progressing. It was weak justification, of course it was, but it was enough for the moment. And what Tom didn't know . . .

Hugo stepped into the street. Tom was still in sight and Hugo watched as he turned into Rue Bonaparte, a quiet street lined with the small shops and boutiques they both loved so much, and a street that would take Tom toward the nearest metro station. Hugo set off after him, softening his footfall and using the few pedestrians as cover.

A large van blocked his view as he turned into Rue Bonaparte, and he had to squeeze between it and an old man with his shopping bags on the narrow sidewalk. As he came past the end of the van, Hugo heard a voice behind him and froze.

"You're so fucking predictable."

Hugo turned slowly. "Ah, Tom. I was just going for a walk."

"For a *follow*, you mean."

Hugo shrugged and suddenly felt ashamed, like a peeping Tom caught in the act. "Sorry, I just thought . . . Well, you know how I worry about you."

"That's sweet, Dad, it really is."

"Fine, I'm sorry."

"That's OK. Like I said, you're predictable. And really quite adorable." He patted Hugo on the shoulder and said, "Just don't do it again."

An hour later, Lieutenant Lerens called. Her voice sounded tired, like she wanted very badly for this to be all over. Investigations, Hugo knew, came with their own cycles of emotion. The initial fizz of excitement that came with a dead body, a murder. Then a sense of trepidation at the realization of how much work had to be done. Exhaustion, like Lerens must be feeling, came and went, settling in with the slog of interviews and paperwork but evaporating, at least temporarily, when a lead revealed itself. She'd be fine, Hugo knew, they just needed a break in the case. That was a cure for all ills.

"Khlapina was dead when she hit the water," Lerens said. "Single bullet-wound to the right temple. The water did some damage but the medical examiner saw stippling."

"Contact shot," Hugo said. "You're thinking suicide?"

"It's possible. If she murdered Raul she certainly had good reason to kill herself. She'd have known we'd track her down sooner or later."

"For sure. You confirmed that she's right-handed?"

"We managed to think of that."

"Sorry, just being thorough."

"We are too, don't worry."

"Did the medical examiner recover the bullet?"

"Yes. And it looks like a .32, the same caliber as the one that killed Raul."

"We're assuming the gun went into the water?"

"We are. If it did, it's as good as gone." She sighed, her voice tinged with sadness. "Fifty bodies a year. That's roughly how many are found in the Seine, did you know that? It's convenient, of course, and with the boat traffic, the currents, and the thousands and thousands of people who live nearby, it's a great way to destroy evidence. Human and otherwise."

"That's a lot of people," Hugo agreed. "So, what's next for us?"

"Right, next." Lerens's voice stiffened. "One of the reasons I called is that we have the Caprons en route to the prefecture. Should be here in thirty minutes or less."

"I'll leave right away."

"Thanks. And bring your friend Tom." She chuckled. "When we mentioned him to the Caprons at the store, you should have seen their faces."

Hugo laughed. "Tom can have that effect, no doubt. But he's out right now. I'll call and see if I can get him." Hugo paused, but figured Lerens had a right to know as she was trusting them to be a part of her investigation. "Look, he's a bit of a lone wolf sometimes. He's used to operating on the fringes, of the law and of decency. Don't get me wrong, he's the finest human being I know, it's just that sometimes he forgets which set of rules he needs to play by."

"I know. Raul told me about both of you, which means I have an idea of what I'm getting into by inviting him to *play*, as you put it." She lowered her voice. "Look, I want to make sure the person who killed Raul Garcia is caught, and if it's Natalia Khlapina I want to be able to tell Raul's wife that I'm one hundred percent sure that his killer is dead. But I also want to be able to tell Madam Garcia why Khlapina killed him, why she wanted to kill you. For her, this has to make some sense, and for me, too. What I'm saying is, if I have someone on my team who can help get me those answers I don't care, not in this case, if he upsets a few people to get them."

"Especially people like the Caprons."

"*Exactement.* I'll see you within the hour?"

CHAPTER TWENTY-FOUR

The Caprons were in separate interview rooms, and both looked terrified. Hugo was able to walk the narrow hallway from one observation room to the next and he did that several times, gauging each man's demeanor. The two rooms had one-way glass that looked into the cramped, windowless rooms where both Caprons sat fidgeting in plastic chairs.

"You want to do this?" Lerens asked. She'd been disappointed that Tom wasn't there, as was Hugo. They knew he could be an effective weapon this evening, though Hugo couldn't help but feel a measure of relief. These interviews would be recorded and any deviation from textbook interrogation could easily find itself in Ambassador Taylor's hands or, God forbid, the hands of someone more inclined to damage his or Tom's career.

"Sure. But tell me what they've said so far."

"Very little. We offered them a lawyer but it turns out they trust lawyers less than cops, so we have that going for us."

"Interesting."

"I thought so. All we know is that the son, Bruno, bought the necklace from Natalia Khlapina."

"Who wound up dead last night."

"Correct."

"Does he know she's dead?"

"No." She gave a wry smile. "Unless he killed her."

"Let's see if we can find out. It's possible the murder–robbery had nothing to do with the Tourvilles, more than possible. Maybe these two are neck-deep in what happened near Troyes and nothing more. Though it'd be some coincidence."

"Agreed." Lerens handed him a manila folder. "Some photos of Khlapina from last night, they might rattle him."

Hugo glanced through them, barely recognizing the bedraggled, sodden body of the girl he'd met at Chateau Tourville. Her face was set like wax, sallow and bruised. Her teeth looked unnaturally white, perfectly so, contrasting starkly with the equally fake-looking bullet hole in her head. The pink streak in her hair looked ominous now, like diluted blood. He closed down any emotion, telling himself he could hate her for killing Raul later, or feel sorry that she was just a victim once her killer was behind bars. "If he's just a thief, or fencing stolen goods, these pictures should do exactly that."

"I think so, too."

Hugo paused. "Before I go in, did you find out where she lives and search the place?"

"Yes and no. She had an apartment but technically it's leased by Alexandra Tourville. I have an officer getting her written permission to go through the place, and once we have it, I want to do that myself."

"I wondered if there was more jewelry in there. And when you do the search, I'll come with you, if that's OK."

"*Mais oui.*"

"Thanks," Hugo said. "Last question: The fingerprint from Lake's room and the murder scene, did they match Natalia?"

Lerens grimaced. "Having a hard time with that. She was in the water for long enough that a quick comparison isn't possible. The scientists have some techniques for dealing with it, and they have instructions to call me when a comparison is done."

"But nothing yet."

"*Non.*" She turned and looked through the one-way glass at Bruno Capron. "So, this one first?"

"Definitely. He's the one with the penchant for stolen property and running from cops. Even if his dad knows something, he's still a dad and will keep his mouth shut to protect his son. Kids, in my experience, are more interested in saving their own skin."

"*Alors*, go get him."

Hugo moved to the door then stopped. "Are you sure it's OK for me to be doing this? You won't get in trouble with your superiors?"

Lerens shook her head. "I can go in there and scream in that man's face. I can lie to him and try and trick the truth out of him. I can make him bored, cold, and uncomfortable. I'm pretty sure I'm allowed to subject him to an American, too."

Hugo smiled. "In that case, I'll get to work."

When he breezed into the little room, Bruno sat up straight, his face a mask but his eyes wary.

"*Salut*," said Hugo. Bruno just watched him, so Hugo went on. "You comfortable? Need anything?"

"To see my father. Take him home."

"Right, apart from that. Something I can actually do for you, I meant. Coffee, a cigarette, something like that."

"A cigarette."

Hugo sat down in the chair opposite Bruno and frowned. "Oh, I just remembered, I don't like to be around people who smoke. I don't mind them doing it, I just don't think I should have to inhale their fumes. Know what I mean? In America hardly anyone smokes any more. Very different here, I'm always amazed how many young people still light up."

The slightest hint of a sneer. "We're not in America."

"No, lucky for you, too," Hugo said. "In America we still have the death penalty, at least in some states. If we were in mine, Texas, you'd be looking at having a needle stuck in your arm. After ten years of solitary confinement, of course, which isn't much fun either."

"No, I wouldn't. I haven't done anything."

"Is that right? See, here's how I look at it, and follow along so you can let me know where I'm stating things incorrectly. We know you bought stolen property from Natalia Khlapina. We know that property was taken after its owner was murdered. We also know that once you were confronted you ran away, and that within an hour a police officer investigating the robbery was himself killed." Hugo paused and looked Bruno Capron in the eye. "And then we know that Natalia Khlapina was murdered last night, likely shot with the same gun that my colleague was killed with."

A shadow passed over Bruno's face, a flicker in his eye as he tried to stay composed and hide whatever emotion he was feeling. With a leisurely hand, Hugo flipped open the manila folder and spread four photos of the dead Natalia Khlapina across the table. Bruno's eyes turned slowly downward, his brow wrinkling as he struggled to recognize the person displayed in front of him. The moment he did, his jaw clenched and his Adam's apple bobbed as he swallowed, the merest shake of his head, almost a shudder, told Hugo plenty.

"Which makes me wonder," Hugo continued softly. "Where were you last night?"

Bruno Capron dragged his eyes up to meet Hugo's. "I was . . . with my father."

"You two," Hugo tapped a photo of Khlapina. "Do everything together, do you?"

"We didn't do this. We are not murderers. I didn't even know that necklace was stolen."

"Yeah." Hugo sat back. "We're not buying that. We've had numerous reports of stolen property going through your little antiques store, and based on this murder and the one in Troyes I'm betting the cops will shut the place down and spend a few months tracing the history of pretty much every single thing you have for sale."

The threat struck home, as Hugo knew it would. Call a thief a thief and he'll act outraged, but threaten to take away his ill-gotten gains, and thereby his income, he'll do pretty much whatever it takes to hang on to them.

"*Non*, monsieur, my father is an old man. He's not well and if you shut down his business it'll kill him." Bruno winced as he used the word *kill*, his eyes almost apologetic. "*Alors*, it's true that sometimes I buy things from people with . . . questionable occupations. Sometimes maybe I suspect the items they sell are not legitimate. But if there's a crime here, it's mine and not my father's."

Hugo didn't believe for a second that André Capron was as innocent as his son made out. At best he was being willfully blind, turning his back as Bruno stocked their display case with the heirlooms of other people, making a profit from crime while pretending he was just like any other businessman.

"Oh, there's a crime here and he's in it as deep as you are. Possession of stolen property, theft, why not robbery and murder? *Qui vole un œuf vole un bœuf,* isn't that the saying?" *He who steals an egg will steal an ox.*

"Stealing is not killing."

"Very true. But you're not denying any of my facts. What some might say are suspicious coincidences, people getting killed around you, and I've still not heard anything resembling an alibi."

"I told you, I was with my father."

"Where?"

"At his apartment."

"Do you own a gun?"

"*Non.* I never have, and neither does my father."

"When did you last see Natalia Khlapina?"

"When I bought the necklace from her. She came in off the street, I'd never seen her before and I didn't see her after."

A hitch in Bruno's voice told Hugo that the young man was lying, or at least shading the truth. Hugo ran the sentence back in his mind and thought maybe Capron had emphasized the word 'see.'

Hugo guessed. "You didn't see her, but we do know that you spoke to her."

"How . . . ?" Capron sat forward. "How could you know that?"

"Tell me about it."

"The store. After I left, I called her."

"Why did you have her number if this was a one-off deal?"

Bruno slouched in the chair, the breath leaving him in a long sigh. "When she came in, I liked her. She was . . . pretty. And it didn't seem like she did this for a living, at least that's what I thought. That's why I didn't think it was stolen, she didn't seem like the sort of person who would do that. She was nice." His eyes slid to the pictures and his head twitched away, recoiling. "I told her I needed to see identification and have her phone number for tax reasons, or for legal reasons. I can't remember which, but I said we did it for all customers. I wrote her name and address down and her phone number. I tried calling it once but it was fake. I used an online service to find her real number, using her name and address, it was easy."

"How sweet. Did she tell you where she got the necklace?"

"I think she said something about a relative leaving it to her in a will. I wasn't listening too closely."

"Because you don't care where things come from, just how much you get for them."

Capron shrugged. "Think what you want."

"Don't worry, I will. So what else did she sell you?"

"Nothing else, just the necklace. As far as I could tell she didn't have anything with her to sell."

Hugo nodded slowly while he thought. The Caprons were small-time crooks, thieves who had no compunction about acquiring other people's treasures and turning a profit from them. But Hugo wasn't convinced they were involved in murder, not Raul's or Madam Bassin's and, if he was right, that meant they were also innocent of killing Natalia. Hugo would never claim to be able to recognize a killer just by exchanging a few words, but he felt confident he could recognize some signs of an innocent man. On a practical level, someone prepared to kill three people wouldn't be so lazy, or stupid, as to sell items stolen from a robbery–murder in his own store. The police had turned up no other connection with Natalia, either, and he hoped a search of her computer hard drive would show she'd hunted online for places to sell the necklace.

Which begged the question: If the Caprons hadn't teamed up with Natalia to acquire the necklace, who had?

"Last question. When you ran from me at the store, you called her."

"*Oui.*"

"Why?"

"To tell her she was in trouble. To warn her, I suppose, in case she didn't know the necklace was stolen. Or to hide if she did."

"Very noble." Hugo thought for a moment. "Where was she when you called?"

"I don't know."

"Anyone with her?"

"How am I supposed to . . . Wait, when she answered, she told me to hold on and spoke to someone else. But I don't know who."

"Man or woman?"

"I couldn't tell. I didn't hear the other person speak. She just said, 'I have to take this,' or words to that effect. That's all, I promise."

Hugo rose. "Thank you for your time, I'll talk to the lieutenant about cutting you and your father loose tonight."

Bruno grunted what may have been thanks as Hugo left. He slipped back into the observation room where Lieutenant Lerens was waiting.

"He's not our killer, is he?" she said.

"No, I don't think so. Doesn't seem like the type, and it doesn't make much sense."

"I agree. In better news, I got a call from the officer assigned to find Alexandra Tourville."

"Don't tell me she's blocking the search."

"She couldn't for long, and I'm guessing she knows that. But the officer said she's in shock over Natalia's death and is happy for us to go over the place."

"That's a relief. She signed the consent form?"

"Yes. There's one slight complication, though."

"She wants to be there," Hugo said.

"Precisely. And in the interests of keeping my job I plan to play along, at least to some degree. I'll let her unlock the door and then stand there while we go in first."

"Actually, having her there might be good, we can do a more thorough interview with her."

"Good idea," Lerens said. "And since you did such a good job with young Monsieur Capron, I'm nominating you."

"I work for you now, is that it?" Hugo smiled.

"*Bien sûr.*" Her face was serious but there was a smile in her eyes. "In fact, earlier this evening I heard you on the phone with your ambassador asking to do precisely that."

"Fine, but let me do one thing before I interview her."

"What's that?"

"Let me walk through the place."

"Profiling?"

"It's not just people themselves who can tell you about a crime or criminal. It's the things they own, the places they put things, the state they keep their home."

"I think you should teach courses in this, Hugo. I would be a diligent student."

"Be happy to, but let's catch Raul's killer first."

"Ah, yes." Lerens pursed her lips. "Madam Tourville cannot meet us at the apartment until tomorrow morning. I've been told to give her that courtesy."

"Politics," Hugo said. "I've been subjected to those myself on occasion."

Lieutenant Lerens nodded and then rubbed the back of her neck. "For once I'm grateful. I could use a good night's sleep." She glanced up. "And no disrespect, but I'm thinking that you could, too."

"Very true."

Lerens turned to go, then looked back at Hugo. "There's a café close by. I'd like for us to talk for a few minutes, I'll buy."

"Talk?"

"Yes. I've found it best to answer people's questions, the ones they pretend they don't have, and to generally clear the air when I'm working closely with someone."

Hugo smiled. He was happy to pretend he didn't have questions, but curiosity was a weakness, and he genuinely wanted to understand Camille Lerens. As best he could, of course.

"Sure, we can grab a drink," he said.

They picked a table at the back, inside and as far away from others as possible. When the carafe of red wine arrived, she poured them each a glass and began to talk.

"I was born Christophe in Bordeaux. My father was a policeman but I didn't join because of that, but because I wanted to." She gave a sad smile. "Of course, even then I would have preferred to join as a police woman."

"You've always known?"

"Yes. This isn't the sort of thing that hits you later in life, as if you get sick of wearing ties or shaving every day. And I think you know it's not a choice."

"Of course not. I can't imagine anyone would choose that kind of . . ." Hugo searched for the right word but didn't find it.

"Torment," Lerens filled in. "Agony. Shame. There are lots of words for it but I've left most of them behind. The funny thing is, my father the macho police man, he always knew. We finally talked about it when I was sixteen, but back then there wasn't much we could do. It was a great comfort to be able to talk to him so openly."

"Your mother?"

"She took longer to come around. But she did and they have always supported me. I think it helps that my father was from Niger and my mother from Egypt. They'd both suffered discrimination for being who they were and they weren't afraid to stand up for me, too."

"I'm glad to hear that. So you joined the police as a man?"

"I did. It was something of a calculated decision. I thought that they might turn me down if I made the gender switch first, but they might have some legal problems if they fired me after I'd proved myself a good policeman."

Hugo smiled. "I have no idea how either of those things would go down in Texas."

"Probably not too different from Bordeaux," Lerens laughed. "My immediate superior almost had a heart attack. But the man at the top, he . . . well, I think he thought it interesting. I also think his lawyers were advising him to play it very low-key."

"I was wondering whether the news media had picked up on it, seems like they'd be interested in that kind of story."

"I don't think anyone really wanted to tell them, not back then, and not in a provincial town like Bordeaux. I didn't want to, of course, and my chief didn't. Plus, the many people above and around me who didn't approve already detested the newspapers so I think they saved their words for me in private."

"Some ugliness?"

Lerens nodded slowly, then took a drink. "The first week I used the women's bathroom, yes. Of course, it was strange for me, too, I felt on the one hand like a trespasser but also . . . also like I was finally in a safe place. Somewhere I belonged and somewhere the men around me, including the man I was, could be excluded."

"I can't image how hard it must have been. You know, Raul told me very little but he held you in very high regard. He respected you for achieving everything you have."

"He was a good man," Lerens said, her voice a whisper. She cleared her throat and looked Hugo in the eye. "Questions?"

"No," Hugo said, "I don't think—"

"Not true!" Lerens laughed. "But it's OK, most people are embarrassed to ask about the mechanics, though pretty much everyone is curious."

"Fine," Hugo said, sitting back. "I admit it, I'm curious. Plus, I have a friend who will pump me for details and if I don't have them, he'll make life unpleasant."

"The great Tom Green?"

"I wouldn't say great, but that's the one."

"Then here are your answers for him," Lerens said, refilling Hugo's glass. "I began with hormone shots, estrogen, and at the same time had my facial and body hair removed with electrolysis. All under the supervision of a doctor, of course. I also had some cosmetic surgery, specifically the breasts men try so hard not to stare at." She smiled, and added: "As you can see, I wasn't greedy. I figured I might still have to chase bad guys and you'd be amazed how much harder it is to run with these things."

"I've never really thought about it."

"No, well, you wouldn't need to. Anyway, that was about it for cosmetics. Nowadays they can do some very clever facial reconstruction, to feminize you, but I didn't really want to change how I look, not in that way. I wanted my body to mirror my soul, and I have the soul of a policeman, not a super model."

"I like the way you put that," said Hugo.

"*Merci*. Anyway, the final piece of the puzzle was the sex reassignment surgery, which is the physical 'sex change' itself. Said good-bye to the parts I'd never wanted, and hello to the part that I did. A lot of surgery and stitches, plenty of bruising and pain, and I'll be glad to never see a hospital again. But the results ... well, Don Juan himself couldn't tell the difference."

"The marvels of modern medicine." It sounded lame the moment he said it, but Lerens just smiled. It was a cliché, Hugo realized, but a true and happy one for her.

"Well, a girl needs her beauty sleep," Lerens said. "Any more questions?"

"No. But if I think of any, I'll let you know."

"I doubt it." Lerens rose. "Still, thanks for coming tonight, being open about all this makes life easier for everyone. And by everyone, I mostly mean me."

"Me too. And I'm grateful that you trusted me enough to tell me."

"Facts are facts, and I am what I am," Lerens said, then smiled. "Especially after hormone therapy and microsurgery." She picked up her glass and drained it. "We should do this again sometime, I make a great wingwoman."

"I'll bet you do."

She turned to leave, then looked over her shoulder. "And on that note, just so you know, I like girls."

Hugo's mouth opened, but nothing came out and he could feel himself blushing, mildly but for the first time in several years. He watched Lerens leave and then sat there, thinking about her and Raul, and how lucky he'd been in his friendships with the French police. Lucky and horribly unlucky.

On his walk home, he pushed thoughts of Raul from his mind and tried to enjoy the Paris night. The soft yellow and white lights in the streets and on the buildings painted the old stone structures around him like a watercolor, there but unreal, which is the way he still felt about living in Paris. He looked up as he walked, glimpsing movement in the windows of the apartments above him and this brought him comfort; those brief glimpses, the shadows flitting across squares of gentle light, told him these people were safe in their homes and going about their routines with their families, their friends, and their lovers.

Tom was still out when Hugo arrived home. He'd picked up a half-bottle of wine for himself and poured a glass. He took out his phone to call Claudia as another need tugged at him, and even though it was after ten o'clock, he didn't hesitate.

"How are you holding up?" she asked immediately.

"You know me," Hugo said. "Get my hugs from Tom when I need them."

"Stop being brave, Hugo. Raul was your friend. Not only that but . . ." Her voice trailed off, but he knew what she was thinking.

"But he took those bullets for me."

"Something like that, yes." Anyone else would have sugarcoated it, but Claudia wasn't like anyone else. "That's not an easy thing to get past, especially for someone like you."

"You're right, it's not." He swirled the wine in his glass but suddenly put it down when the image of blood came to him. "I've put myself in that car, in that parking lot, a hundred times. I wonder whether I would have seen the killer coming, maybe shot first, or been able to somehow capture . . ." He sighed. "But I've also wondered whether that's true. I know how easy it is to sneak up on someone, even if they're being careful. Raul was always very aware of his surroundings, and on something like this he would have been especially alert. Maybe if we'd gone together . . . ?"

Her voice was soft. "A lot of maybes there, Hugo. But I'm glad you're thinking these things and not burying them deep inside."

"Thanks, although the whole repressing thing works fine most of the time. That said, you're welcome to come over and be my therapist."

Her laugh was gentle. "Role-play, huh?"

"Wouldn't be the first time." He sighed. "I really would like to see you, you know."

"I know, Hugo. I would like that, too. It's just . . . not possible, not right now."

"Well, if you change your mind, if it becomes possible, let me know." Something else he didn't want to think about: Claudia with someone new. He lightened his tone. "In the meantime, I'll make like Tom and hire myself someone."

"You should, remember that girl from a while back? What was her name? She seemed very cool."

"Why, because she liked the look of you?"

"Can't blame her for that. Seriously, Hugo, there's nothing wrong with it."

"Oh, I know, it's just not my style. Even if it were, Hugo would not follow where Tom has already trod, if you know what I mean."

"Oh, you are utterly adorable. When things change, I'll be throwing myself at you."

"Good." He wanted to believe her, and he wanted to ask what "things" needed to change, but he was afraid to ask. Partly because he didn't want to hear about a boyfriend but also because he knew how private she could be, and he wanted to make sure he respected that. "Hey, speaking of Tom, have you talked to him lately?" he asked.

"What do you mean by lately? Something wrong?"

"In the last few weeks. No, nothing wrong. I think he's still sober but he's taken to disappearing on me and being all cryptic about where he's going. Once a week he just takes off."

"Um, Hugo, have you met Tom before? That's what he does."

"Yeah, I know. But this feels different. I can tell when it's the CIA or even a hooker dragging him out. But it's Sunday night and he sauntered out of the apartment on his way somewhere specific. He even caught me when I tried following him so he knew I—"

"You followed him?" Claudia sounded mildly outraged.

"Well, you know. Kind of."

"Either you did or you didn't."

"I did until he caught me. Which was almost immediately. Look, I'm just asking. I want to know because I want to make sure he's OK."

"So ask him."

"I did. He told me to mind my own business."

"So mind your own business."

"Very helpful, Claudia, I'm so glad I ran this by you."

"Look, he's sober, happy, and healthier than I've ever seen him. Just be happy for him. I know you spent a long time worrying about him, trying to get him to change. Well, now he has. You got what you wanted, what's best for him, so maybe loosen the reins a little."

"You make me sound like a nagging wife."

She laughed. "Sorry. But you know what I'm saying."

Hugo heard a key in the door. "Well, talk of the devil, he's home. Fingers crossed he's sober."

"It's not even midnight. If he was drinking he'd be out later than this. Anyway, go check on him and call me tomorrow if you like."

If I like. "I will. Good night."

He looked up as Tom swung the door open and staggered in, grabbing the counter for support, his head hanging down like he was going to throw up. When he spoke, his words were slurred, almost incomprehensible. "Hi honey, I'm home!"

A pit opened up in Hugo's stomach. "Oh, Tom."

"Wassamatter?" Tom hiccupped, then burped. "S'all good, man."

"Shit, Tom, what have you done?" He rose and started toward his friend. "You going to throw up? I can get you a—"

Tom suddenly straightened and Hugo saw that his eyes were clear, almost as bright as the grin he was wearing. "Fuck me," Tom laughed, "you're making me feel bad, being all nice and shit even when you thought I'd fallen off the wagon."

Hugo shook his head. "You complete and utter bastard. Jeez, Tom, you just about gave me a heart attack."

"Sorry, amigo." Tom cackled and started for his bedroom. "You deserved that for following me. And you should have seen the look on your face, you sweet, adorable man."

"Fair enough. Just don't do it again. And are you gonna tell me where you went?"

"It's killing you, isn't it?"

"No, I'm just concerned. Fine: concerned and curious."

"Fucking nosy, more like it." Tom stopped in his doorway. "And no, I'm not telling you. Not tonight, anyway."

CHAPTER TWENTY-FIVE

The morning came early for Hugo, but after a better night's sleep than he'd had in a while. It was five o'clock and he considered trying to grab another hour, maybe two, but then remembered the morning's task: searching Natalia Khlapina's apartment from top to bottom, and a few words with her boss, Alexandra.

He reached over and checked his phone for messages. Lieutenant Lerens had emailed just after midnight, offering to pick him up at seven. She'd also given Khlapina's address, which he mapped to see if he could walk. Up near Gare du Nord, so it'd take him an hour or so and give him a chance to eat on the way without hurrying. He checked the weather with a head out of his bedroom window; a soft breeze that would warm before long and a gray sky that would likely stay that way. He dressed in jeans, white shirt, and a jacket, before pulling on his old, slightly frayed Lucchese boots, the best of his three pairs for walking.

As he passed through the living room, he heard a grumble from Tom's bedroom, the door open.

"You up already?" Tom called out.

"Yep. I'm walking up to Khlapina's apartment. Want to join me?"

"Fuck off." A pause. "All due respect, of course."

"Of course. Lieutenant Lerens will be here at seven to pick you up, if you want to be there for the search."

"Very kind. Ask her to bring coffee and food."

"Ask her yourself. See you there."

It was a straight shot, pretty much, but once he'd crossed the Pont des Arts he meandered down side streets whenever he could, taking the smaller ones that ran parallel to busier Rue du Louvre and Rue du Faubourg Poissonnière, avoiding the fumes from the early morning cars and buses carrying their cargo to work. He bought coffee to go in Rue Jean-Jacques Rousseau, rubbing elbows at the counter with the suited workers headed to the nearby mercantile exchange, several cab drivers, and a trio of surly bike messengers fueling up for the morning's deliveries.

As he neared Gare du Nord, Hugo found himself in unfamiliar terrain. The streets and buildings seemed less alluring here, more functional somehow. There were fewer cafés spilling their tables into the streets, and the stores sold more than they displayed, telling Hugo that this was an area where the tourists rarely wandered, a place that working Parisians called home.

That changed, though, when he turned into Rue Cadet, a pedestrian street that reminded him of the quaint streets of the sixth and seventh. A *fromagerie* sat to his right, closed at this time of day but with a gentle orange light burning somewhere in the store, its glow a soft backlight for the wheels of waxed and heavy cheeses. A few steps on he passed a small brasserie with maybe ten tables, the kind of place where the owner would also cook and who, at opening time, would stand on the stoop with a cigarette in one hand and a cell phone in the other, ready to put both behind his back to smile and welcome a new customer.

He moved to one side as a pretty girl on a bicycle approached, pulling a rolling carry-on bag behind her with one hand. She flashed Hugo a smile as she passed, putting an extra bounce in his step for a moment or two.

He chose a large, anonymous café outside the Gare du Nord for his breakfast. He wanted to disappear for thirty minutes, be one of the invisible many so he could think about the investigation and plan some of the questions he'd ask Alexandra Tourville. It wasn't just about the questions, of course, it never was. More often than not it was a person's reaction to his questions that was telling. He didn't kid himself that he was any kind of human lie detector. He knew from dozens of interviews with sociopaths and psychopaths that a lie could slip as easily from some tongues as the truth. Not only that, but a truly good liar could manipulate his listener into either believing or not believing his story, throwing out so-called "tells" whenever he wanted to change the course of his interviewer's belief.

Was Alexandra Tourville an accomplished liar? Hugo had no reason to believe she was any such thing, but he also knew better than to go into a situation like this offering someone the benefit of unquestioned credibility. Her checkered past made that task more difficult, of course, because he didn't want to prejudge her based on ancient indiscretions, whether they were real lapses in judgment or merely dramas conjured up by the media.

He took a last sip of coffee and checked his watch. Time to go.

Lieutenant Lerens was waiting outside the building with Tom and half a dozen men in uniform who would make sure the search was kept secure and undisturbed. She looked better, rested, and Hugo hoped he did too. She wore a sense of purpose about her like a cape, her handshake brisk and firm, her instructions to the uniforms clear and precise. The soul of a policeman, she'd said, not a super model.

"We did a canvass of the place yesterday when we discovered the address," Lerens said. "It's a fairly empty building, but the people we spoke to, including some who work here, told us there's been no unusual coming and going, no strangers or otherwise noticeable people wandering the hallways."

"Good to know."

They turned as Alexandra Tourville arrived in a taxi, watching as the ranks opened as if a red carpet had been laid out for her.

"May I take the keys?" Lerens asked, after the formalities.

Alexandra raised her eyebrows but handed them over without protest. The four of them entered the building, Lerens leading the way and Tom at the rear. Inside, the group paused to take a look, and Alexandra spoke up, as if sensing their surprise at the cavernous foyer.

"It used to be a hotel, very popular in the twenties. Closed thirty years later and has been used as offices, apartments, and pretty much everything you can think of. Five years ago, an elderly couple was running a drugs and prostitution business from the fourth floor."

Hugo looked around him. The dingy reception area seemed to echo with her voice, though he could imagine grand parties being held here, the peeling gold paint and ornate wall sconces now darkened by time and use. Half a dozen fifties-style chairs and sofas littered the space, squared-off throwbacks in mustard and ketchup colors.

The elevator, at the back left corner of the foyer, was new. Clean round buttons that lit up when touched and a gentle slide upwards, barely noticeable.

"Who owns the place now?" Lerens asked. "You?"

"*Mon dieu, non.*" Alexandra Tourville said. "I actually find it annoying that people assume I'm wealthy. My brother is, of course, and he provides a modest stipend for me. That includes four of the apartments here, which are in my name but that I am not allowed to sell."

"How did that happen?"

Alexandra sighed. "If you must know, my past life was marked by a consistent inability to spend money in a sensible way. A lot went to charity, just as much went to expensive parties, and some was stolen by people I trusted." The elevator dinged softly, announcing their arrival on the fifth floor. Alexandra stepped out first, still talking. "I grew up later than most people, Lieutenant, partly because of a sheltered, no, make that *spoiled*, upbringing. And partly because I matured slower than I should have."

They walked down a hallway to a door, number 505. Lerens unlocked it and nodded to Hugo. "All yours. Please, though, don't—"

"Touch anything," Hugo finished her sentence with a smile. "I've done this before, don't worry."

Tom followed directly behind as Hugo entered the tiny apartment. The front hall was two or three steps, no more, and to the immediate left was the windowless bedroom, like a little cave with room for a queen-sized bed against the right-hand wall, and a built-in closet to the left.

"Anything in particular we're looking for?" Tom said quietly behind him. "Besides the obvious."

By "obvious," Tom was referring to the jewelry stolen from Collette Bassin. "Mostly that," Hugo said. He turned and spoke in a whisper. "I'm also curious to see if the senator has been here. No reason to think he has, but . . ."

"Good idea." Tom wrinkled his nose. "Smell that?"

"Perfume," Hugo nodded. "Certainly not a man's."

"But very nice," Tom said with a grin.

Hugo ignored him and went to the closet. He used his elbow to slide it open, crouching to look behind the rows of clothes hanging inside and giving a low whistle at what he saw inside. Tom crouched next to him.

"Someone had a shoe fetish," Tom said, handing Hugo a pair of latex gloves. "Expensive ones, too."

"And most of them barely worn."

Hugo did a quick count, cutting himself off at thirty pairs of shoes, all colors and styles, from the daintiest red stilettos to knee-length boots draped with leather straps and silver buckles.

"How could you wear all these? You'd have to be a caterpillar."

Hugo knew they were both wondering the same thing: not whether Natalia had worn these shoes, but how she'd paid for them.

"Wait a moment." Hugo straightened up, his eyes still on the mass of shoes on the closet floor. "That's odd."

"What is? I mean, apart from the fact she has nine thousand pairs of shoes."

"Yeah, but look at them. Closely." It was a challenge, something they would do whenever they got the chance, whenever one of them noticed something first. Hugo won mostly, but even when he did Tom was never far behind.

"Well, I . . ." Tom grunted as he rested on one knee, inspecting the footwear in more detail. "Ah, look at that. Why would she have two different sizes?"

"No idea. Makes it more interesting, though, doesn't it?" Hugo felt a fizz in his veins, the jolt of adrenaline that came with the discovery of something out of place, out of the ordinary. A shoe fetish was one thing, and might explain why Natalia was dealing in stolen property, but stacks of new shoes in different sizes? That required a more unusual explanation.

He dug through them for anything else, some clue that might lead him toward his answer, up-ending the boots in case they doubled as hiding places, but eventually he stood, empty-handed. He gave the clothing on the hangers a second look, but they were all the same size—Natalia's, he estimated. A quick check under the bed revealed nothing, so Hugo moved out of the bedroom and back into the little hallway.

The bathroom was next, surprisingly large given the size of the rest of the apartment. A walk-in shower lay to his left, a concrete trough sink to his right. Ahead was a washer–dryer, tucked under shelves that held towels and wash cloths.

Hugo did the usual check, noting one toothbrush, one hairbrush, and no obvious missing, or masculine, cosmetics. Hugo rifled through the linens and grunted with satisfaction when his hand bumped into something solid.

"What is it?" Tom asked.

Hugo pulled out a dark wooden jewelry box that had been hidden between layers of sheets and blankets. "I guess she doesn't have a safe here." He opened the lid and Tom peered over his shoulder. "Earrings, couple of antique looking rings, bracelets . . . Nice stuff, but I don't think these are from the murder scene. I'll have Lerens check to be sure, though."

"That they're not from the crime scene, that means something to you?" Tom asked.

"You know it does," Hugo said.

"But you won't tell me until you're sure."

"Right. On to the main living area?"

"Asshole." Tom let Hugo lead them out of the bathroom and the two steps into the narrow living area. "Just so you know, it means something to me, too. Huge clue. Massive. But I'm not telling you."

"Of course not." Hugo looked into the room, getting a feel for the place before invading it fully. The kitchen sat to his left, a few cupboards over a small stove, microwave oven, and minimal counter space that contained a small and an almost-empty refrigerator.

A breakfast bar marked the beginning of the living room, which wasn't much more than a narrow strip of hardwood floor with enough space for a sofa and armchair on one side, a low table with a television on the other, and a thin coffee table in between. Hugo imagined many clipped shins as Natalia and guests navigated their way around. The best feature, and one worth dodging furniture to get to, was an iron balcony overlooking the street, a delicate table and two chairs making a picture postcard impression.

Their search was quick but thorough. Hugo knew he wasn't supposed to be disturbing anything and after a few minutes it was clear he didn't need to. The place was small and tidy enough that stolen property, or anything else worth noting, would have stood out almost immediately. As it was, Hugo headed back to the front door with a fairly complete impression of Natalia's apartment; it was a typically compact but functional city flat, a home kept neat and tidy by someone who didn't spend a whole lot of time there.

The only oddity was the shoes but as Hugo had discovered over the years, an obsession for buying shoes was about as mild a foible as you'd discover when poking around a stranger's house.

Out in the hallway, two more policemen had joined Lerens. One held a camera and a clipboard, no doubt to log the whereabouts of items they found and draw an overall floor plan.

"Check the towels in the bathroom, there's a jewelry box in there," Hugo told Lerens.

"Oh?" Hope rose in her eyes.

"No, I don't think so. Make sure, of course, but I don't think any of it comes from our murder scene."

"Could still be stolen," Lerens said.

"True." He turned to Alexandra. "And now, if it's OK, you and I can go down to the lobby and have a chat while these people do their job."

"*Bien.*" Alexandra turned to Lerens. "Please, be respectful of her things. She was my friend as well as my employee."

"We will," Lerens assured her. "I promise."

"*Merci bien.*" Alexandra turned to Hugo. "Yes, we should talk. There are some things you need to know about Natalia. Some things she would have preferred to keep secret."

CHAPTER TWENTY-SIX

Hugo pulled together three armchairs, and as they sat he pulled a notebook from his jacket.

"Do you mind if I take notes?" he asked. "My memory isn't what it used to be."

"Please, whatever you need."

"Thank you. Now, you said something upstairs about Natalia having a secret."

"Yes. Actually, she had two secrets. Poor girl, she tried to . . ." Alexandra bit her lip, fighting back tears for a moment before she could steady herself. "She had two compulsions. One was for shopping, for buying shoes."

"We saw those, in her closet."

"The second compulsion was a little worse, I'm afraid," Alexandra said. "She would steal. Not a lot, but . . . well, most people don't steal at all."

"Did she steal from you?"

"Yes. Small things, mostly, little pieces of jewelry, cash. And I saw her once stealing from a store. It was a watch, not even fifty Euros, and I made her put it back. She was embarrassed about it, ashamed, and I even offered to pay for her to get help. She refused, of course, said she didn't do it all the time, just sometimes had an urge that she couldn't control."

"Did she steal shoes from you? There were two different sizes in the closet."

"Yes, I'm missing at least three pairs. We have a lot of people coming through the chateau so it was hard for me to accuse her. Plus," she shrugged, a wistful look on her face, "I really didn't care about shoes as much as she did. If taking from me stopped her stealing from stores, where she'd go to jail, then after my initial annoyance I didn't mind so much."

"How long had she worked for you?" Hugo asked.

"Two years, maybe a little longer. It took a year for me to realize she had a problem. She hid it well."

"Madam Tourville—"

"Alexandra, please."

"Of course. Alexandra, did you know that Natalia was in possession of a necklace that was stolen during a robbery near Troyes? A woman was killed during that robbery."

"*Mais non.*" Alexandra put a hand over her mouth in surprise, then shook her head. "She stole small things, from me and from stores. She wouldn't do something like that. Would she?" There was, Hugo thought, uncertainty in her voice.

"Did she have many friends here in Paris?"

"No, not really. I mean, not that I know of. Most of the time she was with me and so, out of necessity, my friends became hers. I suppose a few times a month she might come here for a night or two. I don't know what she did when she was in Paris by herself, if she knew anyone, but she didn't tell me about it."

"Did she have a boyfriend?"

"I think she had someone back home in Saint Petersburg, at least that's what she told me. Honestly, neither men nor women seemed to interest her, I never saw anyone catch her eye."

"And no one pursued her?"

She laughed gently. "Only Felix."

"Felix Vibert?"

"Yes. People think he's gay, but he's not. Bisexual possibly, but he definitely likes women. He has a weakness for them the way Natalia had a weakness for shoes."

"I hope he doesn't keep them stacked in his closet," Tom said. Hugo smiled, but Alexandra didn't seem to hear it.

"He was interested in Natalia?" Hugo pressed.

"At first, very. He fawned over her like you wouldn't believe. It was embarrassing. I told him to back off, even my brother did after a while."

"And did he?"

"Yes. I think he realized she wasn't interested and, in fact, they became good friends. I felt like she confided in him, but I couldn't really give specifics."

Hugo shifted gears a little. "You were talking about your money situation earlier. Do you live off the income from these apartments?"

She stiffened, just a fraction. "I don't know why I mentioned that, and I don't really see how it's relevant."

"I promise I'm not being nosy," Hugo said. "And most of the time I have no idea what's relevant until it hits me in the face." He gestured to his notebook. "I'm not recording this and I won't even write the information down, so if it turns out to be irrelevant I'll keep it to myself. I promise."

That was one of Hugo's strengths, getting people to reveal personal information they'd rather keep hidden. Not through tricks or mind games, but because they felt they could trust him with it.

"*D'accord*. I have the income from the apartments, yes, and what I make myself."

"From teaching."

"That's right."

"Anything else?"

She bristled. "*Non*. And I still don't see . . ."

Hugo waved a hand dismissively. "I don't either. We can leave it alone." He picked up the pen and tapped his notebook, then looked up at her. "Oh, last question on that topic. Sorry, I forgot, but you had mentioned working in the genealogy field?"

"A little. Some private clients, but it doesn't pay much."

"I see." Hugo fished his phone from his pocket as it buzzed. "Excuse me, it's Lieutenant Lerens upstairs." He moved away from the chairs and answered. "This is Hugo."

"You're still with Madam Tourville?"

"Yes. What's up?"

"A thought. Would you please ask her if she'd provide her prints? For elimination purposes, of course."

"Of course. The same thought had already occurred to me."

He rang off and ignored Tom's questioning look. "Before I forget, Alexandra, would you mind letting us take a sample of your finger-prints. It'll make life so much easier when we can eliminate you entirely."

She cocked her head. "You mean I'm a suspect of some kind?"

"No, no, I'm just saying—"

"I know exactly what you're saying. You don't ask him—" she jerked a thumb at Tom, "—for his prints. Why? Because he's not a suspect. Do you have any evidence linking me to any crime?"

"No, we don't, and if we can compare your prints to one found at—"

"Absolutely not. I will not be treated like a criminal. I talked to my brother about this and we agreed that for you to be hounding us and our friends is insulting. It's not even like fingerprinting is an exact science."

"Well, I don't want to argue the science, Alexandra, but it's been pretty exact since the early 1900s."

"Not at all. My brother told me about a study. He said they tested 150 fingerprint examiners in the mid-1990s, a test conducted with the approval of whatever governing body is over fingerprinting. My brother said that one in five examiners made at least one false positive identification." She held his eye, a challenge. "One in five linked a fake crime-scene print to the wrong person. I don't call that science, and I don't like those odds."

"I don't know anything about that," Hugo said, "but I can assure you the way we do it—"

"That's not even the point, for me. These things, science and studies, they matter more to my brother than to me," Alexandra insisted. "Look, I'm aware you're not from here, Monsieur Marston, but in France, in the circles we move, appearances matter. I've had one very heavy and unpleasant crash from grace, so to speak, and I don't plan on letting you orchestrate another."

"But this might eliminate you from the investigation completely."

She leaned forward, her voice low but intense. "I shouldn't be a part of your investigation. I've done nothing wrong, nothing at all. And you say 'might.' You still suspect Natalia of being involved in a crime, and do you have her print from the crime scene?"

"I can't tell you what we have and don't have."

"*C'est des conneries!*" Bullshit! "If you did, you wouldn't be asking for mine. Her print isn't there, I can tell from your reaction, yet you're still investigating her as a criminal. And, my God, she's dead! Do you really expect me to believe that this would eliminate me?"

Hugo sat back, suddenly exhausted. She was right, of course. If comparison showed the print from the crime scenes to be someone other than Alexandra's, she might move to the back of the line, but she'd still be in it.

"We're doing the best we can, Alexandra. We're not trying to cause trouble for you or your brother, we're just trying to find out why Natalia died."

"Suicide. She was stealing and either couldn't live with herself, or maybe..."

"Or maybe she stole from the wrong person," Hugo said. "Which is what we want to know. Like I said, we're not trying to drag anyone's name through the mud, not hers, and certainly not yours."

"I know you don't intend to do that." Alexandra shook her head sadly. "But you still don't understand. My name, my reputation, they are so fragile. And maybe it's my fault that they are, but I have to protect them. To protect myself even if it means being unhelpful to you."

"No one even has to know," Hugo insisted.

"People always know. And if someone asks, am I to lie?" She shook her head, adamant. "No, I'm very sorry. If the people around me knew you'd taken my prints in connection with a murder, *merde*, two murders, then it'd be all over. I've worked so hard to restore my place in the world, to improve my life, I have no reason to risk it all, especially when I know what the result would be. No reason in the world, and I won't do it." She reached down and picked up her handbag, clutching it to her chest as she rose awkwardly to her feet from the low chair. "If you have any other questions, contact my brother and he will refer you to our family attorney. I hope what I've told you this morning is helpful, but I won't become the subject of any witch hunt." Her voice became almost a whisper. "I'm sorry, but I can't afford any more disgrace."

They watched her walk out of the building, waiting by the clear glass door until the officer stationed there opened it for her. Once she was outside, Hugo called Lieutenant Lerens.

"Was she cooperative?" Lerens asked.

"Yes and no. Mostly no. But do me a favor and have a fingerprint guy come to the lobby."

"She agreed to give prints at least?"

"No, she declined and left the building. But she spent the last fifteen minutes sitting in a plastic chair, and while I'm no furniture expert I'm pretty sure it's the kind of plastic chair that would hold fingerprints quite nicely."

"Ah, you are a genius, Hugo. I knew I hired you for a reason. And I have a little discovery of my own to share with you."

Hugo pressed a button on his phone so Tom could hear. "You're on speaker. You were saying, a discovery . . ."

"*Oui*. There's a little crawl space you can access through a panel in the bathroom, leads to some electric stuff. Some sort of maintenance thing."

"Something was up there?"

"You want to play a guessing game, Hugo?"

He thought for a moment, then it hit him: something too big to hide in the apartment itself, but small enough to fit in a crawl space.

"The chest!" Hugo said, springing out of his chair. "Tell me you found the sailor's chest."

Lieutenant Lerens chuckled down the phone at them. "Why don't you come up and have a look for yourselves?"

CHAPTER TWENTY-SEVEN

Camille Lerens and two colleagues, a uniformed officer and an elderly forensic technician, had moved out of Natalia Khlapina's apartment and commandeered a common seating area that held a sofa, two chairs, and large square coffee table. The chest sat on a plastic sheet on the table. Hugo and Tom nodded at Lerens and stood with her, impatient but quiet as the forensic tech dusted it for prints.

"He's almost done," Lerens said. The old man glanced up, frowned, then turned back to his work, lips pursed as he finished up.

"Anything in it?" Hugo asked.

"*Non*. Monsieur Delacroix here searched it, found all the little compartments, but they were empty." Something in her voice told Hugo there was tension between the two.

Delacroix snapped off his latex gloves and shook his head at the lieutenant. "*Rien*."

"Nothing?" she repeated. "How is that possible?"

The old man straightened, his hands on his hips. "I trust you are not questioning my work," he paused before emphasizing the last word, "*Madam*?"

Hugo felt his color rise and he shifted, ready to snap the tech down a peg or two. But Lerens had it covered.

"It was a question, not a criticism," she said mildly. "I apologize if I hurt your feelings, I didn't know you were so sensitive."

The technician clenched his jaw, his eyes flicking over Hugo and

Tom looking for support, but Hugo knew he saw something very different. The old man muttered something to himself and turned to the chest, starting to swathe it in the plastic sheeting.

"Hold on," Hugo said. He turned to Lerens. "I'd like to look inside. Make sure it's empty."

"Absolutely not." Delacroix glared at Hugo. "I am responsible for this and I will not allow some foreigner to paw through a piece of evidence that I have already examined thoroughly." He turned to Lerens. "Unless the lieutenant specifically orders me to do so, in which case I will request another technician be brought in to supervise this . . . superfluous search."

"*Non, non.*" Lerens waved her hand. "You looked inside, it's empty. You're finished here, Monsieur Delacroix, thank you." She gave Hugo a sly wink and mouthed, *later.*

Hugo took out his phone. "I'll just take a few pictures, then."

He walked around the chest, taking photos from every angle. Then he used his sleeve to open the lid, making Delacroix quiver with anxiety. Hugo snapped shots of the inside of the lid and then the interior. He stooped low over the catch. "You saw this, right?"

"What?" Delacroix said impatiently.

"The catch here, like a button. Disguised as a knot of wood. I'm sure you did, I just wanted to . . ."

"Knot of wood? What are you talking about?"

Hugo picked up a discarded latex glove and used it to push the release. Lerens moved closer, too, as Hugo grunted with satisfaction and Delacroix breathed in sharply.

"What do we have here?" Hugo said. With gentle fingers he slid a miniature panel aide and peered in. "Small box. How interesting."

Delacroix, perhaps to make up for his mistake, reluctantly handed Hugo a fresh pair of gloves. Hugo held up the tiny box, undoing the catch and opening it for them to see. Flakes of red wax fell as it opened.

"Hair?" Lerens asked.

"A lock of hair," Hugo said. "A significant lock of hair, I'd have to say."

"To whom?"

"That I don't know," Hugo admitted. "Not yet, anyway. I'm sure your lab people can go to work on it, come up with something."

"You've no idea whose hair it is?"

"No," Hugo said. "I really don't. Looks old, that's about all I can say." He looked at the crime scene tech. "It's all yours. The box, too."

Delacroix nodded and went back to covering up the chest, quick and efficient hands securing the evidence like a disgruntled Santa's helper wrapping a gift. He sealed it with police stickers that he'd already written on, large rectangles of paper that marked date, place, and item. He put the small box and its contents into an evidence bag, sealed it, too, and made a note on an evidence label which he fixed to the front. Then he picked up his bag of tools and signaled the uniformed officer to follow him with the packaged chest, leaving Lerens, Tom, and Hugo with a curt nod and his nose in the air.

"Can you forward those photos to me?" Lerens asked. "As you said, the lab people will work on the hair but I need to confirm it's the chest from the Troyes robbery."

Hugo concentrated as he clicked on his phone until the pictures whirled away into the ether. "Done."

"Thanks. That's strange, don't you think?" Lerens said, perching on the edge of the sofa. "First the hair and then . . . no prints at all?"

"It is," Hugo said, "but it might tell us something important."

"Might?"

Tom groaned and dropped into one of the chairs. "When he says it like that, it means he won't tell you yet."

"Why not?" Lerens looked at Hugo. "We're sharing here, aren't we?"

"Sometimes he only says things when he's sure," Tom said. "It's this thing he does, very annoying."

"Hugo?" Lerens said. "Tell me what you're thinking."

"I think I can make an exception this time," Hugo smiled. "And it may be completely wrong. But I'm thinking it wasn't Natalia who put the chest up there."

"No?" Lerens said. "Why not?"

"A couple of reasons. First, if she has a shoe fetish, why not sell the chest and buy more shoes. It has to be worth something, right?"

"A pair of boots, at least," Lerens agreed. "What else?"

"Well, if there are no prints then someone wiped it clean. And the person who wiped it clean, I would bet, is the same person who put it up there. Agreed?"

"So far, so good."

"Good. Next step, it doesn't make sense for that person to be Natalia because if she didn't want to be connected with the chest, she wouldn't wipe her prints off it, she'd ditch it completely. Sell it or throw it away."

"Or at least hide it somewhere else," Tom said.

"Precisely," Hugo agreed. "What do you think, Lieutenant?"

"We figured she hadn't done the Troyes robbery, certainly not by herself," Lerens said. "You're saying that the lack of prints confirms she has an accomplice."

"Right," Hugo said. "I'd also guess that because our girl was left holding the box, so to speak, and a box without prints that she couldn't sell, Natalia was second in command."

"To whom?" Lerens asked.

But Hugo was staring at the ceiling, nodding to himself. "There is one other possibility, of course," he said.

"What's that?" Lerens asked. "Or should I say, who's that?"

"Hmm?" Hugo looked back at the policewoman. "Oh, just a thought. I probably shouldn't say until I'm a little more sure." He stood and took out his phone. "Excuse me, text from the ambassador. Ah, looks like I'm heading back to the Crillon, our dear senator is safe and sound."

"Wait," Lerens said, "your other idea, the other possibility. What is it?"

"Let me check a few things, first," Hugo said. "Don't want to besmirch someone with idle theories unless I have evidence."

Tom stood and shrugged at Lerens. "See? Didn't I tell you? Very annoying."

Hugo ignored him and spoke to Lieutenant Lerens. "One other thing. Do you think you could track down Georges Bassin's sister? I have a phone number for her and left a couple of messages, but she didn't call back. I really need to ask her something, it's very important."

"Absolutely. Text me her full name and phone number, and any other information you have, and I'll get right on it. We have a unit dedicated to finding fugitives. They're fast and exceptionally good." She paused. "Any chance you'll tell me what you intend to ask her?"

Hugo shook his head. "Not just yet, if you don't mind."

"There, and I'll say it again," Tom said. "Very fucking annoying."

Hugo walked into the lobby of the Hotel Crillon and was met immediately by Felix Vibert. The dapper Frenchman shook Hugo's hand and smiled at the surprised look on Hugo's face. He gestured to an empty couch to one side of the large foyer.

"We should talk before we see Senator Lake," Vibert said.

"Sure." Hugo followed him to the couch and sat. "The ambassador called me; I didn't realize you'd be here, too."

"I know. The ambassador is being smart. He's also had orders from your State Department to try and make the best of a bad situation."

"Which is?"

"All talks about the future of the Guadeloupe Islands have been suspended."

"For what reason?"

Vibert smiled. "Officially, we have been unable to reach an agreement. Which is, of course true."

"And unofficially?"

"Your senator rubs people the wrong way. Since he's been here, the Tourvilles feel like their hospitality has been abused, and that Senator Lake's erratic behavior here in Paris makes him an unsuitable emissary for the United States."

"*Erratic* seems a little strong," Hugo said. "Best I can tell, he's been wandering your beautiful city while he waits for the talks to resume. Nothing wrong with that, is there?"

"You are a loyal man, Hugo. But it's been decided and I'm here to break the news to Monsieur Lake."

"The ambassador didn't mention that, either," Hugo said mildly.

"So call him. Believe me, it's not a duty that I'm looking forward to. I'd welcome the opportunity to leave it to someone else."

"Why you?"

"Henri and your ambassador agreed that if a lower-level negotiator and Senator Lake approve a momentary postponement of talks, it comes across as being informal and therefore more likely the talks will soon resume."

"And will they?"

"Who knows." Vibert smiled. "I'm low-level, remember."

"Right, of course. I guess I'll leave you to your informal chat, though I might wait around down here to see how he takes it."

"As you wish."

Hugo had a thought. "Let me ask you about something else, if you don't mind."

"Of course, anything."

"You remember I asked you about that sailor's chest?"

"I do, yes."

"Good." Hugo pulled up the photos of the chest found at Natalia Khlapina's apartment. He held his phone so Vibert could see each one as Hugo flipped through them. "Do any of these jog your memory at all?"

"Ah, yes." Vibert held up a finger. "I do remember seeing that, and not just before dinner. It was in the hallway at one point, someone had brought it into the house and . . ." he furrowed his brow. "And Henri asked one of the servants to move it. At the time I assumed it was his, obviously, as he told the girl where to put it. Yes, that's right." He looked up at Hugo. "You should ask Henri, I think it's his."

"Thanks, I will. And you're sure it's the same chest."

"Looks exactly like it, but maybe they're all the same. I don't know, I'm not an expert."

"I'm not either, but it looked like the same one to me. I just wanted to confirm."

"What does Henri's sailor chest have to do with anything?" Vibert asked.

"Great question." Hugo smiled and hoped it was enigmatic. "That's what I'm trying to figure out."

CHAPTER TWENTY-EIGHT

At his apartment, Hugo yearned for the familiar warmth of a glass of single malt and a few moments alone to think. He'd considered stopping to buy a bottle, maybe keeping it in his room, but the thought made him feel dishonest and disloyal. When he got in, Tom was sipping milk and watching the second half of a soccer game.

"So did Lake go apeshit?" Tom asked.

"Nope. I waited for Vibert to break the news and hung out just in case, but apparently he took it pretty well. Said he's ready to get back to the United States and do some real work, was actually quite polite about the whole thing."

"That's pretty fucking weird," Tom said. "As volatile as the man is, I'd have thought . . . Oh well, guess we should count our blessings."

"Guess so." Hugo dropped into an armchair and kicked his boots off. "Can I run something by you?"

"Need me to switch the TV off?"

"Sure, if you don't mind." He waited for Tom to find the right button on the remote and kill the screen. "Thanks. Did you see the crime-scene photos or police report on the Bassin murder?"

"I took a look several days ago. Why?"

"I've been thinking about it. I never really analyzed it the way I usually do, just accepted the general consensus that it was a murder–robbery."

"Dude, come on." Tom spread his hands wide. "Stuff was stolen and a woman was killed, that's the definition of a murder–robbery. We all accepted the general consensus because that's what it was."

"I know. But that's the conclusion. I like to make my own because there's more to a crime than a conclusion."

"I never did dig the theory of criminality, all that philosophical shit."

"Shut up, Tom, you had the highest test scores in that class at the academy."

"I did? Cool. Carry on then, I'll see if I can help."

"Look, the point is, just because it ends up as a murder–robbery, doesn't mean it was meant to be one. That the suspect intended to do one or both of those things."

"Sure," Tom said, "he meant to steal but the old lady stumbled on him, and splat. It's still the same crime, whether he intended it going in or not."

"Two assumptions in there, my friend. Sure, most likely the murder wasn't planned, but everyone takes it for granted that the intruder always intended to steal the chest and its contents. What if he intended to take and return it?"

"Return it? I can answer that: thieves don't borrow stuff, they steal it." Tom's eyes widened. "Ah, you think he was after the chest itself, not the jewelry. And once discovered he figured, screw it, I'll keep the whole lot for my trouble."

"Something like that. But there's another assumption, remember."

"Which is?"

"Well, think back to the crime scene. What did they find?"

"An old and very dead woman with a pillow over her face and pieces of a broken vase nearby."

"Which tells you what?"

"Hugo, for fuck's sake, just spit it out. I hate it when you give me the Socratic treatment like this, I have no idea what it tells me. Nothing, except that a woman died from a pillow over her face and the killer didn't like vases."

"I'm just trying to see how this played out. The medical examiner said that the killer probably hit the woman with the vase, fracturing her wrist, and then smothered her."

"OK. And that means what to you?"

"I'm wondering why the killer hit her with the vase. An old woman, weak. She didn't have a weapon."

"She was holding a phone?"

"They found one on a side table, no prints, so possibly she was trying to call for help when she was hit, and afterwards the killer moved the phone and wiped it down. But why hit her with the vase instead of just taking it out of her hand?"

"No clue. Where are you headed with this, Sherlock?"

"To the manner of death. Who gets smothered, Tom?"

"Old people and kids."

"Right. And who does the smothering?"

Tom frowned in concentration, then looked up at Hugo. "Oh. Of course, the vase and the fact she was smothered. Damn, of course."

"Right. The killer wasn't strong enough, or confident of being strong enough, to take the phone away. And not strong enough to kill in the way you'd expect when surprised like that—Collette Bassin wasn't beaten to death or strangled."

"I'd have gone with strangled," Tom nodded. "Old lady, hardly able to fight back, weak little neck. Best choice, most obvious choice."

"Unless," Hugo said, "you're a woman. Much easier to lay on top of her and hold a pillow over her face than strangle, which requires arm and hand strength. Even if your victim's old."

"Our killer is a woman?"

"I think so. And not Natalia Khlapina."

"Damn," Tom said, then smiled. "I bet you could use a drink right about now."

"What about you?"

"Yep. I could always use one but you know what gives me great satisfaction?"

"Waking up sober every morning."

"Well, there's that," Tom said. "But there are also times like this, when I know you'd love a nip of whisky and you can't. Denying you those moments of pleasure is a fine motivating force for sobriety."

"Glad to help," Hugo said, reaching for his phone as it rang on the coffee table. He didn't recognize the number. "Hugo Marston."

The voice sounded distant, but the connection was good. "Monsieur Marston. My name is Marie Bassin. A police lieutenant gave me your number and said I should contact you immediately."

"Madam Bassin, thank you for calling. I'd left you a couple of messages, did you get them?"

"Messages? Oh no, I'm not very good with voicemail. Prefer texting, sorry."

"No, that's fine. I'm investigating the death of your mother, so first let me offer my condolences." Hugo ignored Tom, who rolled his eyes at the formality.

"Thank you, that's kind. Do you have news?"

"Actually, I have a question. Did anyone visit your mother, either when you were there or not, before she was killed?"

"They already asked me that," Marie Bassin said, a note of impatience in her voice. No doubt she'd hoped for news, not duplicative questioning. "My brother and I would take her to dinner on Friday nights—together when we could or just one of us. But other than us and the people who work there, I don't know of anyone who visited her in the weeks before she was killed. Maybe they did, but I wasn't there if it happened, and she never mentioned anyone."

"What about before that, and not just a few weeks. Six months before, maybe."

"I don't know how that could be helpful, but again I don't recall . . . Oh, well, there was someone. Two people, now I think of it. Five or six months before, but that can't be related."

"Who was it?"

"I'm struggling to remember their names, I'm sorry. They were there doing research."

"What kind of research?" Hugo asked.

"Into our family, oddly enough. Some sort of medical people they were."

"Doctors?"

"Yes. Well, medical professors, the older one told me. I spoke to her and my mother spoke to the younger one."

"Her?"

"They were both women, yes. Very nice, too, I'm just sorry I can't remember their names."

"You don't need to, Madam Bassin," Hugo said. "I know exactly who they are."

"Holy shit," Tom said. "Alexandra Tourville? Why the hell would she kill that old woman and steal the chest?"

"It contained something that she wanted. Something she wanted very badly."

"The lock of hair?"

"Now, that I can't answer."

Marie Bassin clearly hadn't known, either. Hugo had deflected her questions about her mother's death by asking about the chest. According to Marie, it had been in the family forever. Her mother used it to keep her jewelry and said Marie could have it once she was gone. A few cryptic comments about it *being* a family treasure as well as *holding* the family treasure, but nothing specific. Marie had known it contained secret compartments, but she'd not known how many or how secret they really were. She'd assumed not very. As for the lock of hair, at first she'd been as surprised as Hugo but then a memory came back to her. "My mother . . . oh, I wish I could remember. She once talked about a man named Louis in connection with the chest. I don't know his surname, I'm sorry, and I don't know if it was a friend or . . . or even a lover. I just don't know. Could it be his, whoever he is?"

Maybe, Hugo had told her. Maybe. And maybe a dead end.

"Even if it's the golden locks of some long-lost lover, or even a bastard child," Tom said, "how the hell do we find out? Is it time to have Lerens pull Alexandra Tourville in?"

"I think she has to. But I want to confirm one thing first." Hugo dialed a number and waited for a moment.

"This is Henri Tourville. Monsieur Marston?"

"Yes. How are you, sir?"

"In the middle of something, I'm afraid. How can I help?"

"I have a quick question. There was an old sailor's chest at your house for that first dinner. Felix Vibert and I were admiring it in the dining room."

"That was a sailor's chest? I thought it was for . . . well, I had no idea what it was for."

"Can you tell me where you got it?"

"No, but only because I didn't get it from anywhere. You looking to buy one?"

"Maybe."

"Then I'll ask Alexie. Or ask her yourself, she brought it to the house. I think she meant to take it to her room but for whatever reason it was in the hallway, in the way. I had someone move it to the dining room."

"Thank you, I appreciate the information, I'll check with her. Is she there right now?"

"No. She's been in Paris for a couple of days. I'll text her cell number to you." He paused, then said. "While I have you on the phone, has Lake said anything about our talks?"

"No, I gather he took it pretty well."

"That's what Felix told me. I'm a little surprised, to be honest."

"We were too," Hugo said. "Relieved, though."

"Definitely, I'm glad that's all over. Maybe the next man they send will be a little easier to work with."

Hugo rang off and looked at Tom. "Alexandra Tourville had the chest, took it to her brother's house."

"Why would she do that?"

"I'm guessing to hide it in plain sight. She might have worried about someone seeing her with it, but didn't want to get rid of it in case she hadn't found everything inside. Keeping it at her brother's place was a smart idea, he told me himself no one really keeps tabs on what antiques or paintings they have or how long they've had them. Maybe she got unlucky that it wound up in the way and catching her brother's attention, but even so, to him it was just another family heirloom."

"I'm still not getting a motive though," Tom said. "Why would a Tourville kill an old woman for an antique chest?"

"Fine question. And add to it, why would she kill Raul?"

"If we're really thinking she did that, too."

"I suppose it's possible she hired someone to steal the chest, and that person killed Madam Bassin and then Raul. But like I said before, I think a woman killed Colette Bassin. Not just that but having talked to Alexandra, I'm not seeing her as someone to trust other people with her dirty secrets."

"Yeah, she wouldn't be big on trust after what she went through, I think you're right."

"Which leaves us with her as a killer, but without a motive. I can only think that she went to steal the chest, got caught red-handed and panicked."

"I know one way to find out."

"Yep," Hugo said, reaching for his phone. "Time for our good lieutenant to bring her in and ask her."

"First thing tomorrow?"

"No," Hugo said quietly. "Tomorrow morning we have plans."

"Ah, right." Tom's head drooped as he remembered. "Tomorrow morning is for Raul."

CHAPTER TWENTY-NINE

Raul Garcia's funeral service was held at a small Catholic church near his home in the eastern suburbs of Paris, the worn-looking and miniscule Eglise de Saint-Therese, which Raul had mentioned to Hugo once before, claiming "attendance under duress" three or four times a year. He'd gone to mark the seasons, Hugo knew, and to please his wife—one of those obligations the policeman had loved to grumble about, but with a smile in his eyes.

Hugo waited outside with Tom and Ambassador Taylor because the church held fewer than fifty people and this service was for Raul's family and close friends, the young and the old who wanted to shed private tears and hold familiar hands for comfort. Outside, all around them, an army of police officers gathered in the narrow streets, the quiet and respectful shuffling into position of men and women who may not have known Capitaine Garcia, but whose mourning for him was as real and sharp as the full dress blues and polished boots they wore in his honor. Hundreds of them would be part of the procession, brothers-in-arms escorting their colleague to his final resting place deep inside the cemetery at Père Lachaise.

Camille Lerens was one of the few police officers inside the church, a friend to Raul as much as a colleague. She and Hugo had spoken at length the previous evening on the phone as he laid out the reasons he was convinced Alexandra Tourville was responsible for their friend's death.

Lerens had resisted at first, demanded more evidence as any good

209

detective would, but finally gone quiet. "At the very least," she'd finally said, "the woman has some explaining to do."

"Agreed. When will you bring her in?"

"Tomorrow. I'll put the fugitive unit to work again tonight, hopefully they can locate and keep an eye on her until I can pick her up myself after the funeral."

"Good. I'll come too, if you don't mind."

"Fine with me." She paused, then her voice was sad. "The cops I send to look for her will be about the only ones not at the cemetery. They'll be mad at missing it."

"Tell them they're helping catch Raul's killer, that should make them feel better."

She was right, and it wasn't just the Paris police force that was devoting so much attention and manpower to Raul's murder and to his funeral. The irony didn't escape Hugo that Raul had done in death what he never would have in life: jumped to the head of a long and exclusive waiting list, bypassing the newly-dead rich and famous for a coveted space in Paris's greatest cemetery. His burial there was inevitable, perhaps, as Raul's rise in status had been easy and immediate. Right after the shooting, Hugo had seen the newspaper headlines and television news stories seething with anger, expressing the fury felt by the people of Paris, putting words to their abhorrence of the murder of a policeman and, at the same time, feeding their macabre attraction to the tragic story of his death. Both of these things, the drama and the tragedy, came together and swept over Paris like a tidal wave, carrying Raul to new heights, elevating the modest police captain into a hero. Something else, Hugo knew, that an alive Raul Garcia would never have countenanced.

"Here they come," Tom said, nudging Hugo with an elbow.

The ripple began near the church doors and spread outwards. The slouched figures in blue, whispering and smoking, straightened up and fell silent as the pallbearers, senior police officers all, exited the church with Raul's coffin held secure on squared shoulders. Hugo's heart lurched and he gritted his teeth, pushing away images of his friend laughing, smiling, the sparkle in his eyes and the dapper appearance that had led Hugo to compare Raul to Agatha Christie's sleuth, Hercule Poirot. *He's Belgian, not French*, Raul would harrumph, but they'd both laugh, always.

Hugo recognized the tallest of the pallbearers as Bartoli Garcia, Raul's brother. In appearance, Bartoli was utterly different from his baby brother: tall, slender, with soft gray hair and matching brush moustache. They had the same eyes, though, sad now, but their color and shape sent a jolt through Hugo as he glimpsed a part of his good friend alive and well. Raul had spoken of his brother several times, shown Hugo a photo from his wallet. They'd been close and were both police officers—Bartoli a senior detective in their home city of Barcelona, Spain. He was now dressed in the finery of his office.

Two minutes later, Hugo watched as the sleek hearse pulled away from the church, four police cars and eight police motorcycles parting the traffic as the procession began the five-mile drive to Père Lachaise. The ambassador hadn't wanted extra security for himself, there were a thousand cops all around them, so Tom drove the embassy car, a black Cadillac with US and French flags sprouting from the hood. Hugo sat in the front seat beside him, and Ambassador Taylor climbed into the back seat.

It felt good to be there, to know that Raul's wife was seeing how many people had been touched by her husband's life, and his death, but Tom seemed to be suffering. Not because he was closer to Raul, he wasn't, rather because he'd lived the last five years burying his stocks of empathy as a covert employee of the CIA, and in his downtime numbing himself with alcohol. Now, sober and on his own time, Tom was feeling his grief and sorrow seep into the light and he didn't know how to handle that. Humor, always a weapon for Tom, was all he had left to fight back the sadness he didn't want to feel, didn't know how to feel. Consequently, he fidgeted as he drove, muttering to himself, not wanting to be inappropriate but eventually not able to help himself.

"Should we put the radio antenna at half-staff?" he said.

"Sure, go ahead," Hugo said gently. He knew what his friend was going through, and didn't want to make it worse by chiding him. They returned to silence, but half a mile later Hugo glanced over at his friend whose eyes were fixed on the road ahead, his hands gripping the wheel as if he were afraid to let go. Hugo saw the jaw clenched tight and looked away as a solitary tear made a slow descent down his friend's cheek.

As they neared the Boulevard Périphérique, the convoy slowed. Cars had pulled to the side to let them pass, drivers and passengers standing and watching, some even saluting. The media had publicized the procession's route and so the bridges overlooking their route were lined with people, some with flags, others with handwritten signs of support, and some even had blown up photos of Raul, the official picture released by the prefecture to the media. Most stood with a hand raised, a wave almost, a signal to every family member, every cop, everyone in the procession, that they were there to lend their support, their respect, their love.

The crowds thickened as they drew up to the cemetery, an honor guard funneling the leading vehicles to the main entrance on Boulevard de Ménilmontant. The three Americans left the car and took their places among the mourners, a slow and silent train led by the pallbearers, silent except for the sound of feet shuffling over the cobblestones of the cemetery and the whispered words of comfort that always accompany the recently-departed to their graves.

After Raul's coffin had been lowered into place and the last words of the priest had been uttered, the mourners straightened their backs and started to move away from the burial site. Hugo's little gathering had been joined by Claudia, who looked like a beautiful widow herself in her black skirt, boots, and jacket. She'd clung to Hugo's arm the whole time and they'd exchanged looks and small smiles, but neither had trusted words just yet.

Hugo put his arm around her as they started to move away, a slow drift in the general direction of their car.

"Monsieur Marston." The voice was from behind him, a woman. He turned and saw Raul's wife standing there, a short and delicate

woman in black. She was stooped, from grief or maybe tiredness, and
the black veil did nothing to hide the redness ringing her eyes. Her
thin hands clutched a tiny black purse, a prop to match the outfit, but
despite the frailty of her appearance, her voice was strong.

"Madam Garcia." He stepped forward, his hand extended. He'd
not had a chance to speak to her, tell her what he was feeling, because
the ranks of family and the Paris police had closed her off from the
world, protected her while she suffered through the first bouts of grief.
And Hugo hadn't pushed, that wasn't his way, but he'd wanted to speak
to her in person. "I'm so sorry," he said. "Raul was a friend, a truly wonderful man."

"*Merci bien*. He spoke to me about you often." Her tone was
reserved and Hugo suddenly wondered if she was angry, if she blamed
him for not being in that parking lot, for putting her husband there
instead. "He said you always got him into trouble."

"Never on purpose, of course, he was always there for me. He was
a great policeman."

The corner of her mouth twitched. "He said the same about you.
He used those exact words."

"I didn't know that." Mourners filed past, parting around them like
water, giving them space to talk. "Please, if there's anything I can do.
Anything at all."

"There is something. I know that you were working together when
he was killed. I don't know the details of the case, he would never tell
me. But he did tell me, always, bragging like a child, when he got to
work with you. He liked his job, Monsieur Marston, but he loved the
few cases he had with you. It was like he was young again, chasing bad
guys with the American cowboy."

"We worked well together, we really did."

"What I'm trying to say, is that he didn't die because of you. If
everything he told me about you is true, you will try to blame yourself for what happened. I know that could have been you in the car,
not him, but please remember, always remember, that you did not kill
Raul."

Hugo's throat closed on him and tears stung his eyes. "Thank you," he whispered.

"If you had been in the car, Raul would have given his life to change places, to save you. And I know you would have done the same. You have seen a lot of death in your job and, if you're like Raul, you have spent many hours telling the family of victims that they are not responsible, that the only person at fault is the one who pulled the trigger."

Hugo nodded sadly. "Yes, I have."

"Then you need to remember that is true here, too. It doesn't change because you are involved, because Raul was involved." She reached out and put a hand on his arm. " You are not responsible for his death. You were a good friend to him and you brought him great joy. The thing you can do for me is to remember that. Please."

Hugo opened his mouth but couldn't speak, silenced by her words that were so unexpected and generous. Madam Garcia gave him a small smile and squeezed his arm, nodding as she moved back into the flow of people, loved ones reaching out to take her arm.

Hugo stood still for a moment, then moved away from the path, away from the main entrance and from the gentle crush of people. He wanted a moment by Raul's grave, a chance to recover and then say good-bye, and maybe a few other words. As he waited, he saw Lieutenant Lerens approach, with purpose in her movements, which told Hugo she had news.

"How are you, Hugo?"

"Same as everyone here. Sad and pissed off."

"I heard what she said, Raul's wife."

"An amazing woman."

"He wouldn't marry anyone else."

"No." They stood in silence for a moment, then Hugo said, "They were having trouble, you know. Their marriage."

"Ah, Hugo. Everyone has trouble in their marriage. Does that bother you, that he died while they were having problems?"

"A little. He was working too much, too late. She didn't like that."

"Why would she? If they were arguing about that, it was because she wanted to see more of him, not less. That's good, Hugo. A good thing."

"I suppose so. And thanks for trying to make me feel better. Anyway, you have news?"

"Let's walk." They joined the stream of people heading back to the entrance, and Lerens kept her voice low even though most around them were police officers. "We found her place, but not her."

"She has an apartment in Paris?"

"Doesn't everyone with a country home?" Lerens was joking, but barely.

"Where is it?"

"I'll give you one guess."

Hugo glanced across as it hit him. "The same building Natalia lived in."

"Right. She told us she owned apartments there, and said she rented them out. Just forgot to mention that she kept one for herself."

"How convenient. And no wonder your canvass of the place didn't turn up any unexpected visitors."

"Right. Anyway, she's not home and they've sealed the place off. I have someone meeting us there with a search warrant."

"Based on?"

"The circumstantial evidence that we talked about before. And a fingerprint match from the plastic chairs in the apartment building to the one taken in Lake's room. Nice work, Hugo."

"Thanks. No match to the Bassin crime scene?"

"We didn't get a full set from the chairs, so no."

"Damn. The prints you have won't hold up in court, you know that, right? She'll argue that she could have left them at different times."

"Of course she will." Lerens smiled. "But I said search warrant, not trial. You coming?"

CHAPTER THIRTY

They staged outside the building, two officers on each corner wearing tactical gear and carrying automatic weapons. Another four men stood in front of the main doors awaiting breach instructions. Behind them, uniformed officers formed a cordon to keep curious Parisians out of harm's way. Someone had made the decision to go in heavy despite the impossibility of clearing out the area, a show of force and a direct, highly visible, and very lethal response to the death of a police officer.

Hugo and Lieutenant Lerens ducked under the yellow tape, a uniformed *flic* saluting and holding it up so they could pass. They headed straight for the main entrance where they shook hands with the SWAT captain, whose cloth tag on his chest read *Moreau*. Hugo recognized him from a previous encounter, one that had resulted in Hugo being cuffed, and from the slight narrowing of the captain's eyes, the recognition was likely mutual.

"She's definitely not here?" Lerens asked.

"Definitely. Undercovers went up and knocked, then cleared out the apartments either side of hers. The neighbors saw her go out about an hour before we got here."

"So we can get in the main doors?"

"Correct. Just a matter of getting in to her apartment."

"Then let's do exactly that."

She let Captain Moreau lead the way with three of his men, the burliest carrying a tactical Mini Ram device that he'd use to smash open the apartment door. They left one man to secure the elevator and took the stairs. Halfway up, Lerens stopped and grimaced, lifting her left foot and shaking it a couple of times.

"All OK?" Hugo asked.

"Comes with the territory," Lerens said. "The things you'd think would be a problem, boobs, bras, and other girly stuff, are easy. It's the feet."

Hugo looked down. Lerens wore black shoes, feminine but functional, the kind he'd seen policewomen wear all over the world. "They look comfortable enough."

"For most women, they are." She started up the stairs again, keeping her voice conspiratorial. "Problem is, men and women have different foot structure, in terms of density, flexibility, and goodness knows what else. Never found a pair that didn't give me trouble sooner or later. These ones sooner, apparently."

"I had no idea. Couldn't you just wear men's shoes? They look pretty much the same and for work, who'd even notice?"

"Oh, Hugo, and you were doing so well." She cast him a disappointed look. "I'd notice, that's who."

They caught up to the SWAT team and followed them to the third-floor apartment belonging to Alexandra Tourville. Hugo and Lerens stood back as the SWAT officers positioned themselves on either side of the door and knocked loudly. They waited in silence, Moreau's eyes intent on his watch. After thirty seconds, he nodded and an officer knocked again, louder this time. Hugo shifted on his feet as another thirty seconds ticked by. One more knock, then a wait of fifteen seconds. Moreau gave the thumbs up and then the door crashed open under the Mini Ram. It took less than twenty seconds to clear the small apartment, at which point the SWAT team stood down to let Lerens and Hugo make an initial search. Two crime scene technicians waited in the hallway, ready to come in and photograph, bag, and catalogue anything collected as evidence.

The apartment was exactly like Natalia's, and it wasn't until they moved from the bedroom to the living area that Hugo's found anything of interest. Instead of a table bearing a television, Alexie's apartment had a long desk covered in paperwork. Hugo began sifting through it as Lerens looked in the kitchen cabinets.

"A few dishes, cups, but not much in the way of food supplies," Lerens said. "You finding anything?"

"Research papers. To do with her genealogy business, I think. Some articles about DNA testing, too, and a lot of internet searches."

"That's the modern way to trace ancestors," Lerens said. "Easier than combing through boxes and boxes of municipal and church files. And the DNA makes it more certain, too."

An open packet of buccal swabs seemed to confirm her theory, but Hugo was looking for something more definite, something relating to the case. He thumbed through several well-used books on French history and noticed several more on the floor. Hugo wasn't surprised at Alexie's interest, the nation's most controversial queen was another woman whose reputation had been tossed about on the sea of public opinion like so much flotsam.

He put the books down and looked through a stack of computer printouts.

"Camille, I think I have something," he said. She walked over and looked at the paper in Hugo's hands, the rows of boxes and lines.

"What is it?" she asked.

"A family tree," Hugo said. "And unless I'm much mistaken, it belongs to the Bassin family."

They completed the search, slow and painstaking, in less than an hour and the results were largely disappointing. Lerens had hoped to find the gun used on Natalia and Raul, or at least some ammunition, but those were at the bottom of the Seine, Hugo assured her, nestling in several feet of mud. She'd known that, of course, but once in a while a search turned up a smoking gun, quite literally. Just not this time.

They convened at a café nearby. The crime scene people had photographed the printout of the Bassin family tree, as well as two pages of notes made by Alexie, then printed out copies in their van for Hugo and Lerens to study.

"What does it all mean?" Lerens asked.

"Not sure yet. The notes are mostly in shorthand, probably her own form of code. I can't make much sense of them."

"We've got people who can probably crack it, if you think it'll help." She toyed with her coffee, stirring it, tapping the spoon dry, then stirring again.

"Me too," said Hugo, thinking of Tom. "And cheer up, this is a good lead. Another connection with the Bassin family, it's good evidence."

"I know. It's just frustrating that I don't know why any of this is happening. I feel like I'm two steps behind every step of the way."

"We *were* two steps behind," Hugo said. "Now we're just one. And closing in."

"You promise?"

"Sure," said Hugo. "Why not."

"Very encouraging. In the meantime, I'm not sure what else we can do."

"Me neither. Your people will find her, we've both seen them do it time and again. No one can move around without leaving some sort of trail, especially someone not used to living in the shadows. They'll find her."

"Waiting for them to do it is the hard part. That and not really knowing the why of all this."

"Agreed. On that score, do you mind if I send this stuff to a friend? I haven't spoken to her in a while, but she's big into genealogy and may be able to make sense of it."

"Go ahead. Someone local?"

"England, actually."

"As long as she's a professional and quick."

Hugo smiled. "She's a professional, all right."

"What does that mean?"

"Don't get me wrong," Hugo said. "She's one of the brightest, most honest, and hardworking people I know. She does the genealogy stuff part-time, but when I spoke to her last year she said her other business was a little more lucrative."

"I could use a lucrative business. Especially if Alexandra Tourville disappears and I don't solve this case. What is it?"

"She's a professional dominatrix."

"Well," Lerens said, laughing for the first time that day. "I wasn't expecting you to say that. Now, I'm absolutely the last to judge someone else's lifestyle but I have to say, I'm very curious how the upright and respectable Hugo Marston came to be friends with a pro domme."

"Who says I'm upright and respectable?"

"Fair question, and one shouldn't take people at face value. So, something you want to share with me?"

"My friendship with Merlyn," Hugo said, before taking a slow sip of coffee, "is a story for another day."

CHAPTER THIRTY-ONE

He'd not had a moment alone with Raul since his friend's death. A crowded open-casket viewing had been at his home, a long line of men and women in black paying their respects, a sad and silent shuffling past that left no real time for words. When Hugo's turn came, the only real thought he had was about the incredible job done by the funeral home, their patches and make-up remodeling Raul into angelic, if contrived, serenity.

The taxi dropped Hugo off at Père Lachaise in the late afternoon. He'd already called Merlyn and they'd caught up after a year of no contact, then he'd explained the situation and texted the photos. She had down time, she'd assured him, and would get right on it. Hours, she promised, not days.

Here, the day seemed to have held still for him, the wind dropping and the sun hovering just above the old chestnut, oak, and plane trees that sheltered the stone tombs and kept the summer heat from scalding the tourists. On the path outside the cemetery, a few people came and went but the media had packed up their trucks, their stories wrapped up and ready to go. Hugo used the smaller entrance in the northwest corner, near Avenue Gambetta, and as he trotted up the narrow stairs two uniformed policemen stood aside to let him pass. Paying their respects to a fallen colleague, possibly, or maybe just looking for a quiet place to smoke and pass an hour.

Hugo took the cobbled Avenue de l'Ouest toward the heart of the cemetery, feeling the calm of the place settle about him. He wasn't a man of faith like Raul Garcia, and much of the time they'd spent at this cemetery together, on the case of the crypt thief, had been passed in good-natured banter, their jousts and jests a thin disguise for a probing interest in the other's beliefs.

But a belief in God or the afterlife wasn't necessary for a conversation with the dead, not in Hugo's book. Just as funerals were staged to indulge and assuage the sadness of the living, so could a quiet talk to a stone cross or a mound of earth provide balm for a mourner's grief. A few minutes alone just sitting might be enough, a time for some memories of a short but distinct friendship to wash over him, to dilute the sorrow that Hugo was afraid to let himself feel too deeply.

But when he got to Raul's tomb, a waist-high stone casket garnished with a hundred bouquets, he saw that he wasn't alone. On a bench opposite, a woman sat looking up at him. Her eyes were dry but the tissue in her hand said she'd been crying, and because it was Claudia, Hugo was very glad to see her.

"How are you?" he asked gently.

"Very happy you're here." She took his hand as he sat. "There were too many people this morning, too much fuss. I can't help thinking that he'd have hated most of it."

"True, but it wasn't just for him."

"I know. Even so, I wanted just to sit with him for a while." Her voice quavered but she threw Hugo a sharp look. "And don't you dare give me some nonsense about how he's not here anymore. Don't you dare."

"How could I?" Hugo squeezed her hand. "I'm here too, aren't I?"

"I suppose so."

They sat quietly for a moment, then Hugo said, "I think he'd have liked it that we were here together."

"He would." Claudia turned slightly to face him. "Hugo, I know what happened, how it happened. I want to know that you're not blaming yourself."

"Then I have to disappoint you, because I am. Not . . . all the time, or too much. But I wish people would stop pretending that those bullets weren't intended for me."

"They were intended for anyone who got in the way. You, Raul, whoever."

"Nice try, and I'll get over it, Claudia, so please don't worry. I think for me it's just part of the grieving process." He gave her a small smile. "I call it the *blaming* process."

"Then blame the person who shot him, who wanted to shoot you." Claudia slumped on the bench and sighed. "And tell me you're doing OK, truly OK."

"You know me, I'll be fine. This sucks, all of it, and I don't have the words to say how much but . . ." He shrugged.

"I know. But remember what I said. Blame the right person, and that's not you."

"That's the thing about feelings and emotions, they aren't always logical. And I'm a police officer at heart, so I'm always going to wonder what I could have done to stop it from happening. I can't help that, and part of it is wishing I'd been there instead of him. And I could have been, should have been."

"Stop, Hugo. Please." She entwined her fingers in his. "He wouldn't like it that we're arguing."

Hugo chuckled. "Are you kidding? He'd love it. He'd come right over and put his arm around you and tell me I'm a fool. He'd love it." By the time he'd stopped talking, Hugo realized she was crying again, so he put his own arm around Claudia and pulled her tight. "We were lucky to have known him. Let's stick with that for now."

She sniffled and nodded, then straightened up. "My derriere is sore, I've been here almost an hour," she said. "Can we go for a walk in here, then I'll let you two boys have some alone time."

"Sure, that sounds wonderful." They stood up and strolled up a slight hill toward Avenue Feuillant, not paying attention to anything but the feel of the stones under their feet and the soft rustle of the trees overhead. "You know, the last time I was here, it was with Raul. We were trying to find the scarab, figure out what that murderous little bastard was up to."

"I know, I was with you one of those times. And kept bugging you both for the story."

"Like I could forget. Of course, you ended up *in* the story, which you have a habit of doing, don't you?"

"Tough to get rid of me."

They walked on in silence, eyes passing over the names of the long-dead and a few belonging to the more recently interred. It was its own city, this place, with its rows of miniature houses in differing states of repair, some gaping open thanks to rusted gates, others sealed tight and impenetrable. They approached a young man who'd tucked himself inside a weathered sepulcher like a sentry, his pen at the ready and a rough blond beard pointed down at the notebook in his hand. As they passed, he showed them the lines of poetry that he'd scratched across the stark white paper in blood-red ink. Hugo and Claudia exchanged soft smiles at the exchange, and he knew she loved this aspect of Paris, the convergence of death and art that appeared in front of your eyes like a very real ghost, the inspiration that came to those who sought it, art springing to life on the hallowed ground filled with the dead.

"He believed in God, didn't he? Raul, I mean," Claudia said finally.

"Yes. But if you're going to tell me he's in a better place, I'll throttle you."

She gave a gentle laugh. "No, I wasn't going to say that. I was just going to ask you to see it from his perspective, to understand the way he would have seen it."

"Which is?"

"That God, his God if not yours, had some sort of plan in mind."

"Killing a good man is a shitty plan."

"I agree. But remember that Raul may not have."

Hugo didn't feel like arguing. He felt like sitting on someone else's grave holding Claudia's hand, drawing comfort from her and sharing a grief that he suppressed just as much as Tom did, letting it out in dribs and drabs for Claudia to soak up or wipe away. They sat in silence for a minute, then Claudia asked, "So you found who killed him?"

"We're looking for her."

"I can't believe it's Alexandra Tourville."

Hugo looked at her sharply. "Who told you that?"

"Camille Lerens." Claudia smiled. "Don't worry, she told me unofficially. We're friends, did you know that?"

"No, I didn't."

"I wrote an article about her when she joined the force from Bordeaux. She liked that I wrote as much about her career as her gender."

"I had no idea you even knew her."

"Yep. She's fed me stories now and again, she trusts me not to write things I shouldn't."

"Smart woman," Hugo said.

"Me or her?"

"Both, as far as I can tell."

"Why did Tourville kill Raul? Try to kill you?"

"I think for the same reason she killed her assistant, Natalia Khlapina. She was tying off loose ends, severing all connections between herself and the Troyes robbery, the murder of Collette Bassin. Self-preservation, pure and simple."

"But why did she rob that house? What was in the chest that she needed so badly?"

"I'm not sure." He couldn't tell her about the lock of hair, for some reason it seemed like the key to this. If Camille Lerens hadn't told Claudia about it, Hugo felt he shouldn't, either. "I've been thinking about it, though, and I'm sure it has to do with the family's history."

"The Tourvilles?"

"No, the Bassin family."

"Tell me why you're sure it's her. I have to be honest, Hugo, I have a hard time believing it, despite her past."

"I know. And this reminds me of Senator Lake, the way everyone was judging him."

"Deservedly, no?"

"I'm beginning to think so. But when it comes to character flaws and personality defects, people's judgments go from zero to one hundred in a flash. Like with him, and maybe with most politicians, you either love them or you hate them. And if you hate them, you pounce on some aspect of their personality and magnify it. We all do it, all the time. The same way new lovers ignore each other's defects until they can't anymore."

"You're losing me. I thought we were talking about Alexie Tourville."

"We are. See, her behaviors before she supposedly turned her life around are pretty telling. She was selfish, in constant need of stimulation, and irresponsible with money. Now she's broke and resentful that she has to rely on her brother. How else would you describe her?"

"Charming when she wants to be. Sexually promiscuous, if we're to believe what we read."

"The photos help on that score," Hugo said. "And related to that, she has this ability, or drive, to reinvent herself."

"I get the feeling those traits mean something."

"They do. And bear in mind, she doesn't exhibit them to a sharp degree, but they are all behaviors exhibited by someone with sociopathic tendencies. When we talked to her about Natalia's death, she acted sad but I didn't see any tears, no real sorrow."

"Wait, that sounds like you're justifying her being the bad guy."

"And that's because she's not your psychopathic killer from Hollywood. Sociopathy is a continuum. It exists in corporate CEOs, politicians, people who are successful but who have enough empathy to fit right in with the people around them. Forget the idea that every sociopath or psychopath gets off on killing, they don't. You and I live alongside them, they can be our neighbors and our bosses. Most are relatively harmless, getting off on furthering their careers, making money, or achieving positions of power."

"So what's her motive in life, what's her goal?"

"That," Hugo said, "is where I'm not caught up yet."

"Personality aside, go back to why you think she killed Madam Bassin."

"Well, there's the chest. It was found in Natalia's apartment but

Alexie obviously has access to it: she's the landlord. And she said Natalia only went there a couple of times a month, so getting in unseen would have been easy. The whole apartment building is practically deserted."

"OK, what else?"

"No one can definitively say Alexie had possession of the chest, not yet, and it's true that Natalia could have taken it to the Tourville Chateau. But Natalia doesn't make sense as the killer, and I think Alexie lied to me about her."

"How?"

"She belabored the fact that Natalia was a thief, essentially a klepto-maniac with a shoe fetish. But those things don't necessarily go together. And the jewelry in Natalia's apartment, it was older. Beautiful, but old. Kleptomaniacs are like magpies, they like shiny new things. They don't steal objects that are old, used."

"Camille told me that she had a lot of new shoes."

"A lot of women own a lot of shoes. Which brings us to the shoes that were the wrong size, that would likely fit Alexie."

"She stole them from her boss?"

"That's what Alexie told us, what she wants us to think. But again, someone stealing new shoes doesn't also steal almost-new ones that are the wrong size. I think Alexie either kept shoes at the apartment for when she stayed, or piled some in to make her thief story stronger."

"Fingerprints on the chest?"

"None, and as I told Tom, that tells me it wasn't Natalia who put it up there. Someone else did, and the only someone else I can think of, the only someone else who we can put at the Bassin residence, is Alexie Tourville."

"Is it killing you, not knowing what was in that chest?"

"Of course." Hugo grimaced. "But I'll figure it out." *That is, figure out what else was in the chest.*

He stood and stretched, looking around. He realized that he'd not paid attention to the direction they were walking and, looking for markers, his eye settled on a tomb across the pathway, no more than thirty feet away.

It belonged to Oscar Wilde, and Hugo remembered the discussion he'd had with Alexie Tourville and Lake about Hugo's hobbies, his love of books. She'd asked which authors he liked, and Oscar Wilde had been one of the first to come to mind. Now here he was, a few steps from the man's grave.

He moved closer, the first time he'd seen the glass wall that enveloped the tomb, a measure implemented to keep the red-glazed lips of fans away from the crypt itself. Their kisses had become a headache to clean and had even started to erode the flying nude angel wrought by sculptor Jacob Epstein. Hugo stood in front of the sculpture, as snippets of Wilde's work and his life history drifted through his mind.

Claudia walked up behind him and rested her head on his shoulder. "Wilde, eh?"

"In every sense of the word. It came back to haunt him, of course, and the poor man died penniless here in Paris. In fact, the first time around he was buried somewhere else, Bagneaux cemetery just outside the city, and was moved here almost ten years after his death."

"I didn't know that. How long did he live in Paris?"

"Two or three years, I think. Prison ruined him," Hugo said, "he was never quite the same after that. You know, to try and escape that time, to get past it, he even . . ." Hugo straightened, his eyes wide.

"What, Hugo? He even what?"

"He's just given me an idea." A slow smile spread over Hugo's face.

"What idea? All this has something to do with Oscar Wilde?"

"Yes. But mostly no." Hugo took out his phone. "Thanks to old Oscar, though, I think I might know what's going on."

CHAPTER THIRTY-TWO

They shared a taxi back into the city center, Hugo impatient and Claudia frustrated. He'd left a message with Merlyn but she'd not responded, and he spent the car ride deflecting Claudia's questions, her demands for an explanation.

"No, you're in reporter mode," he said finally.

"I'll turn that off. Stay in Claudia mode."

"Nice try, but we've been through this before. Cops and journalists don't have that on–off switch."

Hugo stopped the cab on Rue de Rivoli and kissed Claudia on the cheek. "I need to stop in at the embassy, but I'm out of cash. Would you mind?"

"Seriously?" she said, and he was unsure if her indignation was real or feigned. "Are you turning into Tom now?"

"It's a cab, not a call girl," Hugo said with a wink. "Have the driver take you home, I'll pay you back later."

"You better. And, seriously, call me when you can."

"I will, I promise." As he climbed out of the taxi his phone buzzed and he waved it at a departing Claudia before answering. "This is Hugo."

"Hey, it's Merlyn. S'up?" Merlyn, the friend he'd made out of the blue in England while trying to keep track of the movie star he was assigned to protect. The beautiful yet waiflike goth girl who was more worldly than most people twice her age. Her directness had caught Hugo by surprise back then, and she'd accorded his position of authority no automatic respect but helped him because she was a good person, and because she believed that Hugo was, too.

"S'up yourself. I've been trying to call."

She chuckled. "You might want to remember what I do for a living before you get too stroppy with me, Marston."

Hugo grinned despite himself. "Not my cup of tea, as you might say, but fair point." He cleared his throat and adopted as formal a tone as he could. "So, lovely Miss Merlyn, does your wonderfulness have anything for me?"

"Oh, Hugo, you're such a dork sometimes. I do miss you."

"Thanks, I think."

"Welcome. Anyway, as far as this little task goes, it would've helped if I'd known what I was looking for. But I found out a few things, so how about I info dump and you use what you want?"

"That'd be perfect, thanks."

"Sure. Tell you now or email it?"

"Give me the highlights, then email whatever else you have. And thanks, Merlyn, I owe you."

"Yeah, you do. Coming to England any time soon?"

"Not that I know of. Visit me in Paris, it's prettier than London."

"Can't argue with you there. All right, here's what I know. The Bassin family is as old as the hills. And they've lived in that house for a couple of hundred years, exact numbers will be in the email. Nothing out of the ordinary, a kid here and there, marriages and deaths, but only one blip, so to speak. I think that something dodgy happened toward the end of the 1700s."

"What do you mean, 'dodgy'?"

"Hard to tell. But if I had to guess, there was some kind of family dispute or something. One branch of the Bassin family up and moved out of the house, and another moved in. No idea why, of course. Anyway, two interesting things related to that. First, the ones that moved out changed their name."

"How can you tell?"

"Well, after the revolution in France the new regime conducted an exhaustive census. Actually they got the idea from us Brits, basing it on the one in 1086 ordered by William the Conqueror."

"Which produced the *Domesday Book.*"

"Right, same idea. Interestingly, it was much less well organized, to the point where the same towns and villages got recorded twice within months of each other. Most of the information was the same, of course, but if people moved about in that time, well, it was essentially recorded. That's what happened here."

"And those records were kept?"

"It's so weird how Americans think two hundred years ago is a long time. I mean, we have the *Domesday Book* from a thousand years ago, so yes, those records were kept."

Hugo smiled. "Thanks for the lecture."

"Welcome. Anyway, the ones that moved out were a husband, wife, and their son. They moved to Marseille and filled out the right forms which got put in a box for a hundred years, then got put onto microfiche, and finally scanned into a computer sometime in the modern age. And for the record, whoever made that family tree that you sent me had figured it out, I'm guessing. So many records are digitized now that if you have the right access, you can trace people quite well, even that long ago and especially when they move countries."

"Wait, you're telling me the Bassin family left their house for Marseille, and then moved abroad?"

"That, my Yank friend, is interesting part number two."

The moment he got off the phone with Merlyn, he called Tom, leaving a hasty message when his friend didn't pick up. "Where are you? I need some help. Listen, find Senator Lake and stick with him. I don't care if he throws a fit or not, just keep eyes on him. And call me when you get this."

He then tried Lieutenant Lerens, who answered immediately. "Hugo, I was about to call. Where are you?"

"Heading to the embassy. Did you get something on Alexie Tourville?"

"Yes. We tried pinging her phone after getting the number from her brother, but had no luck. However, one of our junior detectives was going through the papers we collected from her apartment and found bills for a second cell phone. You'll never guess who she's been in contact with?"

"I'm ahead of you on that one," Hugo said. "Senator Lake."

"Yes, how did you know?"

"It's a long story, but we need to find both of them as soon as possible."

"Well, Lake left yesterday evening. He flew to London so he could get on the *Queen Mary II*."

"He's taking the boat back to America?"

"Yep. Doesn't like flying, apparently. I spoke to Ambassador Taylor, he said Lake had talked about the romance of a transatlantic crossing. Mysterious and romantic, he said. He's a strange man, your senator."

"He's graduated from strange, I'm afraid. But his leaving is not good news."

"Why not?"

"Long story. You were saying that Alexie Tourville has a second phone."

"Oh, right. We got the number from the bill and we're pinging it. As we speak, quite literally. I wanted to make sure you were available in case we got a hit." She paused. "And here we go . . . hold on, I think it's the tech people." She went quiet for a full minute, then came back. "Still with me?"

"I am."

"Good. We're on the way to the embassy to pick you up. She's heading south. We should be able to catch up with her before she gets too far, but we need to hurry."

"I'll wait outside. Just open the door and I'll jump in."

Tom called back as Hugo stood on the Place de la Concorde, waiting for Lieutenant Lerens.

"The *Queen Mary*, eh? Nice," said Tom.

"Can you get someone on board, security, to check on him?"

"Probably. What are you afraid of?"

"I just want to make sure he's safe." Hugo waved an arm as a procession of three white police cars, lights flashing but sirens quiet for now, split the traffic and headed toward the sidewalk where he stood. "And Tom, if you can wave your magic wand and get yourself on board, do it."

"I'm not following."

"And I'm not going to be any less subtle. Nice day for a boat ride, Tom. Take a hint." He hung up as the passenger door of the middle car opened. He slid in and the three cars immediately took off again.

"Ready for a chase?" Lerens asked.

"Always."

Lerens nodded and picked up the handset for her radio. She spoke to the cars in front and behind, using a number code Hugo didn't recognize. In unison, the sirens began to wail and the growing rush-hour traffic slowed and parted in front of them, promising a fast-track exit from Paris.

"Do you know how far she is?" Hugo asked as they swept alongside the river, the magnificent cathedral of Notre Dame looming to their right.

"Not far. She made a stop just a few minutes ago in the Thirteenth, was there a while. We're keeping tabs with a police chopper. If she gets too far south we'll use local cops, too, just have them stay a couple of miles back. The chopper is high enough she won't see or hear it, and the pilot has been told to report in every five minutes with her location."

"Do we know why she stopped?"

"Underground garage, so no, but we have officers headed there to see what they can find. She's been back on the road about ten minutes."

The lead car turned right on the short Pont d'Austerlitz, taking them south toward the main arteries that led out of Paris and toward the road known as the *autoroute du soleil*, which so many Parisians used to begin their vacations, the highway of the sun that ran down to Lyons and connected it with the sprawling and industrial port city of Marseilles. The highway that now carried Alexie Tourville out of the city and, Hugo assumed, to some place of perceived safety. Given her demonstrated ruthlessness and undoubted resourcefulness, he knew that losing her was not an option.

The radio came alive and they listened to the exchange.

"Air One." The pilot, Hugo assumed.

"Go ahead, Air One." The dispatcher, a woman's brusque and efficient voice. She'd be charged with coordinating the converging forces and making sure information was shared.

"Subject continuing south on the A6," the pilot said, "just past the split with the A10. Maintaining coverage, will report again in five minutes unless a change of course."

The dispatcher repeated the information then signed off.

"How far back are we?" Hugo asked.

"It's twenty minutes or so to where she is now."

"What is she driving?" Hugo asked.

"She has a black VW Golf. It's a 1998 but it's a GTI, so it'll be quick if we have to chase."

"Do you have a plan for when we catch up to her?"

"No, Hugo, I'm making this shit up as I go along and I've simply no idea how to stop a bad guy in a moving car."

Hugo held up a hand in surrender, or apology. "I wasn't questioning, I was asking."

Lerens took a deep breath. "Sorry, I didn't mean to snap at you. As you might guess, this is about as high profile as it gets—Alexandra Tourville is a cop killer, maybe a serial murderer, and on the run. I have a lot of eyes on me and a fair few of them wouldn't weep if I screwed up."

"No need to apologize. Looks to me like you're doing everything right so far."

"Thanks. And to answer your question, once we get close I'm going to have local units shut down the road behind her to give us some space, then the three of us will do the stop. I'd considered having some more units line up in front but if she sees them she might run. I'm going for the element of surprise, but we'll have local police mobilized in case she doesn't stop. Suggestions?"

"Nope. Sounds like a good plan."

They feel silent as the radio hissed again.

"Air One."

"Go ahead, Air One."

"Subject is stopping for fuel. I don't have a visual, there's a roof over the pumps but I'll see when she leaves."

After the dispatcher had confirmed the message, Lerens said: "That'll get us pretty close to her. We'll give it five more minutes then turn lights and sirens off."

A minute later the pilot came back on, urgency in his voice. "Air One."

"Go ahead," the dispatcher said.

"Something happened down there, I can't tell what. She just took off from the pumps and a couple of people ran from the main building to where she'd been. If I had to guess, I'd say she drove off without paying."

"*Merde.*" Lerens picked up her handset. "Thanks Air One. Which direction did she go?"

"Back on the autoroute, same direction, south."

"Got it. Dispatch, please notify local law enforcement not to engage if someone calls police." She dropped the handset in her lap and pulled a map from the side pocket of the car. "Here, see if this is any use."

Hugo studied the map, though the one on his phone would have been as useful and probably more up to date. "Fuel stops are all marked, I see the one she was at." He looked out of the window and saw a sign for the east–west A86, then checked the map again. "We're getting close to the split, might want to kill the sights and sounds."

"'Sights and sounds,'" Lerens smiled. "I like that." She hit two buttons on a panel beside the rearview mirror and in seconds the cars in front and behind followed suit. They remained, however, at a steady ninety miles-per-hour. She picked up the radio again. "Dispatch, please contact the rolling block, have them move onto the highway. I want to pass them any minute and when I do, they need to be ready."

"Will do."

Lerens swore, tapping the brakes as the forward car suddenly slowed, then honked at a camper that was in the fast lane and shouldn't have been. It eased over and the trio sped up.

"There," said Hugo, pointing forward. Four police cars were entering the highway, nose-to-tail on the hard shoulder and doing no more than twenty miles an hour.

"Perfect," Lerens said, picking up the handset: "Lerens here. We're passing the road block, have them take up position."

Hugo turned and saw the cars move into the slow lane, then fan slowly across the highway. They'd maintain a sped of fifty or so, their roof lights alerting the traffic speeding up on them, then after five minutes they'd slow everyone down to a crawl, and then a stop, creating a safe zone between the public and her team as they pulled over Alexie Tourville. That, at least, was the theory.

The police car in front of them moved to the center lane, letting Lerens take the lead before moving in behind.

"A black Golf GTI," Lerens said—to herself, it seemed. Trucks dotted the road in front of them, blocking much of their view and she leaned forward as if by doing so she could see past them.

"You drive, I'll watch for it," Hugo said.

"Not a chance."

They sped past a double-decker coach in the center lane and almost missed the Golf. Hugo spotted it as it disappeared behind the smoked glass and shining body of the huge passenger vehicle.

"There, let the coach get ahead, she's in the slow lane."

Lerens tapped the brakes and used the speeding behemoth as cover. She picked up the radio handset, her message for the drivers behind them, but heard by the entire team.

"Visual confirmation of the suspect. She's in the slow lane. I'll get right behind her, Cabret stay to my left, Sorelle use the shoulder in case she dumps and runs."

They drifted out from behind the coach like fighter planes, swinging across the road to position themselves behind the enemy. They cheated left a little, ignoring the white lines of the road to cover it more fully and making sure the car with two wheels on the shoulder wasn't too close to the retaining wall. Lerens clenched her jaw in concentration, one hand on the wheel and the other on the radio, ready to give the order. Hugo squinted as he saw movement in the black car that was thirty yards ahead.

"Looks like two people inside," he said.

Lerens grunted acknowledgment, then glanced at her wingmen. She held down the call button and said, "Two suspects in the target vehicle. We're going now."

She dropped the handset and pressed a button on the overhead panel, the car's siren beginning its insistent wail, joined immediately by those either side.

CHAPTER THIRTY-THREE

The brake lights on the Golf flared red for a second and the car jigged left, as if the driver had twitched involuntarily. Hugo could see the two people in the front of the car turning to look behind, then ahead again.

"Looks like she cut her hair," Hugo said, though it was hard to be sure. The rear window had a dark tint to it and it may just have been a hat or even a pony tail changing her profile.

"I would, too," Lerens said, "but then I'd also ditch my phone and use someone else's car. Maybe she didn't have time for all three." They both stiffened as the car signaled an intent to pull to the shoulder on the right. "Here we go."

All four vehicles slowed in unison, the VW sliding to the hard shoulder.

"They're planning to run," Hugo said. Lerens glanced at him, inviting an explanation. "They undid their seat belts already," he explained.

Hugo looked left and right, gauging the terrain. Open fields lay to both sides, so either they'd come to their senses or he was in for a long, muddy run. As the cars came to a halt, Lerens killed the siren and the two either side of them did the same. The steady beat of the police helicopter was audible, now, and getting louder. Hugo leaned forward and looked up. The chopper swung overhead, no more than a hundred feet from the ground, wheeling in the air so its nose pointed down at them like a bird of prey waiting to swoop down on its meal. Hugo hoped its sudden appearance would be added deterrence for Alexie and her partner, the final assurance that running would be futile.

Lieutenant Lerens flipped the gear into park. She and Hugo pulled their weapons as they stepped out, shielding themselves behind the open car doors as their colleagues, two in each car, did the same on their flanks.

"Let's go," she said. "My guys will back us up, they know what to do."

"OK, but be careful. We've seen how far she's willing to go," Hugo said. He licked his lips, his heart hammering in his chest as he fought to control his breathing. He kept his gun leveled at the figure in the passenger seat and started forward. They moved, one careful step at a time toward the little black car while, flanking them, the uniformed officers sighted their standard issue SIG SP handguns toward the front windows, just in case.

Lerens reached the back of the car. She slowed and her left hand came away from her gun for long enough to touch the trunk of the VW. It was an instinctual movement, one drilled into officers during training and practiced daily on the streets, an officer leaving behind fingerprints and maybe DNA in case the traffic stop went wrong.

She moved forward and on opposite sides of the car they drew level with the back windows, still unable to see the occupants clearly. Lerens rapped her gun butt on the glass and shouted, "Windows down and hands out. Now."

Slowly, agonizingly, Hugo watched the windows on his side scroll down and a pair of small hands poked out. A woman, he assumed, and so the question flashed through his mind: If this is Alexie, who's driving? Hugo drew level with his suspect and crouched to look into the car, at the exact moment that Lieutenant Lerens did the same thing. They both stared at the occupants for a moment, then their eyes met.

"Not exactly what I was expecting," Hugo said.

"Me neither," Lerens agreed. She yanked open the driver's door and Hugo opened the passenger side.

"Both of you," Lerens ordered, "out now."

The little boy on Hugo's side didn't move. Tears rolled down his face and his eyes were glued to the end of Hugo's gun. Hugo put it back in his holster and reached in for the boy, pulling him out gently but firmly. Lerens did the same with the teenage boy who'd been driving, and they met at the back of the VW. Two of the officers stepped forward with handcuffs and secured the kids' hands behind their backs.

"Where's your phone?" Lerens asked the trembling boys.

They looked at her for a second, then each other, and they shook their heads in unison. "We don't have a phone," the driver said. He was the braver of the two, and looked slightly older. "We were just taking a trip."

"A trip?" Hugo asked. "You have a license?"

"*Non.*"

"How old are you?" he asked.

"I'm thirteen," said the driver, then nodded at his companion. "He is eleven." The passenger glanced at Hugo and nodded his head.

"Why are you driving this car?" Lerens demanded.

"I found it." The driver was defiant.

"Found it? Explain that to me."

"The windows were down and the key was in it. What was I supposed to do?"

"How about wait until you get a license, and then buy your own," Lerens snapped. "Where was it?"

"Bois de Boulogne," the kid said sulkily.

"Did you see who left it?"

"*Non.* I watched for a while before I got in. I didn't see anyone."

"So you just took it and picked your friend up?"

"He's not my friend. He's my brother." The boy's eyes softened as he looked at his slumped and wet-eyed sibling. "It's his birthday and I wanted to see him. We're in foster care, but they didn't put us together. I just wanted to see him, take a trip somewhere with him."

"OK." Lerens tone softened. "Go with these officers, wait by my car while I talk to my colleague for a moment." She gestured for the uniforms to take the boys to the back of the police cars.

"If you're going to leave a car to be stolen, the Bois is as good place as any," Hugo said. Over the years, authorities had worked hard to clean up the Bois de Boulogne, Paris's second largest park. They'd mostly succeeded, but after dusk it could be a hair-raising, and sometimes actively dangerous, place to be. The nearby drug dealers and prostitutes who lay low in the daytime would abandon their lairs and drift through the park's many lanes and secluded spaces looking for customers. Sometimes they'd look for each other, and the next morning police or an unlucky jogger would find the remains. Parking a car there was a bad idea, walking away from it even worse. And, as Hugo and the young car thief both recognized, leaving it unlocked with the keys inside was an invitation.

Lerens nodded. "Agreed. And I assume this means her phone's in here somewhere."

"Check inside, I'll look in the trunk."

"*Bien.*"

He peered into the rear window of the hatchback but the parcel shelf obscured any view. "Pop the release for me, will you?" Hugo said as Lerens opened the driver's door.

"Want me to cover you while you open it?"

Hugo gave her a wry smile. "You think she's hiding inside?"

"You never know."

Lerens chuckled and popped the trunk release. Hugo put his fingers under the metal rim and swung it open, his gun ready just in case.

It took a moment for his eyes to adjust to the dark interior of the trunk, but when they did he saw a huddled shape that turned his blood to ice. He opened his mouth to tell the lieutenant, but at first no words would come out. Then the adrenaline kicked in and he called out.

"Camille!"

She heard the urgency in his voice and backed out of the front seat. "What is it?"

"I was wrong." Hugo nodded to the open trunk. "She's here after all."

"Seriously?" Lerens moved slowly to Hugo's side, her gun back in her hand.

"Yes, but you won't need that." He reached in to double check her pulse, but Hugo had seen enough bodies to know the difference between unconscious and dead, and her battered face wore the plastic gray pallor of forever-gone.

"Those boys didn't kill her," Lerens said. "Not for a car."

"No, I'm betting they'd faint if they knew she was in there. They didn't do this."

"Then who?" Lerens ran a hand over her face. "*Pute!* There's someone else out there killing people?"

"Looks like it," Hugo said. He shook his head sadly. "I was afraid this would happen but I didn't think . . . I really didn't think . . ."

"*Attends.* Hugo, are you saying you know who did this?" Lerens looked incredulous, and her eyes flashed with anger. "I want to know what's going on, and I want to know *now.*"

"Of course. Call your crime scene people, get them here as quickly as possible. To be sure I'm right we'll need to know how she died—as best they can tell us out here, anyway. Call them and I'll tell you everything I know."

As Lerens got busy, Hugo took out his phone and dialed Tom, but again had to leave a message.

"It's me. This just turned ugly and our little lady is dead. Do whatever you have to do to secure Senator Lake, Tom, I don't care what strings you have to pull but get to him as soon as you can. If you have to evacuate that boat by calling in a hoax bomb threat then do it, because I'm not kidding when I say this is a matter of life and death. And, yes, I mean his."

CHAPTER THIRTY-FOUR

Hugo rang off and watched the lieutenant as she worked. She was on her car radio and he listened as she had the dispatcher get the crime scene team rolling. Then she requested extra units to help with traffic because their stop had blocked one of the busiest motorways leading out of Paris, and if they didn't set up a diversion soon there'd be a riot. France's motorists were accustomed to being inconvenienced by striking farmers and their roaming flocks of sheep, but everyone involved in this operation knew those same motorists wouldn't tolerate a mere crime scene blocking their southward escape from the city.

Orders issued, Lerens escorted each boy to a separate police car, helping them into the back seat and lingering a moment to talk to them. Then Lerens turned to the uniformed officers and told them to put on gloves and find Tourville's phone, with minimal disturbance to the body's position. Good idea, Hugo thought, it may contain recorded or photographed information related to her crimes or, of more immediate interest, evidence of her killer.

Hugo almost jumped when his phone buzzed and he saw it was a text from Tom.

Took your advice. On a helicopter. Got your VM but can't talk. Obviously.

Hugo smiled and wondered just how close Tom was to the ship, whether it had set sail and if so, how far it had gotten.

Lieutenant Lerens caught him smiling at the phone. "Something funny at last?"

242

"Tom. Always funny, even when he shouldn't be."

"Ah. So, you want to tell me what's going on?"

"Sure," said Hugo. "But let's sit in the car, this could take a while."

"*Bien sûr.*" They settled into their seats in her car and Lerens half-turned and looked at him. "Now go."

"*D'accord.* But I'd ask you to remember that some of this is fact, and some is . . . well, let's call it deduction. Or guesswork, if you prefer. I think we can prove most of it, eventually, but for now—"

"Hugo," she interrupted. "Just tell me."

"Right, sorry. I'll start with Alexandra Tourville. Obviously we all know about her past. I think that all of this has happened because she was trying to resurrect her career. Not so much make a name for herself—that door closed a while back—but I think she was seeking enough money to become independent from her brother and maybe grab a little power to go with it."

"What kind of power?"

"Political. The power thing may have been an afterthought, but I think she stumbled across her chance and decided to take it. If I had to bet, I think she started down a path without knowing exactly where it would end up, or how, and it all snowballed. Became one of those things that once you start, you can't stop or back out of."

"Well," Lerens said, "I'd know a little something about that, wouldn't I?"

Hugo laughed softly. "I suppose you would. Anyway, she'd started her genealogy business. She was working for a client in the United States, she told us that. My friend in England, she's tapped into that community and found out who. A political rival of our good Senator Charles Lake."

"Why would a political rival hire a genealogist?"

Hugo shrugged. "These days rivals will dig up any dirt they can. Maybe they were hoping to link him to a mobster, a child molester, Adolf Hitler. Don't ask me to explain the devious mind of a politician. Point is, she dug into Lake's background and obviously found something. I'm willing to bet that she found a dead end."

"What do you mean, 'dead end'?"

"That his family tree was stunted. No more information." Hugo held up a finger. "That would have told her to check immigration records. Merlyn said that's the obvious move when a trail dies, especially if it's between 1800 and 1900. She also told me that a lot of those records have long since been lost, but a lot still remain."

"So she found out Lake's family were immigrants, big deal."

"Correct, on both counts. Everyone in America is an immigrant, right? But Alexie Tourville had a few suspicions, given her knowledge of history, the timing of the immigration, and the names on the immigration paperwork."

"Suspicions? About what?"

"I'm not sure, not entirely. I'm coming at this from the opposite end, unraveling what she created so it's hard for me to know what she knew, and when. But at some point she figured out what I did at Père Lachaise today."

"Which is?"

"That when people want to hide their past, when they want to bury some part of themselves, one of the first things they do is change their name. Oscar Wilde did it: he even had business cards made up with his new name of Sebastian Melmoth. But, like Oscar Wilde and pretty much everyone else who changes their name, they hang on to some variant of their old one. In Wilde's case, he picked the names Sebastian and Melmoth after Saint Sebastian and the titular character of *Melmoth the Wanderer*, a Gothic novel by his great-uncle. But it's the same for everyone, Martin Smith will call himself Mark Simons. Julie-Ann Jones will call herself Anne Johnson. I've seen it time and again." He smiled. "Look at you, Christophe became Camille."

"That's true." She nodded slowly. "But I still don't get it. Who changed their name?"

"That's where Merlyn worked her magic. She told me that a family called Fontaine moved to America a couple of hundred years ago. In 1796, I think she said."

"So?"

"Think about the names," Hugo said.

Lerens rolled her eyes. "Tom said you did this. Fine, the names. Fontaine, Tourville—"

"Forget Tourville. The other players."

"Fontaine," Lerens tried again, "Bassin, and . . . oh my goodness, Lake."

"Wrong order but otherwise right. A 'bassin' can be an ornamental pond, right?"

"Yes, of course . . ."

" Pond, Fountain, and Lake. Same family from start to finish, from then until now."

"So . . . Senator Lake is descended from the Bassin family?" She thought for a moment. "You know, that would be pretty embarrassing for him. I mean, the man hates foreigners, especially the French."

"True, although like I said, pretty much everyone in America is descended from somewhere in Europe. But yes, he'd look a little silly if someone proved he was of French descent."

"Someone like . . . Alexie Tourville."

"Right."

"She was blackmailing him?"

"Not about that. Not just about that, anyway. But along those lines, because that first night at the chateau she was pressing Lake about his rich donors, asking what would happen if they suddenly didn't like him anymore. I thought at the time she was referencing her own past, but I think she was testing him, consciously or not she was showing her hand or obliquely pointing to the writing on the wall."

"Which said what?"

"That there might come a point where his wealthy isolationist friends would turn their backs on him. And I think that's where the robbery at the Bassin house comes in."

"Explain it to me."

"I can't," Hugo said apologetically. "Not entirely, anyway. And without proof, my little theory is going to sound . . . far-fetched. But it has to do with the lock of hair we found in the chest."

"Hugo, this whole thing is far-fetched. Every step of it has been insane, so try me. And how many times do I have to point out that life has taught me to be a little more open-minded than some people?"

"I keep forgetting, sorry. But since you insist, Merlyn used the family tree and the notes I sent her and saw that one branch of the Bassin family left that house around the time we're talking about, and some others moved in. Siblings, cousins, I don't know. But Georges Bassin had mentioned something similar. My theory is that whoever moved out headed to Marseilles where they changed their names to Fontaine, and then moved to America where they, like so many who came, changed their name again. A twofold attempt to cover their tracks. The husband, wife, and their son. I also think they weren't so much emigrating as escaping."

"Explain that."

"Because they didn't *need* to emigrate. These were people with a big house, money, and who lived far enough from Paris and politics that the craziness of the revolution had passed them by."

"The revolution?"

"Yes. Bear with me. Merlyn knows plenty about that period and she said it didn't take much digging to find out that the Bassin family were friends with some powerful people, people who wanted to end the bloodshed and put France back on an even keel."

"You're all over the map, Hugo. The historical map."

"Yes. But I'm trying to connect what was in the chest with Senator Lake, and make sense of it. You remember at the Tourville place, the stranger in his room?"

"The imagined stranger."

"No, it was real. I realized that he'd been telling the truth when he insisted he'd not been drinking much. And yet he was totally out of it. I think Alexie slipped something into his drink—I do remember that she brought us glasses of champagne right before we sat down. Easy to do."

"But why?"

"In her apartment we also found buccal swabs, for taking DNA samples."

"That's right." Lerens thought for a moment. "Didn't Lake say someone was leaning over him?"

"He did, and she was. Taking his DNA."

"So you think . . . the hair in that chest, whose was it?"

"Ah, now that's where my theory really does become guesswork. If she was blackmailing him, and I think she was, it had to be someone both French and royal."

"But I thought you said everyone in America was descended—"

"Yes, but imagine it from his point of view. He has French blood, royal blood in his veins. He's descended from kings. The people that keep him in power, that would have financed his presidential run, even if they might have looked the other way, he couldn't be sure of that. And think about his personality. Think about how he'd suddenly see himself and the paranoia we've all seen in him that would, surely, convince him his political coffers would soon be empty. You know Claudia Roux?"

"Yes, I do. For a reporter, I like her very much."

"She covered a story recently. A man who tried to kill his wife because he believed she was having an affair, convinced himself of it. This reminds me of that, where someone's reality doesn't mesh with the truth."

"Yes, I read that." Lerens nodded. "And similarly, it didn't matter to Alexandra whether or not his donors would withdraw support. She'd be pretty safe betting on Lake's paranoia, that he'd be convinced they would."

"Right. This is a man who's suspicious and insecure enough to bug his phones, his own office. He wouldn't think about this the way you or I would because he already assumes his political career is teetering on the brink. His reality isn't yours or mine, and in his fragile world his all-American image brings him power. And, like I said, money. Without an image or money, it's over."

"And so Alexandra decides to claim some of that political money, most likely, and maybe even a hold over the most powerful man in the world."

"If he became president."

"Right. And that's the beauty of it. He might survive as a senator if all this came out, but no way he'd make it to the presidency. This anti-Europe thing is his shtick, it's defined his political career and so this revelation would make that a joke. In Washington, and I'm sure it's the same for you in Paris, there's always someone waiting to pounce on stuff like this. He probably wouldn't make it through the primaries. Even more than that, there's his blue-collar image. He basically told me that if that was undermined his grass-roots following would not only disappear, but take the deep pockets with them. He called it a double-whammy."

"If you're right about this . . ." Lerens shook her head. "Then Lake is the one who killed her."

Hugo nodded. "I'm afraid so."

They sat in silence for a full minute, then Lerens shifted in her seat and said, "One thing, though. Who exactly is it you think he's descended from?"

Hugo gave a sad smile. "That's the other beautiful part of her scheme. If I'm right about this, he's descended from the one French royal every American has heard of. The royal responsible for making one of the most callous and reviled statements toward the working people of France. The person who's image, even today, is the polar opposite of his own."

The lieutenant's eyes widened. "You think . . . you think he's descended from Marie Antoinette?"

CHAPTER THIRTY-FIVE

They both jumped at a knock on the car window. Lerens opened the door, muttering under her breath at the uniformed officer.

"Lieutenant, I found her phone but we'll need the code to get in, if you have it. Otherwise the forensic people will have to work on it."

"*Merci.* Bag it, please, and make sure you note exactly where you found it."

"*Oui,* Madame."

When he'd gone, Lerens turned back to Hugo. "We're missing something, aren't we?"

"Yes. There was something else in that chest, the answer to all of this. The proof that connects the Bassin family to French royalty."

"Good, because I'm not sure I understand the implication of the name-changing and sudden moving."

"I don't think . . ." Hugo frowned. "Me neither, not completely. It's like I'm seeing shadows moving through the fog and I can't quite make sense of everything." He looked at Lerens. "But I'm convinced there is more evidence, something that solidifies that connection."

"You think Lake has it?"

"I do," Hugo said. "I think Alexie Tourville confronted him with it and he killed her for it."

"And Natalia Khlapina?"

"You heard what Bruno Capron said when I interviewed him."

"I did. When he called Natalia, she was with Alexie, wasn't she?"

"Yeah, I think so. I'm betting Natalia really did steal that necklace and resell it on her own. She probably confessed it all to Alexie and maybe asked where the hell it came from."

"Which meant," Lerens said, "Natalia made herself a new and very direct link from the Bassin robbery to Alexie Tourville."

"And for self-preservation, Alexie had to kill her."

Silence descended, as did the darkness of the evening. As the sun bled red on the horizon, the crime scene team arrived and set up their flood lights, painting the bizarre image in Hugo's mind of an outdoor operating theater. Men and women in scrubs, faces covered and moving with deliberate speed, circular lights on wheels being adjusted as gloved fingers probed and tugged at the body, emptied the car. The starkest difference was the ceremonial five minutes devoted to the first of the professionals, the photographer, who leaned in close then wandered further away, angling and zooming as his soft shutter-clicks marked the start of the preservation of evidence, which was itself the formal acknowledgement of the demise of Alexandra Catherine de Beaumont Tourville.

CHAPTER THIRTY-SIX

Tom provided little information, just a vague cover story relating to potential threats, a suspect passenger, and national security (British and American, to cover all angles). It was a story easily swallowed by Captain Youree McBride of the *Queen Mary II*, and made more palatable by Tom's deliberate reference to the captain's beloved US Navy, and his own dramatic arrival in a Bell UH-1 Iroquois helicopter, familiar to McBride from his navy days as a "Huey."

Tom's descent onto Deck 13, the highest on the ship, was less than impressive, however. Despite being made of steel, the upper decks were not built to cope with the stress of helicopter landings and take-offs, something the pilot informed his passenger a little too late in the proceedings, as far as Tom was concerned. Fortunately, the ship's flight deck officer was there to guide his visitor's feet to the floor and unhook the cable that had dropped the twisting and cursing visitor from the Huey.

"Keep your head down, sir," the officer shouted, "and follow me."

Free from his tether, Tom ducked beneath the downdraft of the rotors, glancing up as he felt the pressure ease to see the winking lights on the belly of the chopper disappearing into the night sky. He stumbled and decided to pay attention to where he was going, looking for the line his host was taking. Just ahead, a crew member manned a heavy metal door and swung it open for them. Inside, the hulking officer turned and shook Tom's hand.

"Welcome to the *Queen Mary II*, sir, I'm Staff Captain Lawrence Nicoletti. People say I don't look like a Lawrence, though, so just call me Nick." An American, which surprised Tom.

"Thanks, Nick. Tom Green."

"Yes, sir. I'll take you to Captain McBride, he's a little curious as to why you're here."

"Don't get too many late-night visitors coming in by helicopter?"

"Not too many, sir. This way."

Captain McBride worked out. A lot. That was the first thing Tom thought when he saw the man, his white shirt crisp against a broad chest and tucked in around a waist Tom had owned in his teens. A firm handshake emphasized the man's physique, and his buzz cut and square jaw screamed *marine*. British Royal Marine, in this case. On the flight over, Tom had taken the time to read the man's bio, learning that McBride was born in the small northern city of Shreveport and spent more than thirteen years in the navy's Fleet Protection Group before leaving the military. Oddly, he'd tried his hand at acting, landing roles in London as Peter Pan before returning to the sea. He'd joined Cunard Cruise Line, working his way up the ranks in the organization. He was impressive in more ways than just physical, with intelligent, watchful eyes, and a calm demeanor that came from years of facing crises at sea and dealing with them. After the handshake and name-swap, McBride waited for Tom to explain his presence on the ship.

"One of your passengers may need a friend," Tom started. He handed the captain his credentials, the ones for today anyway, that put him in military intelligence. It was an in-joke in the Company that the only time you used CIA credentials was to get into one of their buildings for a staff meeting. In the field, you either acted like a civilian or had some fake identification related to your mission. Tom had a box full to choose from, and this had fit perfectly.

"Yes, sir," McBride said. He took his time looking at the name, photograph, and seal on the ID card. "Mind if I ask a couple of questions, sir? I have a boat full of passengers I'm responsible for."

"Ask away, and I'll answer if I can."

"Very good, sir. Can you tell me who this person is?"

"His name is Lake."

"Who is he?" McBride asked. "Is there someone out to hurt him?"

Tom ignored the first question. "Ah, you want to know if there's a maniac or terrorist on the ship who might be here to hurt other people, am I right?"

"Correct."

"Not that I'm aware of." Tom held up a hand as Captain McBride furrowed his brow. "Look, I'm acting on pieces of information, I don't have the full picture myself." *Thanks to fucking Hugo,* Tom thought. "My understanding is, there's only one person at risk. You have the passenger manifest?"

"Yes, sir, I pulled it up on my computer."

Tom stood behind the captain who perched on a high seat and adjusted the screen of his laptop. The truth was, Tom didn't know what to tell this man. Going into a life-and-death situation was not unusual for Tom, and going into it with minimal information was common enough. What chapped his hide, though he'd not admit it, was that Hugo almost certainly knew exactly what was going on and declined to share. There was, quite simply, no more irritating man on the planet than Hugo Marston, particularly when the shit was starting to fly and you only had seconds to decide which way to dive for cover. Where Tom would inevitably dive head-first into a pile of deeper shit, Hugo always managed to find safety and come out smelling like roses. And the most irritating thing of all was that it wasn't luck, it was the cool head Hugo kept no matter what, and the big fucking brain that kept ticking away inside that cool head every moment the man was awake.

Tom knew that his own brain was pretty efficient in a crunch, and the truth was that Hugo had been one of the first guys he'd known to keep up with him on that score. And Tom was fine with having an intellectual equal. What he wasn't fine with was the fact that this particular equal looked like Cary Grant and acted like James Bond, but didn't know how to be anything but modest. Very fucking annoying, and a complete waste of chick magnetism, as far as Tom was concerned.

And here he was, the chubby wingman swooping onto the deck of the fanciest ship in the world on the say-so of a dude who wouldn't tell him the whole story. Here, in the dark and dangerous sea with fake credentials in his pocket and making shit up to save a man's life. Maybe.

"Last name, Lake," Tom said, "first name, Charles."

McBride directed the cursor to a search box in the top right corner of the screen and began to type. "Charles. Lake." He twisted in his seat. "Wait, this isn't *the* Charles Lake? The politician?"

"I was hoping you wouldn't notice."

"I'm smart like that, it's why they made me the captain." He smiled and looked back at the computer. "Balcony stateroom, number 4081. Last-minute reservation."

"Rooms like that are available last-minute?" Tom asked.

"Sometimes, but usually not. I imagine he just got lucky. He certainly didn't tell anyone who he was when he called, even though that can sometimes help."

"How do you know?"

"Trust me, if a Yank senator was on board several people would have taken the trouble to tell me. And cruise liner captains, me included, get a list of, shall we say, notable people on board. Writers, actors, politicians, sports stars. He'd definitely qualify and would be receiving an invitation to dine at the captain's table, at least one night and probably two."

"Makes sense."

"Which makes me wonder why he's playing it so low-key."

"I'll ask him and let you know."

"I'd prefer to escort you down there. I've seen your credentials and don't doubt your intentions, but he's my passenger and I could probably hold you up for hours arguing about jurisdiction." The captain's tone was friendly, but Tom knew he meant every word.

"I probably don't have any," Tom said. "I rarely do. I also don't have very much time so if you insist, then come with me. But just you. I don't want a cavalcade of civilians thumping down the hallway letting everyone and their granny know we're coming."

"Just me is fine. And maybe on the way down you can explain a little more about what's going on."

They walked, Tom on the shoulder of the big captain who led him out of the bridge and along a succession of short hallways to an elevator. "I appreciate the cooperation, captain. Are you armed?"

"Do I need to be?" Captain McBride pressed the down button.

"Nope." Tom smiled innocently. "I am, so we're golden."

"Yeah, had a row with my superiors over that. They told me you would be and I'm not wild about the idea of an American whatever-you-are carrying a gun on my ship."

"I'm not planning to use it, don't worry. My mouth is bigger than my gun, and usually better at getting people to surrender."

"Wait, are you here to protect Lake or arrest him?"

"Precisely," Tom said. He checked his phone but saw no message. *Fucking Hugo.*

"Cell phones don't usually work out here, if you're getting your instructions that way. Intermittent at best."

"Great. Then we'll keep making it up as we go along."

They entered the elevator and stood in silence, and when the doors reopened Captain McBride led the way. The hallway that serviced Lake's room was as long as any that Tom had seen, stretching out for what seems like a hundred meters either side of him.

"We're close," Tom said, eying the door numbers.

"Very."

"Describe the room to me."

"Narrow. The premium balcony staterooms, which this is, have a panoramic hull balcony with chairs and tables, a king-size bed, and a compact bathroom. That'll be on the right as we go in."

"As I go in," Tom corrected. "If you don't mind, captain, hang here a moment. You'll have a good view of any fun and games."

"He may not be in there." McBride handed Tom the card key.

"I know, but I don't want your people hunting high and low, letting him know we're looking for him. Not yet."

Tom paused in front of the door to cabin 4081 and knocked. He stood to one side so Lake couldn't spot him through the peephole. He knocked a second time, louder, and waited another ten seconds before slipping the key card into the door slot and letting himself in.

A quick glance told Tom that Lake wasn't in the room itself, and he cleared the bathroom in three seconds. But the sliding door to the small balcony was closed, as was its curtain. Tom put his hand inside his jacket and hesitated. He considered applying Hugo's scruples to the situation but rejected the idea and pulled his gun. A quick glance over his shoulder to make sure no one was in the corridor, then Tom moved slowly forward. He passed along the foot of the bed, and his stomach tightened as movement from the balcony caught his eye. He took four quick steps to the sliding door and pulled it open, stepping out onto the metal deck with both hands training the gun at the flash of white he'd seen from inside.

The balcony was empty, except for the furniture and a white towel that lay over the back of a chair, its corners flipping up at him as the sea breeze ran over the balustrade and swirled in the little space. Tom reached over and touched the cotton, damp from the wind and spray, but otherwise clean. He looked out toward the ocean, but saw nothing but blackness. The sea and sky had joined at some invisible horizon and the dark of the night seemed to seep over the metal guardrail toward him, surround the steel hull of the ship, and make its bulk brittle and weak. He shivered and took one more look at the two empty chairs and the lone table, small, round, and white, and as bare as the rest of the balcony. Or as Hugo would say in this context, "Silent."

He walked back through the cabin and put his head out of the door. "Captain. You can have your crew look for him now, if you don't mind."

"Will do. And if they find him?"

"Have someone chat him up until I get there. Don't get handsy with him though, no need for that."

"Got it." Captain McBride lifted his radio to his lips and gave specific instructions, then turned back to Tom. "That was the control room, our communications center. Most crew members will have a radio, and depending on their job it'll be tuned to a certain channel. The control room will make sure the message is put out to each channel so that every employee on my ship will know to keep an eye out for the senator."

"Thanks. I'm going to poke around in here for a bit, if you don't mind hanging out with me in case he comes back."

"Happy to. Looking for anything in particular?"

"Nope."

The room was immaculate, the bed made and the senator's clothes stashed neatly in the drawers and closet. His toothpaste, toothbrush, and shaving kit was laid out in the bathroom and his empty toiletries bag hung on a hook beside the bathroom door.

Tom took out his phone and tried calling Hugo. He wanted to check in, and hopefully he could get more information, like a clue as to what he should be looking for. The signal faded once but came back strong the second time, and his friend picked up on the third ring.

"Hey, Tom, I've been trying to get through. You're on board?"

"Yep. In his room, as a matter of fact."

"Not there, I'm guessing."

"Correct. I'm going to have a poke around but I'd appreciate some idea about what to look for."

"Sure. Anything that connects him to Alexie Tourville, for one. Also, and I know this will sound weird, but anything that has to do with Marie Antoinette or her son."

"Seriously? Like a guillotine, or a piece of cake?"

"I'm not kidding. Something that would fit inside a sailor's chest."

"Guillotine's out then. I'll look for cake."

"Tom."

"What? Look, tell me what the fuck's going on and maybe I can expand my search parameters."

"Alexandra Tourville was blackmailing Lake over his past. His ancestors. I think the man himself is a descendant of Marie Antoinette, through her son. Anyway, he decided that instead of paying, he'd kill her."

"Jesus, are you sure?"

"I found her body, so I'm sure about that part of it. And the rest, too."

"She's dead, huh?" Tom whistled through his teeth. "And that's some theory."

"Yep. Now I need the evidence to back it up, which is where you come in."

"OK, I'll see what I can find." Tom paused. "Lake didn't kill Raul, did he?"

"No, that was Alexie Tourville trying to cover her tracks."

"And he killed her?"

"Yes."

"Then maybe he deserves a fucking medal."

"Maybe, Tom, maybe. But that's not our call, is it?"

"Never is." Tom looked up as Captain McBride appeared in the doorway and jerked his thumb toward the hallway. "Gotta go, looks like our dear senator came home."

Tom hung up and saw the captain stand to attention in front of the cabin door. The angry voice of United States Senator Charles Lake barreled down the hallway.

"Who the hell are you, and what the hell are you doing in my room?"

Tom stepped out, next to Captain McBride. "Hello, Chuck. I think we need to talk."

CHAPTER THIRTY-SEVEN

Charles Lake brushed past Tom into the cabin and looked around. His eyes settled on his briefcase, which lay unopened on the small desk near the balcony door. He started to move toward it.

"Please don't, Senator," Tom said.

"Don't what?" Lake paused. "This is my cabin and I'll do as I damn well please."

"I just want to talk for a moment." Tom tried the friendly route. "Sit on the bed for me, would you?"

Lake didn't move but Tom saw a tiredness in his face he'd not noticed before, a weariness that showed in wrinkles at the corners of his eyes and a slump in his shoulders. On the left side of his neck, a dark red streak about three inches long hid behind his collar. "Who are you? I mean, who do you work for?"

"All kinds of people. CIA, FBI, the Mormon Church..." Tom shrugged.

Lake's eyes narrowed. "The Mormon—"

"I'm joking. About the last one, anyway." Tom checked over his shoulder and saw Captain McBride standing in the doorway, seemingly entranced. "Seriously, sit down. Let's talk."

Lake sank on to the bed, his eyes on Tom and still wary. "About what?"

"Alexandra Tourville."

Lake's eyes flicked toward the desk again, then back to Tom. "So talk."

"She's dead." Lake didn't respond, so Tom went on. "Our mutual friend Hugo thinks she killed the old lady at the Bassin place, then her own friend Natalia, and then my friend Raul Garcia."

"The policeman."

"That's the one."

"I don't know anything about that."

"Well, that may be the case." Tom nodded slowly. He turned and looked at Captain McBride. "Would you give us a moment?"

The captain started. "A moment? You mean . . . is that proper?"

"Ah, you English." Tom smiled. "Yes, it's proper. Two people having a chat in a cabin. It's just that part of the chat needs to be in private."

"But if he's a suspect in some kind of crime, shouldn't any interview be witnessed? I mean, that's how we do things in England and I assume—"

"We're not in England, captain. This is two Americans having a nice talk in international waters. We're in international waters by now, aren't we?"

"Even so, this is my ship and I'm not comfortable with—"

"With what? We're not going to fight, for fuck's sake. We're going to talk, and if it makes you feel better," Tom reached into his pocket and pulled out his phone, flicking at the screen and showing it to McBride, "there you go, I'll record our conversation, how's that? I'm even recording me telling you I'll record it."

The captain took a step back, then hesitated. "I'm going to head upstairs, make a few phone calls. If someone up the chain of command tells me this is improper, I'll be back down. And probably not alone."

"Perfect," Tom said. "I don't want anyone getting in trouble with the chain of command."

"That makes two of us," McBride said. He stepped out of the cabin and pulled the door closed behind him.

For the first time in years, Tom was unsure what to do. According to Hugo, he was alone in a room with a killer. He was also alone in a room with a US Senator, and a man who had realistic ambitions for even higher office. There was no script for this situation, no training exercise welling up from his CIA or FBI days telling him what to do next. His experience in the field, undercover and in the uniform black suit and sunglasses of those agencies, had left him unprepared. Tom was old-fashioned in that he liked his bad guys obvious and identifiable, he liked a clear red line between them and him, and the idea that Hugo could be wrong tugged at him like an invisible specter.

Tom held up his phone to reassure, or maybe remind, the senator that their conversation would be recorded, and moved to the desk. He laid the phone beside the briefcase, careful not to touch it. Then, not having a plan or even a full grasp of the facts, Tom resorted to doing what he did best. He talked.

"Beautiful ship. You know, I've never been on a cruise before. Though is this a cruise or a journey? Seems like cruises are for old couples in flowery shirts who drink too much and like to island-hop in the Caribbean." Tom paused but Lake just stared at the carpet between them. "Anyway, I was hoping you'd want to tell me what's been going on."

"I don't know what you mean."

"No? How'd you get that scratch on your neck?"

"No idea." His tone was flat, final.

"Then let's move on to the sudden disappearances in Paris. Or if you prefer, why you're here on this ship."

"I don't like flying. No sin in that."

"Yeah, true, but it was a bit of a rush to get here, wasn't it?"

"I decided last-minute, after the talks fell through. Seemed like it'd be a relaxing way to get home, even if it meant hurrying to get here."

"I'm sure it is. Don't like flying, myself, not much." Tom looked around the cabin. "I can see how this'd be preferable. Although we both had to fly to get here, which is kinda weird."

"Please," Lake said. "It's late and I'm tired. Just tell me what you want and go."

"Sure." Tom leaned casually against the wall, his pose matching his tone. "We can be honest with each other, right?"

Lake nodded but said nothing.

"See, you know Hugo Marston. He's a smart guy. Super smart. Pisses me off sometimes and he has this really fucking annoying habit of not telling me stuff, making me guess and wallow around in the dark like a blind pig in mud. He does that a lot, and it's only when he's absolutely sure of something that he tells me. Like I said, it's annoying, but there is an upside."

"Oh?" Lake seemed like he was paying attention now but struggling to follow along.

"Right. The upside is, when he tells me something, the odds are he's right. Which kinda makes sense, when you think about it. I mean, if he made me wait and was wrong every time, that'd be pretty dumb. Anyway, he made me wallow around on this case, right up until a few minutes ago."

"Is that right?" Now, Tom thought, the senator was pretending not to care, but there was a tension in the man's throat that suggested otherwise.

"Yeah, it is. Couple minutes ago he told me that you killed Alexandra Tourville. And I figured, you know, he made me wait, so it's gotta be true."

"Ridiculous." Lake finally held Tom's eye. "Why would I do that?"

"I'm not sure, not yet. Hugo said something about your ancestry. Marie Antoinette or some shit." Tom waved a hand. "I didn't get all the details, to be honest."

"That's insane." But the firmness had gone from his voice, as if the discovery of a motive was more powerful than any piece of physical evidence, a reason for murder more revealing than his prints on a bloody knife or smoking gun. "I would never kill anyone, not . . . premeditated, not unless provoked."

"Maybe." Tom looked down and to his left, at the briefcase. "That locked?"

"Yes." Lake looked up. "But please don't. You need a warrant, right?"

"Not if you give me permission. It's called a consent search, and I'm thinking there's something pretty damning in there."

"Damning? I'm already damned. You're going to see to that, aren't you?"

"I'm just trying to find the truth," Tom said. He hesitated, but then said what he was thinking. "And part of the truth, Senator, is that if you killed Alexandra Tourville, and if Hugo's right that she killed Raul Garcia, you deserve a fucking medal."

Lake smiled thinly. "They don't give medals to murderers," he said.

"Sometimes they do. But yeah, probably not in your case." Tom tapped the briefcase. "So I have your permission to look inside?"

"No. In fact, I think you need to leave and that I should speak to a lawyer before I talk to you or anyone else."

Tom sighed. "OK then. That's your right, of course, though fuck knows where we'll find a lawyer in the middle of the ocean. I mean, there's probably a stack of them on board, but in my experience the guys who do criminal defense don't make too much money. They're the ones crammed into coach class, assuming they can afford to fly at all. The attorneys on board this tub, I'm betting they can tell you a thing or two about oil and gas law or how to sue someone for trademark infringement, but not so much on criminal law."

"I can wait until we get back to America."

"America?" Tom amped up the surprise in his voice. "Oh, no, Senator. If you want to take a look outside, maybe look behind as best you can, you're going to see a nice wake bubbling in the moonlight. Be all romantic if, you know, you hadn't killed someone."

Lake's voice sharpened. "We're turning?"

"Sure are, and we're headed for Brest." Tom smiled. "And not the good kind, no, the kind that has a harbor on the northwestern tip of France, where good Captain McBride will weigh anchor and the French police will send a boat out to pick us up and take you to a jail cell. That kind of Brest."

Color drained from Lake's face and his jaw dropped open. "No. No, not that."

"Yeah, I can see why that'd suck for you. I mean, all those things you said about the French and now you're going to be . . . I mean an American prison would be bad enough, but a French one?"

"No, please, we have to go back to America. Arrest me there, give me a chance to ... if I have to go to jail at all, there. Please, be reasonable."

"What do you expect? You killed a French chick on French soil." Tom shrugged. "Also not my call. Look on the bright side, you've got to think the food will be better. Finally, a stereotype that might work in your favor."

"But immunity. I have diplomatic immunity!"

"I thought so, too, but apparently your mission was over when you throttled dear Alexie to death, which means you were on your own time, as it were. Funny how these things work, isn't it?"

The life went out of the senator and he folded almost in half, his head sinking to his knees and his hands wrapped in desperation around his head. "I can't go to prison," he whispered. "I can't, I just can't."

Tom was quiet for a moment, and when he spoke his voice was gentle. "You know, there is one possibility. One other option we could discuss."

CHAPTER THIRTY-EIGHT

Hugo and Lieutenant Lerens had made the drive back to Paris as part of a small convoy of cars that included the medical examiner's van containing the body of Alexandra Tourville. Earlier, Lerens had requested Dr. Alain Joust attend, and the ME had set off from his apartment in the Fifteenth Arrondissement immediately, not minding being dragged out of bed to drive almost an hour down here.

"Even if it's night, I do like to get out of the city occasionally," he'd said as he hefted his bag of tools to the trunk of the little black car. "And so much more interesting than the usual gang stabbings and beatings."

"Yep," Lerens said, "this one's classy all the way."

"Well then, let's have a look at her."

Blunt force trauma and/or strangulation had been Dr. Joust's initial opinion. "Usual disclaimers, of course, it could change once she's on the table. But my best guess right now is that she made someone very, very angry."

Joust had promised to get to work right away, so Hugo and Lerens waited in her office at the prefecture. He'd spoken to Tom on the way back into Paris, interrupted when Lake returned to his cabin, and Hugo now thought about calling him back. But he figured Tom would ring once he had something, or once he'd searched and found nothing.

In the meantime, he called his second-in-command at the RSO's office, knowing he'd be home and wanting to help. Ryan Pierce had joined the Bureau of Diplomatic Security straight out of Tulane Law School, where he'd graduated at the top of his class. He was an athlete, too, the starting pitcher for Louisiana State University. He was from Bossier City, Louisiana, and had the southern accent to go with it, as well as a love for catfish and gambling. But he was also one of the nicest and brightest men Hugo had ever worked with. He answered his phone almost immediately, and in the background Hugo could hear children shouting.

"Ryan, it's Hugo."

"Hey boss. Need me to come into the office? Please?"

Hugo laughed. "Nope. I need some help but you can take care of it from home, I think. Once you've brokered peace between your kids."

"That'll never happen." Ryan had two boys and a girl, all high-energy and loud. "What do you need?"

"Two things. First, check with TSA and see when Alexandra Tourville last visited the States."

"Easy. Next."

"Hang on." Hugo stood and excused himself from Lerens's office, smiling enigmatically at her quizzical look. He closed her door before speaking again. "I'm back. And this one you might want to do in private, out of earshot of your wife."

"Oh really? Top secret?"

"Not in the slightest." Hugo chuckled again. "Come to think of it, delete your internet history once you're done, too."

"Why?"

After Hugo had ensured Ryan knew what to do, he sat back and waited with Lerens for Tom to call. They chatted amiably, Hugo with a million questions he didn't dare ask. Over a carafe of wine, maybe, where he knew she wouldn't mind, but they wouldn't have been appropriate in her office. Instead they swapped war stories and Lerens was recounting the first time she arrested someone, a well-known Bordeaux vintner who was driving drunk, when Hugo's phone rang. They both looked at the display and saw it light up with Tom's name. Hugo answered and put him on speaker.

"Hey Tom, I'm with Camille, what news?"

"You go first."

"Nothing much. Tourville was either beaten to death or strangled. Maybe a little of both. The ME's doing an autopsy right now to make sure. He took swabs from her neck and face at the scene so we may have DNA to match with Lake."

"DNA. There's an irony," Lerens said.

"Why's that an irony?" Tom asked. "You fuckers better fill me in when I get back."

"We will," Hugo assured him. "You have Lake?"

"Senator Lake, you mean? Senator Charles Lake?"

"Tom."

"Why's it only you who gets to withhold information? It's not fair."

"Don't you remember your mommy telling you life isn't?"

"You as my mom, that's about right."

"It's worse for me than you," Hugo said. "Now answer the damn question and tell me Lake's in custody."

"I always wondered if these fancy ships had jails. You know, just in case."

"On a ship, they're called *brigs*," Hugo said. "And I'm hoping the *Queen Mary's* is occupied by a US senator."

The line went quiet for a moment, then Tom's voice came on. "Gonna have to disappoint you there."

"Tom, explain. Where are you?"

"I'm in Lake's cabin. Hold on a sec, the captain just came back. Need to tell him something."

Hugo shook his head and smiled at Lerens, who stared wide-eyed at the phone, her palms facing up and disbelief on her face. "What's he playing at?" she asked.

"Have patience. I have a sneaking suspicion things haven't gone to plan and he's stalling for some reason."

"You think Lake's persuaded him he's innocent?"

"Maybe. I doubt it, though."

Tom came back online. "Sorry about that. Now then, where were we?"

"Senator Charles Lake," Hugo said. "You were about to stop being an ass and tell us what the situation is there."

"The situation, yes. Well, that can be described quickly and easily. In two words, as a matter of fact."

Hugo felt a rock sinking in his chest. "What two words, Tom?"

"Man overboard."

Hugo and Lieutenant Lerens exchanged glances.

"Tell me you're joking," Hugo said.

"Nope."

"He was right there with you, Tom, what the hell happened?"

"Well, we were talking for a while. You know, me asking questions, him not really answering them."

"Jeez, Tom, tell me you didn't . . ." Hugo didn't believe Tom would harm the senator, but his methods had always been off the grid.

"No, no. Don't worry your pretty little head about that. I don't kill US senators, Hugo, that would be insane. Not without written authorization, anyway, and who had time for that?"

"So what happened?"

"Hang on, I was going to ask how you knew he'd be on the boat."

"Lerens told me, but also something he said at that first formal dinner. He hated flying and had this romantic view of sea travel. Even dying at sea had romantic undertones for him. I'm sure he needed some time to think, to figure out what to do, and taking the *Queen Mary* fits his inclinations and his mindset perfectly."

"Shit, Hugo, you guessed he'd kill himself, didn't you? That's why you said it was a matter of life and death. His life and death."

"Is that what happened?"

"Well, I didn't throw him overboard."

"He jumped?"

"Flying leap, actually."

"Are they looking for him?"

"Yeah. I gave him a few minutes in the drink, had a poke around his cabin, then let the captain know. They dropped some boats to look but I can't imagine they'll find him."

"Why on earth did you wait?"

"Dude, he wanted to go out with a splash. Sorry, didn't mean . . .
Anyway, he chose his exit and how frickin' embarrassing for the guy
if he makes this grand final gesture and we drag him out of the ocean
soaking wet and gasping for air like a half-drowned kitten. Only for
him to be slapped in the brig and taken back to France. And let me tell
you, a French prison was absolutely the last thing that man wanted."

"I can see why," Lerens said drily.

"Precisely. And that's why," Tom went on, "if you're about to ask,
I didn't try very hard to stop him. In his shoes I would have done the
same. That and he's a big dude, I didn't want to be hanging onto his legs
as he went over the balcony else I would have gone too. No thanks."

"So he admitted to killing Alexie Tourville?"

"Oh yes, he most certainly did. Wouldn't tell me why, though. Just
sat there saying mean things about her."

"Did you record your conversation with him?"

A slight pause. "Well, there's the thing. I thought I had, using my
phone. Turns out none of it recorded."

"That's not good, Tom. Not good at all."

"It makes no fucking difference to anything, as it happens. He sat
on the bed, cried, confessed, jumped off the balcony."

"OK, fine." Hugo rubbed his forehead, trying to think through the
fog of tiredness. "Did you call anyone else?"

"No, sweetie, I always call you first. I expect the captain panicked
and phoned everyone up his chain of command, so you might want to
check the newspapers in a few minutes."

"Great. When we're done, will you call the ambassador? We should
tell him as soon as possible. There's going to be a media shitstorm and
he'll appreciate a few minutes to pull on a coat and open his umbrella."

"Nice image. I sure will."

"Thanks. Hey, you said you'd searched the place. Before or after he
jumped?"

"Well, I didn't have time before he showed up and he wasn't wild
about me poking through his stuff. He has this briefcase, he kept it
locked and seemed very protective of it."

"You looked inside?"

"Hugo, really? Are you serious? I mean to say, a representative of the people of our great nation tragically takes his own life in front of me, and you think I'm breaking the locks of his most personal and private possessions—"

"Knock it off, Tom, what was in there?"

"Hey, come on. What was in there will blow your socks off. In fact, if it's what I think it is, it'll make historians do strange things to each other before ending up on display in some museum in Paris."

"And that gives you the right to torture me a little?"

"Yes, and here's why. If you'd been here instead of me, you would have jumped on Lake and wrapped him up tight, stopped him from taking a leap from the ship. Then you would have catalogued and inventoried his belongings and waited for a search warrant or court order to open his briefcase. Which, by the way, would then have been in the custody of the French police or subject to an ever-lasting international dispute over jurisdiction. The briefcase would have sat in a large plastic bag, in a locked storage facility, and we'd spend the next two years wandering around guessing at why all this shit went down."

"Are you done?"

"No. Now, instead of that nightmare taking place, I am able to decisively solve this bizarre crime and have the paperwork to back me up."

"Paperwork? What's that supposed to mean?"

"OK, now I'm done. And yes, paperwork, because the only significant thing I found in his briefcase was a letter. A letter that was written in 1795."

CHAPTER THIRTY-NINE

C her Monsieur,
I hope this dispatch finds you in good health and, please, do forgive
me for dispensing with further formalities but time presses in on me and
I have come to think that perhaps more than one life depends on your
receipt of, and trust in, my words. One life, for certain.

I know that you left our shores perturbed by the bloodshed. More
than perturbed, perhaps. You are not alone there, of course. But it has
become increasingly clear to many here that we need the support and
cooperation of your nation as we rebuild. You can be a model for us, and
a source of very real sustenance and this is why many who now hold
power here fear that you will cut all ties.

This letter, and the small box that comes with it, are gestures of
good faith, ones that I hope you will take as proof that the bloodshed is
ended.

You know of the young man to whom the hair belongs. He is a
symbol for us because he has survived the killing and I hope that he
is now a symbol to you, of our dedication to restore France to the civi-
lized and respected nation you love. I cannot go into detail, for obvious
reasons, but through friends we managed to take him safely from the
temple and send him to the countryside to live with a loyal family. They
even have a son of their own, he is the same age, so perhaps a friend.

The sad news, though, is that he was not treated well in the temple and has been very ill. The young man looking after him has promised that he will travel to your shores with his family, and bring his new charge, as soon as he is well enough. For now, then, a chest containing his clothes, this letter, and a lock of his hair are all I can offer. And my promise. For these items come with a promise that he, a symbol of the old France you wanted to see changed, will live on and his life spared will be a symbol of the new France, one that has moved past violent times toward a new start, and a new partnership with your own young and great nation.

This promise, mon cher Thomas, is made with my own blood.

Your friend,
Albert Pichon

CHAPTER FORTY

Lerens's voice was barely a whisper. "The Dauphin. He's talking about the son of Marie Antoinette."

Tom had photographed the letter and sent it to their phones and they sat in Camille Lerens's office reading and rereading it.

"The letter, it was in the chest with the hair. That's the missing piece we were looking for." Hugo shook his head in wonder.

"*Merde*. The Lost Prince," Lerens said. "The Dauphin's death has always been a mystery."

"Apparently a myth. He was locked away and official records said he died in the Temple prison in Paris in 1795, when he was ten. Tuberculosis, apparently, which was rampant back then, but a lot of people refused to believe the official version. They said he didn't die at all, but was spirited away to safety and another child put in his place." Hugo smiled. "Don't look at me like that, I flicked through a book about her and King Louis just last week. Guess where?"

"Don't tell me it was while you were at Chateau Tourville."

"Good guess." They acknowledged the significance with a shared look. "Anyway," Hugo said, "I remember reading that a doctor assigned to treat him died under strange circumstances the week before the Dauphin's alleged death, and the doctor's widow said that he'd refused to take part in some irregular practice to do with the patient."

"Over the years several people have claimed to be descended from him, but no one's had any proof. Until now."

273

"Right," said Hugo. "This Pichon, he was planning to smuggle the Dauphin to America as a show of good faith, a royal life spared. He mentions the Temple, he's referring to the tower of the Temple, the prison where Louis Charles was held until his supposed death. And remember, Marie Bassin, she told me her mother had mentioned the name Louis in connection with the chest. It must have been some kind of family story, a legend that seemed too outrageous to be true. One that even the Bassin family didn't take seriously."

"Hugo, this is . . . *incroyable.*"

"It is. Truly history."

"Who is the letter being sent to? He says, *mon cher* Thomas, but who would that be?"

Hugo smiled. "That's what makes this so remarkable. It was sent to the man who was the US minister to France from 1785 to 1789, the year the French Revolution started. That man was Thomas Jefferson."

Lerens shook her head and let out a low whistle.

"If I remember my history correctly," Hugo continued, "Jefferson was pretty much in favor of the French Revolution. He was hoping for a democracy to spring up but he got sick of the executions, he felt like people were being massacred for no reason. Or not good enough reason. Anyway, he left with a very sour taste in his mouth. You can see that from Pichon's words."

"Saving the Dauphin, sending him to America . . ."

"A show of good faith, indeed."

"And the family he was supposed to go with?"

"The Bassins. I think he was spirited away to that house, the same one we visited."

"*Alors*, wait a moment," Lerens said, sitting forward. "Did you say they left that place, and sailed via Marseilles to America?"

"With one child."

"The letter," Lerens furrowed her brow. "It said . . . there should have been two sons on board."

"Yeah. And we know from all this craziness that the Dauphin made it there. I can only think that the Bassins' real son died. When that happened, I don't know, maybe they decided to change the plan and keep Louis Charles as their own. That would explain the sudden move away from their home, the name changes, and the fact that Louis Charles was never known to have come to America."

"Because he came as the Bassins' son, not as the deposed King of France."

"Right." Hugo's mind was racing, imagining the death of the young Bassin boy. "You know, Camille, and I don't know if you'd want to do this but . . ." He trailed off.

"What, Hugo?"

"If we're right that the Bassins' son died. Well, they couldn't tell anyone. They had to keep it a secret, right?"

"Of course. Otherwise the switch with Louis Charles couldn't have worked."

"Which means that . . ." Hugo sighed. "I think it's likely the little boy was probably buried by his parents somewhere on the Bassin property. And all this stayed a secret, Camille, which means his grave is still there."

CHAPTER FORTY-ONE

They assembled on the lawn behind the Bassins' rambling house, forced to wait until Sunday morning because that was the soonest Georges Bassin could be there. Hugo had worried that their purpose might upset the church-attending Georges, but the old man had shaken his head and said no.

"It may be a little gruesome," Georges said, "but it's necessary. And it strikes me that given what we're doing, well, it's perhaps appropriate to do it on the Lord's day."

He'd consulted his sister Marie as soon as Hugo had called him to explain the situation, and they'd agreed, and informed the investigators, that there was only one place on the property a grave could be. Most of the land had been leased for years to neighboring farmers, ploughed, planted, and harvested over and over for decades. The only untouched, unmolested spot on the Bassin's land was a stand of trees on the nub of a hill, half a mile from the house and at the intersection of three ancient footpaths. A stand of trees taking up a few thousand square feet, no more than that, and as far as George and Marie knew, pretty much untouched since the day their family moved in.

Hugo stood with Georges on the lawn, looking over the open field toward the copse. They stood beside a bed of rose bushes, bare now and clipped, made ready for winter by the gardeners who tended them.

"I bet this garden is something in the spring and summer," Hugo said.

"*Certainement.* I hope you'll come back and see for yourself. The scent is sublime, and that little circle of grass in the middle has been a picnic spot for the Bassin children forever."

"The rose garden's been here a long time?"

"Long before I was born. It's always been the pride and joy of our family's matriarchs, and now that Marie plans to move in, I'm sure she'll keep it that way."

A grumble of engines caught their attention, and they looked toward the driveway where a truck was coming to a stop with a backhoe in its trailer bed. Tom, Marie Bassin, and Camille Lerens looked as a tall woman climbed down from the cab of the truck.

Jennifer Winkler was the prefecture's leading forensic anthropologist, someone who'd worked with both Lerens and Raul Garcia in the past. Rail thin, she stalked toward them in khaki pants and matching jacket, a blue police cap on her head. She'd spent two days in the copse before summoning the investigators to brief them. And by briefing them here, Hugo assumed she'd found something.

"*Bonjour,*" she said, as her audience closed in around her. "I'm Jennifer Winkler, as most of you know. I need to tell you what I've been doing and what I've found. Just don't get your hopes up too high just yet, *d'accord?*"

Hugo and several of the others nodded, waiting for her to continue.

"You asked me to find a grave two hundred years old. There are a number of techniques I use to try to locate a burial that old. The first is ground penetrating radar, or GPR, but the results are often inconclusive or full of false positives." She looked at Hugo. "The FBI doesn't even use this technique any more, that's how unreliable it is. I did use it here, only because the search area is small and therefore we can tolerate a few false positives. Now, another method is simply to walk the area and see if there are any signs on the ground surface."

"For a burial that old?" Georges Bassin asked.

"Seems strange, but yes. The soil will settle over time and there can be a slight depression visible to a trained eye." She shrugged. "Actually, you can see it yourself if you walk through a cemetery, just look for the depressions that often show up in front of the headstones. Of course, it's harder here because there's a lot of debris on the ground, sticks, branches, leaf litter. But with a small search area you just need to clear the area to see the ground surface. Questions?"

"Yes," said Lerens with a smile. "Did you find something?"

"I'm getting there," Winkler said. "The last method is to use a backhoe. We refer to it as 'the forensic backhoe.' Forensic anthropology joke, there. Anyway, we use that to slowly remove the soil, like they do at an archeological dig. We usually start by removing maybe six inches to a foot from the search area. It sounds clumsy, but a skilled backhoe driver can remove an inch of soil at a time if need be. Once the upper layers of soils are gone, that's when the fun begins. That's when you can sometimes see the burial shaft."

"I don't understand," said Georges Bassin. "Isn't there just more soil there?"

"Yes, of course, but the soil within the burial will be a different color and have a slightly different texture than the undisturbed surrounding soil. That difference may be very subtle, especially after so much time, but it will be there. As long as the area hasn't been disturbed since the coffin was buried, of course."

"What would be left of the coffin, or skeleton?" Hugo asked.

"Out here, and after two hundred years, the wood coffin will probably be gone."

"And the bones?" Hugo pressed.

"Whether or not bones survive depends on the soil type and water drainage in the area. If you have an area that frequently floods or an area where the water table fluctuates, the bone would disintegrate faster. If the climate is relatively dry and/or the soil has good drainage, the bones could still be in great condition, you would be able to pick them up and they won't fall apart in your hands. In fact, I've excavated burials that dated back to before Classical Greece—so around 550–500 BCE— and some were in great shape, while others turned to dust in your hands."

"The copse is pretty elevated," Georges Bassin said.

"It is," Winkler agreed. "So I think we might be in luck, assuming we can find the right spot."

"And the odds of that?" Lerens asked.

"Ah, yes. I apologize, I didn't mean to toy with your hopes," Winkler smiled. "But I think I already did. Shall we go dig?"

The procession behind the backhoe was slow and silent, but Hugo knew that everyone's nerves were keyed high. Finding a skeleton, a little boy's bones, would confirm his theory and add to the evidence supporting the idea that Alexandra Tourville had blackmailed Charles Lake.

But Hugo also knew that everyone in the group saw this mission as more than just a collecting of evidence. Rather, they were in search of a child abandoned to his grave by his parents, a mother and father who in simple terms had replaced him with the kidnapped heir to the throne of France.

As they started up the last rise to the stand of trees, Hugo looked over the fields and saw the lines of police officers holding back the throng of media. News trucks and reporters' cars filled every available lay-by and field entrance, the tiny bodies of reporters milling around each other looking for the best angle, the best shot toward the woods.

Jennifer Winkler led them into the trees on a grassy path just wide enough for the backhoe. Dr. Alain Joust and two evidence technicians were in attendance; they'd help Winkler photograph and preserve whatever they found for analysis back in Paris. Marie and Georges Bassin had already given DNA samples, eager to help identify their long-dead ancestor if at all possible.

The site was near the eastern edge of the trees, the place with the best view of the Bassin house and the surrounding countryside. Winkler had cleared the area by hand and the depression in the soil was plain for them all to see. They stood to one side as the backhoe operator took off a layer of dirt, peeling it away like a strip of bark from a tree. Winkler stood closest, supervising and directing the operator with hand signals, having him strip out another inch-deep layer, and then another. She held up her hand for him to wait, then knelt to study the soil.

"Look, you can see," she said to the group, who inched closer. "The soil here in the burial site is darker. Even after so much time, it's less compact than the lighter soil around it."

She stood and gestured for the operator to resume, and Hugo could see the concentration on his face as he took off more layers of soil, inch by inch. Winkler's eyes were glued to the ground, and as the bucket of the hoe dipped into and out of the hole she held her arms in a cross, telling him to stop altogether.

She knelt by the grave and waved the investigation team over. "Look closely, see how the soil is slightly lighter?" A soft mumble as that fact was acknowledged. She leant in closer. "And look here, see the very faint red lines in the dirt?"

"That can't be blood," George said, "surely not after—"

"No, no," Winkler said. "They must have used nails to hold the coffin together. I wondered if they'd still be here, and we might find some still. But what you're seeing here are stains in the soil were the nails resided after the coffin disintegrated.

She was, Hugo saw, a teacher as well as a technician, enjoying her work and appreciating a good audience. But now she went to work in silence, Hugo and the others drifting away to give her space. She spread a square blanket of canvas by the hole, to lie on and to collect evidence, Hugo assumed. She began working by hand, at first kneeling beside the hole and then lying on her belly before finally stepping gingerly inside, digging and scraping with a hand-trowel and some other tools Hugo couldn't name. She dug around like a surgeon, with gloved and careful hands, to find what she knew to be in there and Hugo continued to watch, fascinated. Beside him, though, Tom was getting antsy, and if he couldn't do anything physical then he wanted to talk.

"So you think Lake knew he was a Frenchman?" he asked Hugo, keeping his voice low, as if they were in church.

"I doubt it. He thought he had native American blood, and I suppose he may have. But the French thing, no, his reaction was too extreme."

"You mean, killing Alexie?"

"Right, killing Alexie. That makes me think it came as a shock, made him totally rethink who he was. Plus, if he'd known about his heritage I don't think he'd have been so anti-Europe. Of all the bad things you can say about Lake, I never really saw him as a hypocrite."

"Fair point."

"So you tell me something." Hugo watched his friend closely. "The *Queen Mary*'s captain told me you turned your voice recorder on, he saw you do it. Yet five minutes later, Lake confesses to everything and jumps from the ship. And somehow none of that is preserved."

"Ah, Hugo." Tom pursed his lips. "Everything that happened in that cabin, from his confession to his going overboard, all of that was his doing, one hundred percent voluntary."

"And that's all you can tell me?"

"Are you worried about his demise, or the state of my conscience?"

Hugo chuckled. "Well, let's just say I'm glad to hear you acknowledge a conscience."

Tom raised an eyebrow, then leaned in and lowered his voice to a whisper. "Fuck you, Marston. I'm a goddamn saint."

They both looked up as Winkler pushed herself to her knees and called out, "I have something!"

The investigators moved in closer and two of the evidence technicians joined them, one firing up his video camera to record the actual excavation. The other held a stack of paper bags into which the bones would go, the paper absorbing any moisture and preventing formation of mold or fungi.

It took two hours, but one by one the bones of a little boy came out of the soil and into the light. Hugo found the scene bizarre, like a funeral in reverse; awed and respectful watchers gathered around the lip of the child's grave, holding onto their emotions as his bones were freed from the muddy and anonymous hole that had held him in death as his fragile remains were raised from the dark and brought back into the light, into the land of the living. The last piece to come out caused Camille Lerens to utter a prayer and Tom to rest a hand on

Hugo's shoulder, the communion necessary to withstand the sight of a mud-encrusted skull lifted from the grave and placed like a holy relic on the canvas, where it sat looking at them in wide-eyed surprise before another set of gloved hands picked it up and gently placed it in a cardboard box.

Hugo, Tom, and Camille Lerens stopped on the way back to Paris at a restaurant that Tom had read about somewhere, an article declaring it world-beating for its champagne coq-au-vin.

"Don't worry," Tom said as they sat down, "the alcohol burns off in the pot."

"I'm not worried," Hugo said. "Just wondering which wine to order."

"Hey, go for it. Be a good test, and you can't go on martyring yourself forever."

"Just for that, I'll drink sparkling water."

"You hate sparkling water."

"That's what martyrs do," Hugo said. "Anyway, the stuff helps me think."

"Idiot. The case is over, you don't need to think." Tom nodded to a shopping bag Hugo had brought into the restaurant. "Don't tell me you grabbed a souvenir out there."

"Nope, but that reminds me, I got some help from my colleague Ryan Pierce. First of all, he confirmed that Alexie Tourville was in the States at the time Jonty Railton was essentially bullied out of the talks. I'm thinking she slashed his tires and made the threats, figuring Lake was next in line. Which, Ryan tells me, was no surprise in Washington and something she could have known given her connections."

"A careful planner, that one," said Lerens.

"Careful and cold," Hugo said.

"No doubt, but I was asking about your bag?" Tom prompted.

"It's a present for Camille, thanks in part to Ryan's shopping abilities."

Lerens looked at Hugo. "Present? It's not my birthday."

"I know. But you did solve the case and that warrants something, don't you think?"

Lerens laughed. "I thought you solved the case? I just kept you company."

"Team effort," Hugo said. "You're the case detective so you get the credit but, sure, the Americans helped. Which brings me to the present." He brought the bag out from under the table and handed it to Lerens. "Go ahead, open it."

Lerens peered inside the bag and shrugged. "OK, I'm game. Thank you."

Hugo and Tom watched as the lieutenant dug in the bag and pulled out a rectangular box, placing it carefully on the table. She opened the top flap of the box and moved aside some tissue paper, a smile spreading across her face as she saw its contents.

"Shoes!" she said.

"There's a company in the United States," Hugo said, "that makes shoes for transgender people, that's all they do. I guess they spotted the hole in the market that you identified when we were climbing those stairs. This pair is designed for people on their feet all day. My resourceful deputy researched them and tells me they received excellent reviews."

Lerens shook her head slowly. "Hugo, you're a thoughtful man. A kind man, thank you."

"You're welcome. There's a gift certificate in there, too, you can get another pair."

"A Godsend. A lifesaver. Thanks again, from the soles of my feet."

"Ahem." Tom cleared his throat. "You guys aren't gonna kiss, are you? I'm about to eat and that would totally fuck up my appetite."

"Bullshit," Lerens said. "You'd love it. I've heard about you and your appetites." They laughed as Tom blustered and pretended to be embarrassed, then Lerens patted his arm. "And like I told Hugo a few days ago, I like girls. Always have, always will. In fact, I make a very good wingwoman."

"Now you're talking," Tom said, looking at his watch. "We can be back in Paris in an hour, shower up and . . . Oh, wait."

"Already have plans?" Lerens asked.

"As a matter of fact, yes."

"What are you doing on a Sunday night?" Hugo asked.

Tom grinned. "Same as I did last Sunday. Going out and not telling you where."

"Oh, right." Hugo took a sip of water. "Maybe I'll have to follow you again. Except I'll do a better job of it this time."

"Try it," said Tom. "I dare you."

"Fine, I will."

"Oh, leave him to his secret plans," Lerens said. "Why do you care so much, Hugo? You're not his mother."

"It's not that," Tom chuckled. "Oh, don't get me wrong, he's a sweet and caring man, he proved that with the shoes. But it's not some weird parental or protective motivation driving you, is it Hugo?"

Lerens looked back and forth between the two friends who sat silent, smiling at each other as if communicating by thought alone. "Then tell me," she said, "what is it?"

"Simple," Tom said. "It's a mystery that he can't solve. Back when he was in London, only a few years ago, he found himself a murder-mystery that no one had solved. A woman killed in an alleyway that some people attributed to Jack the Ripper, and some didn't. Hugo had his own theories and visited the scene of the crime, oh, how many times?"

"Just a couple," Hugo said.

"Yeah, right. Anyway, he never did solve it and my guess is he'll never stop trying." Tom grinned. "Nothing Hugo hates more than a mystery he can't unravel, and now he's facing one that *I* created. Ain't nothing worse than that, is there Hugo?"

Hugo smoothed the table cloth in front of him and leaned back to catch the attention of a passing waiter.

"*S'il vous plaît, monsieur*," Hugo said. "When you have a moment could you bring me some water?"

The waiter looked at the table, then at Hugo. "*Mais monsieur*, you have some already."

"Yes," said Hugo with a smile. "But I think I need some sparkling water, too. Perhaps you could bring a whole bottle. *Merci bien*."

ACKNOWLEDGMENTS

Sincere thanks once again to my posse of beta readers, Jennifer Schubert, Theresa Holland, Elodie, Nancy Matuszak, and Donna Gough, whose insight and honesty were invaluable. I am extremely grateful for your time and your wisdom.

Thanks also to Susan Garst for her guidance on forensic archeology (again!) and to Philip Breeden, who has the impressive title of Minister Counselor for Public Affairs (Information and Cultural Affairs), but who I know as the kind person who made time to show me around the US Embassy in Paris and tell me what I was getting right and wrong in Hugo's world. Likewise to his colleague, who must remain mysterious and anonymous, my thanks.

As this journey progresses, my friends continue to impress and assist me with their support and encouragement. I can't name you all but need to mention the likes of Sareta Davis, Johnny Goudie, Andy Baxter, Michelle Pierce, Caro Dubois, Ed and James Frierson, Jeniffer Barrera, and Mike Luna. A special thank you to Ann and David Hillis for letting me hideaway in their Hill Country retreat, a place of natural beauty and calm with just a hint of danger to keep a writer sharp. Likewise, but on the other end of the process, much gratitude to Scott Montgomery and his crew at BookPeople in Austin, including Raul Chapa, Colleen Farrell, Sarah Bishop, Emily Rankin, Consuelo Hacker, Kathleen Allen, Mandy Brooks, Carolyn Tracey, Elizabeth Jordan, and Julie Wernersbach. I need to mention, too, my friends at APD, the guys in Charlie Sector who give me inspiration (and protection) when I ride shotgun: Lawrence 'Nic' Nicoletti, Steve Constable, Bob Miljenovich, John Mosteller, Andrew Morris, Dave Nickel, Nick Draper, A.

J. Carrol, Joe Strother, Jason Cummins, Dan Kessler, Will Johns, Jamie Byrnes, Brent Cleveland, Brian Yarger, and Michael Whitener. I know I forgot someone there, so to every APD officer: my thanks!

There are many professionals in my world now, people who are more to me than their job title, people whose dedication and enthusiasm have brought Hugo to life for my readers. Dan Mayer, my editor; Jill Maxick; Meghan Quinn; Melissa Raé Shofner; Mariel Bard; Catherine Roberts-Abel; Ian Birnbaum; and my wonderful agent, Ann Collette.

And as ever, I am eternally grateful to my wonderful, understanding, enthusiastic family who cheer my every success and give me the time, space, and inspiration to write.

ABOUT THE AUTHOR

Mark Pryor (Austin, TX) is the author of *The Bookseller* and *The Crypt Thief*, the first and second Hugo Marston novels, and the true-crime book *As She Lay Sleeping*. An assistant district attorney with the Travis County District Attorney's Office, in Austin, Texas, he is the creator of the true-crime blog DAConfidential. He has appeared on CBS News's *48 Hours* and Discovery Channel's *Discovery ID: Cold Blood*.

Visit him online at www.markpryorbooks.com, www.facebook.com/pages/Mark-Pryor-Author, and http://DAConfidential.com.